LIE IN PLAIN SIGHT

ALSO BY MAGGIE BARBIERI

Maeve Conlon Novels

Murder 101 Novels

LIE IN PLAIN SIGHT

MAGGIE BARBIERI

MINOTAUR BOOKS ✖ NEW YORK

LIE IN PLAIN SIGHT. Copyright 2016 by Maggie Barbieri. All rights reserved. Printed in the United States of America. For information, address St. Martin's Press, 175 Fifth Avenue, New York, N.Y. 10010.

www.minotaurbooks.com

Designed by Omar Chapa

The Library of Congress Cataloging-in-Publication Data is available upon request.

ISBN 978-1-250-07344-0 (hardcover)
ISBN 978-1-4668-8519-6 (e-book)

Our books may be purchased in bulk for promotional, educational, or business use. Please contact your local bookseller or the Macmillan Corporate and Premium Sales Department at 1-800-221-7945, extension 5442, or by e-mail at MacmillanSpecialMarkets@macmillan.com.

First Edition: March 2016

10 9 8 7 6 5 4 3 2 1

In memory of my father, Kenneth J. Scarry
(1940–2015), a true gentleman and a lover of justice.

LIE IN PLAIN SIGHT

CHAPTER 1

"You've changed."

Maeve hoped so. The last few years had taken a toll on her, both emotionally and physically, and change was welcome. She wondered if it was for the better.

She lay on her back, one leg thrown out from under the down comforter on her bed, and considered the observation as well as her feet, sorely in need of a pedicure, not that she had ever had or desired one. If she was getting back into the game, so to speak, it might be worth the effort. The time. The money. The last two she had little of, and that presented a problem. "You think so?"

"I think so," he said, rolling on top of her and smoothing her hair off her forehead, their faces nearly touching.

"How so?" she asked, knowing that this was a bad idea, going down this road, both the one that had their limbs entwined and the other about how she was different now. This time.

"Do you really want to know?"

Game playing. Her least favorite relationship tool. But she played along. "Yes. I'd really like to know."

He thought for a moment, kissing her while he did, stalling. "You're calmer. More confident. You know what you want now."

"You could say that about any woman past the age of forty. Forty-five maybe. We all fall into those categories." She thought about herself at younger ages. Scared as a child. Terrified as a young teen. Tentative as a young adult, finding her way after the abuse. Exhausted from the beginning of motherhood until about five years ago when the girls had gotten old enough to fend for themselves, for the most part. Then, enraged. It came out of nowhere and held her in a viselike grip, a hand around her throat until she did something to release the tension.

After that, she was free.

She was ready for him to leave, the point proven. She could still have him, still make him happy. He had other ideas, though, their bodies becoming tangled once again, the down comforter flying off the bed at one point, a feather coming free and landing on her sweaty skin.

"I love you," he whispered in the middle, just like he always did, taking the fun out of it for her, ruining her moment. She couldn't say it back; she wouldn't. That would take things to a new level, make the whole relationship more complicated than it needed to be. She didn't think "you're lucky I still like you" was an appropriate response, so she stayed silent, or as silent as she could, given what was happening in her bed.

It was twenty minutes before she could convince him to leave. She ushered him out of the room and down the stairs, telling him at the top, "This can't happen again."

He smiled just like he had that first time, repeating what he had said then. "But it will." When he got to the bottom of the stairs, he turned back. "I sent Rebecca a check for her textbooks, so she's covered. Don't worry about that."

"Thanks, Cal." She watched him leave, thinking about how strange it was to have an affair with the husband of another woman, particularly someone who had once been her husband. She was cheating on the man she loved with the man she once loved and would never love again, even if she missed him, if only a little bit.

CHAPTER 2

At back-to-school night, Maeve learned that every other student in Heather's senior class either aspired to or was definitely going to go to Cornell.

Or Harvard.

Or Yale.

Or Georgetown.

But mostly Cornell.

The graduating class four years hence would be busting with students from Farringville High School, if their parents had anything to say about it.

There was nothing lower than a semi-Ivy on the list, with her older daughter's school, Vassar, making the list with three or four students applying; she lost count after a while, her mind going elsewhere. All of the applications would go out soon and be "early decision" or "early action," a student's acceptance a binding commitment on the former. Maeve started to sweat. Heather had shown no interest in writing her application essays, culling her list of schools, or signing up for the retake of the SAT.

"Leave me alone!" was the oft-used response to Maeve's inquiries regarding anything having to do with college. That and a door slam.

When it was her turn to tell the guidance counselor, running a session at back-to-school night about the college process, about Heather's plans, Maeve lied. She wasn't sure why, but she did.

"Cornell, too," she said, looking at the mother of one of Heather's more academically focused classmates, who returned an affirming nod, "and maybe some schools out west."

The guidance counselor, an older woman on her way out the door after this year, her retirement date looming, looked at Maeve expectantly. "Such as?"

The lies came easier this time. "UCLA. Berkeley." Maeve felt like a *Jeopardy!* contestant presented with a category on the mating habits of lemurs; after that list, she was almost out of schools. She almost said "Gallaudet" before remembering that the school catered to deaf students, and Heather definitely wasn't deaf; Maeve knew that because her daughter often told her that her voice was "ear-piercing." Drama, thy name is Heather Callahan. "Johns Hopkins," Maeve said finally, remembering too late that that wasn't in the West but in the mid-Atlantic region, south of where she lived in the Hudson Valley.

The guidance counselor continued to look at her, and in that look, Maeve saw the question: Are we talking about the same girl? It was clear that Mrs. Demke had met Heather and knew that she didn't have a clue about where to go, what to study, or how to execute a plan to get into college, despite having more of an interest just months before.

Maeve wasn't sure what had happened to change Heather's desire to get out of Farringville by any means necessary, college being the likely choice for escape, but over the summer, something had imbued her with a deep apathy for the college process. Maeve's oldest,

Rebecca, had tackled the job of finding and getting into a college with a zeal that Maeve envied. She had been ready for the next step and the challenges that came with it, and despite telling her sister repeatedly what a great thing it was, going to college, being away, Heather had sunk into some kind of black hole about the whole thing, staring at Rebecca as if she had lost her mind.

Did she now want to stay in Farringville? Maeve wondered about that and shuddered at the thought, even though when Heather left, she would be alone. Heather's former boyfriend—someone Maeve had hated with the passion of a thousand burning suns—was gone from the picture. Maybe his disappearance from her life had Heather in an emotional free fall that hadn't ended yet. Maeve decided that as she did with most things, she would wait it out. Be patient.

The litany of superior schools was interrupted by one comment that fell into the category of attainable. Reasonable. Maeve looked over at the mother who proclaimed that her daughter would go to "whichever state university takes her and gives her money" and smiled. The mother smiled back, pleased with the hush that fell over the room at her revelation that her daughter was average and that she had limited funds for education. Maeve found that refreshing. She recognized the mother as Trish Dvorak, someone she had known better when the girls were small, before she had started her business and thrown herself into it full-time and without rest.

The guidance counselor, at a loss in the face of such averageness and honesty, hastily went through her PowerPoint slides and concluded with a question-and-answer period that quickly became specific to each parent's child and his or her chances of getting into his or her dream school with a varying number of Advanced Placement classes.

At the end of the session, Maeve left the room and walked down the hallway that housed the trophies from years past, the glory days of Farringville High School and its student athletes, mostly from the sixties, when the football team was huge and no one really cared about the lasting effects of concussions. Farringville now had a football program that was on its last legs, its punter a kid who'd never held a football prior to being recruited to the team but who exhibited some impressive high kicks during the spring musical, *Oklahoma*. At the end of the hallway in a large open area, tables were set up, one asking parents to join the PTA, another selling tickets to the fall drama, and another with a sign showing down-on-their-luck children in Mississippi with the plea PLEASE HELP. Two male students stood behind the table taking donations.

"Ma'am, can you help?" one of them called out, a tall, handsome boy in pink Bermuda shorts and a bright green polo, a little out of sync sartorially with the rest of the Farringville High students, who tended, Maeve had observed, toward the hipster look more than the preppy look. An older man stood off to the side, watching carefully as people approached the table and the kid made his pitch.

Maeve knew that she had an empty wallet because she always had an empty wallet. "Sorry, guys," she said. "I didn't bring any money." That was one way to put it, far less pathetic than "I don't have any money right now."

The shorter of the two, a kid who looked like an older version of one of Heather's preschool classmates and probably was, walked around from behind the table and handed her a pamphlet. "We're raising funds to go to Madison, Mississippi. A very poor town," he said. "We're building a school."

"And we'll have a table at Founders Day if you want to donate then," the taller one said, flashing a smile. "We don't leave for another eight months."

"Starting early?" Maeve asked.

"Yes," the shorter one said. "It costs each one of us over one thousand dollars to go and spend the week there, so we're trying to raise some money so we can cut that cost a little bit."

Maeve thought of Heather at home, sulking in her room, the thought of building a school for Mississippi children the furthest thing from her mind. "Is the trip full?" Maeve asked. "Can other students go if they want?"

They looked at each other.

Maeve walked closer to the table. "I'm Heather Callahan's mom. I'm asking on her behalf." Might do the girl good, Maeve thought. Maybe her home life wouldn't seem so terrible if she was doing something for someone other than herself.

The preppy kid held out his hand. "I'm Jesse Connors. And this is Tim Morehead. Tell Heather to come find us if she's interested in going. We'll give her all of the details."

Maeve shook both of their hands. "I will. Thanks. And if you want a donation, come by The Comfort Zone. If I'm not there, I'll leave an envelope."

The older man came forward. "Thank you very much," he said, holding out his hand. "Charles Connors."

"Maeve Conlon."

"Whatever you can give will go a long way toward making this trip a reality," he said. He pointed to the kid in the Bermuda shorts. "It was my son's idea. To give back to a less fortunate community."

Maeve thought of the cluster of broken-down double-wide trailers that sat on the east end of town, and of the school lunch program that had been in effect for kids who couldn't even afford to bring their own lunch, and one of her late father's old sayings jumped into her brain: Charity begins at home. After the closing a few years earlier of one of the bigger businesses in town, a stonecutting yard that had been in existence for over a hundred years, Farringville had become a town of the haves and have-nots.

Maeve folded the brochure and put it in her back pocket. Regardless of her feelings, they were the nice kids, the good kids, the ones she wanted Heather to be around and to socialize with, not the crowd with which she currently ran. That crowd was looking for the next party, the next reason to be rowdy, not a way to help people half a world away. Where had she gone wrong as a mother? she wondered as she wended her way through the throngs of people in the school, the din of their excited chatter bouncing off the institutional cinder-block walls.

Trish Dvorak found Maeve in the cafeteria after the first session of the night. "Do these people really think that every kid is going to go to Cornell?" she asked, surveying the cookies and slices of cake that had been put out on a table next to a big coffee urn.

"Or Harvard?" Maeve asked, handing her a macaroon from The Comfort Zone.

"Delicious," Trish said after taking a bite. "How do you do what you do all day and stay so thin?"

"Not so thin," Maeve said, grabbing the hunk of flesh that sat above the waistband of her jeans. "But I'm on my feet all day, so I suspect that burns a bunch of calories. I do eat a lot of cake," she said, smiling. "So Taylor is going to a state university?" she asked.

"That's the hope," Trish said. She herself was rail thin, her clavicles poking out from beneath the striped T-shirt she was wearing, skinny jeans on her thin legs. "Her father isn't contributing toward the tuition, so it's a SUNY, financial aid, and hopefully some kind of merit package." Trish took another macaroon. "He's a douchebag, in case I didn't make that clear."

Maeve raised an eyebrow. She thought of her own ex as a lot of things but would never verbalize them in polite society, and in particular on back-to-school night. "Some ex-husbands are."

"Oh, we were never married. And he barely acknowledges that she's his, so I've kind of given up," Trish said. "Shocking, right?"

Maeve put another cookie in her mouth. People sleeping with ex-husbands shouldn't throw stones or live in glass houses or . . . whatever. She wasn't sure so she stayed silent.

"State schools are a lot harder to get into now because everyone has realized what a great deal they are," Trish said.

Maeve knew Taylor from soccer, but barely; she had played with Rebecca. She knew Trish worked several jobs and hadn't seen her at many games. But she knew nothing about her academically. Hell, she knew next to nothing about her own daughter academically and held her breath every time a progress report came in the mail. There was a school for everyone, right? That's what the guidance counselor had said. "I'm sure it will work out," she said, grabbing a cup for coffee. Trouble was, no decaf. She'd be up all night if she had coffee this late. That was another side effect of being in her forties, and not one of the welcome ones. Hell, what were the welcome ones? She didn't have enough time to spend thinking up what they might be.

"I haven't seen you in ages, Maeve," Trish said. "When was the last time we really spoke? The Museum Village trip? Third grade?"

"Probably," Maeve said, wondering why Trish had decided to let her know about Taylor's father now instead of back then when they had spent real time together, trying desperately to keep a group of little kids from wandering off. "Or maybe Ellis Island in eighth grade? Wasn't that the one where Heather split her lip open?"

Trish nodded. "Yes."

"You were so nice to her," Maeve said. "I remember that you were the only mom who had Neosporin in your pocketbook."

"Always prepared," Trish said. "Former Girl Scout."

"I remember having a purse full of cookies. And old receipts. But you? A whole medical kit," Maeve said, laughing. She tipped the coffeepot; three drops of coffee fell into her cup. "What's our next session?" she asked, looking at the clock and seeing they had five minutes to get where they needed to go.

"Tips on How to Pay for College," Trish said, laughing. "I wonder if one of the tips is 'rob a bank'?"

Maeve was lucky; Cal had started college funds the day each girl had been born, and though the price of college escalated faster than he could save, he paid for any shortfall himself. Maeve was on the hook for the meal plans, according to their agreement, and that was enough to shoulder financially. She looked at Trish. Sure, there was financial aid, and maybe there would be merit money, but it seemed like it would be a stretch anyway. "Trish, I hope I'm not out of line here, but I'm looking for someone—"

"Yes," Trish said.

"You don't even know what I'm going to ask you," Maeve said.

"I need a job, Maeve. I was just too embarrassed to ask," Trish said. "That's why I came over here. I don't care if you need someone to wash dishes all day. I need to do something. I lost my job taking care of the Lorenzo kids. Do you know them?"

Maeve did. She might have been the reason that Trish lost her job, the father of the two children she had taken care of being someone Maeve had taken care of herself. In her mind, she had committed a public service that night a couple of years before.

Trish continued. "Terrible thing that happened back at the dam. Not sure you remember. The dad died."

"Yes. I remember," Maeve said, an image of his eyes as he went over the railing, the belief in them that he would make it until about three-quarters of the way down and then the realization that the choice he had made—to take his chances—had been the wrong one. Rather than feel sadness at that, Maeve felt happy and resisted the urge to let a little smile break out on her face. As she got older, it was getting harder and harder to act, to make believe that she was sad when bad people died, people others didn't know the truth about.

Trish was still talking. "They're moving." When she saw Maeve's blank expression, she figured it was because Maeve had lost the thread of the conversation, not that she was thinking still about that night at the dam, Lorenzo falling onto the riverbank below, his body twisted and awkwardly posed, the life draining from him as she watched. "The Lorenzos."

"Right," Maeve said, taking a cookie from a tray and popping it into her mouth before thinking. Too much nutmeg. Always a sign of a bad baker. Less is more, especially with certain flavors, nutmeg being one of them. "Yes. I remember." She needed out of this conversation, and fast.

"I'm cobbling stuff together," Trish said, pleading her case. "I clean houses, something I swore that I would never do again. Almost killed me and I was young back when I first started. But people are cutting back. I need to add something to make ends meet."

Maeve didn't consider herself a soft touch; far from it. She was a single mother, for all intents and purposes, but one who had support, both financial and sometimes emotional, from her ex. She looked the woman over, taking stock, thinking about Taylor's father, his reluctance to pony up for her tuition. Did she have to add a new person to her list, the one she kept in her head, of people who needed to be eradicated from the world? She tried not to let it show on her face when thoughts like that went through her mind. "Ten dollars an hour. I'll need you to do deliveries, some counter work. If you're interested in baking, I'll train you on some items." She picked up a napkin and, pretending to wipe her mouth, surreptitiously got most of the cookie out and wadded up the paper.

"Off the books?" Trish asked.

"Most definitely on," Maeve said. The last thing she needed was a run-in with the IRS. She was dating a cop and had slept with her ex. She needed to keep her nose clean in at least one area of her life.

Trish was disappointed, something she unsuccessfully tried to hide. "Okay. When do I start?" she asked.

"Tomorrow. Seven?" Maeve said. "We'll basically be a two-man operation, so the days are long, but I'm now closed on Mondays, so it's Tuesday through Sunday."

"That's great, Maeve." Trish leaned in and gave Maeve an awkward hug. "Thank you."

Maeve watched her go, a trace of cigarette-smoke smell in her wake. That was the shortest job interview in history. She hoped she hadn't made a mistake.

CHAPTER 3

The Fitzpatrick twins were being christened on Saturday, and Donna Fitzpatrick had been in no fewer than four times making sure that Maeve had gotten the pink icing for their cake the correct shade. Maeve pulled a piece of bakery paper from the stack underneath the counter and grabbed her piping bag, the one she had at the ready, knowing that Donna would come in exactly at twelve-twenty after dropping her older son off at preschool to see if the color had changed, even the slightest, since the day before.

Maeve squirted a little squiggle of icing onto the paper. "See? Same as we discussed when you placed the order. It's a cross between salmon and Thulian." The latter, Maeve had had to look up. *What the hell is a Thulian?* she remembered asking herself as she sat in bed with her laptop. She still wasn't sure she knew, but she had figured out how to create the color, and Donna almost seemed to be pleased, despite the curl of her lip indicating that maybe it wasn't exactly the shade it had been the day before or the one she wanted. "Yes? Good?" Maeve asked, Donna's ability to speak seeming to have left her.

"Yes," Donna said. "Just like that," she said, pointing to the farthest end of the paper, where a little dollop had hit the air and already discolored.

Maeve's sister, Evelyn, a few years older and developmentally challenged, was wiping down the café tables in the front of the store, quietly eavesdropping on the drama at the counter. Maeve prayed that she wouldn't say anything to Donna Fitzpatrick—she had a tendency to be a "truth bomb," as the girls called her—but she just kept wiping the same table over and over, humming to herself. Maeve recognized it as her favorite Kelly Clarkson song. Evelyn had a job in another part of the county but loved being with Maeve; Maeve brought her up every couple of weeks to spend the day in the store since that was where she herself spent most of her time. Evelyn, as it turned out, was helpful on busy days, doing the things that Maeve's former employee and best friend, Jo, had never done with any regularity.

Maeve was relieved to hear the phone ring so she could excuse herself from Donna's observation of all things fondant and pink. "The Comfort Zone. Can I help you?"

"Maeve? It's Judy Wilkerson."

The school nurse. This day just kept getting better and better. Behind Donna, the bell over the door trilled, and in walked a crowd of Maeve's regulars, six guys from the railroad who had discovered that at $7.95, Maeve's lunch special of a healthy slice of quiche accompanied by a small salad and a drink was one of the best deals in town. They clustered around the drink case, loud the way men in groups can be, particularly men who had just left the deafening machine shop at the station, where one had to scream to be heard.

"Judy, hi," Maeve said. She walked into the kitchen with the phone to get some privacy. "Heather, right? She was complaining of a sore throat this morning when she left. But she also had a history test, so I didn't make much of it."

"No, not Heather," the nurse said. "It's Taylor Dvorak. Is Trish available? I tried her cell, but she's not picking up."

"No, she's out on a delivery," Maeve said, picking up a dirty knife and putting it in the sink, which was now overflowing with dishes.

"Okay, well, you can give permission."

"For what?" Maeve asked.

"To send Taylor home. Her mother put you down as her emergency contact when she started working for you last week."

News to Maeve. That would have been good information to have. "Oh. I wasn't aware of that."

"You and every other person in town who either has their own business or works from home. I have one gal who works from home who has no fewer than thirty kids that she's emergency contact for. The last five—all of whom got the stomach flu at the same time—were kids she barely knew." Judy let out a chuckle. "Anyway, I have Taylor here, and she said she has a nasty headache. She gets migraines and wants to go home before it gets any worse."

Maeve walked back to the front of the store, where Donna Fitzpatrick was hitting the bell on the counter, impatiently awaiting Maeve's input on the pink frosting. The railroad guys were also making noise, and Maeve could see the front door opening and closing, a steady stream of customers entering. "Do I need to come get her?"

After a quick conference with her patient, Judy returned to the call. "She's walking distance from school, and she said she's going to go straight home to bed. Just let me know if that's okay, and let her mother know as well, if you don't mind?"

"Are you sure? Do you think it's okay to let her leave? Trish should be back shortly," Maeve said.

Judy laughed. "She's almost eighteen, Maeve. I could keep her here, but then she'd have to sleep in the office all day. She's almost technically an adult. I think it's okay."

Maeve mulled that over, wondering what she should do, what someone else might do if the situation were reversed and it was Heather. Would she be comfortable letting Heather go home on her own? Last year, definitely not. This year? Probably. "I guess it's okay," Maeve said, going back into the front of the store. It was filled with both happy and unhappy customers, Donna Fitzpatrick leading the charge on the latter. "Yes, go ahead and send her home."

"You'll let Trish know?"

"I'll let Trish know," Maeve said before hanging up. She needed more help than just Trish could offer and was relieved when Jo came out of the kitchen, a cup of coffee in one hand, her toddler on her hip. Maeve pulled an apron out of the box beneath the counter and handed it to Jo. "You're a sight for sore eyes. Can you give me fifteen minutes until we get done with the rush?"

Jo looked at the coffee in her hand, the squirming baby in her arms. "You're kidding, right?" She readjusted the baby, hoisting him higher on her slim waist. "This was a social call."

"Not kidding. Can you put him in the stroller and give me a hand? Fifteen minutes. I promise." Before Jo could protest, Maeve pushed her gently through the swinging doors and started waiting on one hungry customer at a time. Jo joined her, and even with Donna Fitzpatrick quizzing Jo on the various shades of pink and testing her on salmon versus hot pink, they managed to empty the store in less than fifteen minutes with two minutes to spare.

The baby, despite the noise and raucous laughter of the railroad guys, had fallen asleep in his stroller, his thumb hanging limply between his lips. He was named after Maeve's father, a secret she had to keep; Jo's devoutly Jewish mother thought that he had been named after a deceased relative.

After they cleared the store of customers, Maeve and Jo took seats across from each other at one of the café tables where customers sat who wanted to eat in. Jo lifted the lid from her coffee cup and took a long sip. "Oh, hiya, Evelyn," Jo said, noticing Maeve's sister behind the quiche case. She was shorter than Maeve by a few inches, a tiny sprite of a woman.

"Hi, Jo," Evelyn said. "I love your baby," she said, as she did every time she saw Jo and her son.

"Thanks," Jo said. "How are things at home?"

Maeve appreciated that Jo treated Evelyn like anyone else, not falling into the trap of speaking loudly and slowly to the woman. She was challenged, yes, but not deaf. Evelyn smiled, happy to be part of the conversation. "My friend Debbie is going to a wedding this weekend! She's wearing a sparkly dress!"

"That's fantastic!" Jo said, keeping up the conversation until it was clear that Evelyn was done talking about Debbie and her dress.

Maeve took in the dark circles under her friend's eyes. "Baby not sleeping again?" she asked.

"It's been a rough week," Jo said. "Just when it seems like we'll get a solid eight hours, he starts with the feeding-every-hour bullshit." She clapped her hands over her mouth when Evelyn admonished her for cursing.

"You know what I say, right?" Maeve asked.

"Yes. Let him cry." Jo had heard Maeve's thoughts on getting a baby to sleep a thousand times, or so it seemed. "I just can't do it."

Maeve understood. She had been much more agreeable about feeding Rebecca all night, her first, than Heather, her second. Maybe that was why Heather was such a crab all the time. Too much crying and not enough breastfeeding as a baby. Maeve knew one thing: It was always the mother's fault, no matter what happened, no matter that Cal had been the biggest "let her cry" proponent in the house. No one would ever know that because to the outside world, he was a doting father, along with being a cheating husband, two things that hadn't changed.

Jo looked over at the baby. "He's a good baby, though. Don't get the wrong idea."

"I know he is, Jo," Maeve said. She hoped she could get a few minutes with Jo; between the baby taking up all of Jo's time and the business taking up all of hers, they rarely had more than a few minutes to catch up.

Evelyn asked Maeve if she could have a muffin. "Sure, honey. Eat it in the kitchen, okay?" she said. She watched her sister go into the kitchen and then turned back to Jo. "So, what's going on? Besides Jack, the sleepless wonder over there?"

Jo had dirt. Gossip. The straight skinny. Maeve could tell by the way her face brightened at the thought of spilling some juicy tidbit about someone in Farringville, most likely someone Maeve didn't know, knew tangentially, or didn't care about at all. Still, it gave Jo a thrill to be in possession of village intel, and Maeve was happy to hear it, if only to offer a diversion from the occasional drudgery of the bakery.

"Want to hear this one?" Jo asked, amping up the drama. "This is a good one. Better than you'll hear from anyone else."

Maeve hadn't seen Jo this excited about a juicy, gossipy morsel in a long time. And who didn't love a good piece of gossip? Maeve had to admit that she did and felt just the slightest pang of guilt over it, barely enough to notice. "Sure. What is it?" Maeve asked, looking at the clock over the counter. Trish had been gone for over an hour, and the delivery was only on the other side of town. Maeve wondered where she was and, again, if this precipitous hire had been a mistake, a few days into it.

"Cal."

"Cal Callahan?" Maeve asked. The hair on the back of her neck prickled at the thought that the gossip she so eagerly awaited was about her and her ex.

"One and only. Your ex-husband. The father of your children. Cad-about-town Cal Callahan."

"What about him?" Maeve asked. They had been careful. He'd had every reason to be at her house that night. He had walked in without hiding and left the same way. There was no way that any-one could know that they had had a tryst, if that's even what you called sleeping with your ex-husband, the one who had run away from you only to come running back like a dog that finds his home after being lost for years.

"Affair."

Maeve was nothing if not a good liar with a great poker face. Those two things had served her well. "Really? Any idea who it might be?"

Jo narrowed her eyes, studying Maeve's face. "That's it? That's all you've got? I thought you'd be thrilled to hear this news, or at least disgusted. One or the other."

Maeve shrugged. "He's a big boy. He can do what he wants. And I don't really care." She shrugged again for good measure. Clearly she was losing her touch, not having the proper reaction to the situation.

"That's it? 'He's a big boy'?" Jo narrowed her eyes. "What gives?"

"Nothing gives. I don't care."

"You don't care."

"Nope."

"Not even a little schadenfreude? Some satisfaction in the fact that he's cheating on Miss Gorgeous? The Brazilian knockout?"

Maeve started to sweat. She didn't want to have this conversa-tion. Jo needed to drop it.

It took her a few seconds, but Jo eventually figured it out, standing and knocking over her bar stool, the metal clanging when it hit the floor and jarring the baby awake. "*J'accuse!*" Jo said, pointing her finger at Maeve, a smile spreading across her face. "It's you." Jo leaned over and picked up the chair, replacing it gently in front of the table while glancing over at the baby, who was asleep again. "Well, I'll be damned."

"No," Maeve said. "I will." *And I think I'm okay with that,* she thought.

"You are the worst liar," Jo said.

No, I'm not, Maeve thought. *If you knew some of the things I've done and lied about, we wouldn't be friends.*

Through the small window in the door that separated the kitchen from the front of the store, Maeve saw Trish standing by the door, then turning quickly to talk to Evelyn when she saw her boss. Maeve stood. "Listen, it was one time. It was a mistake." She held one finger up, letting Trish know she'd be right in. "I'd hardly call it an affair."

"You don't seem terribly guilty about this."

"I'm not," Maeve said, feeling the same way she had when it was over: satisfied. Content. A little reckless.

Happy? The score had been settled, one that had remained one-sided since Gabriela had upended her life all those years ago.

"We're not done," Jo said, following her into the kitchen.

Maeve turned. "Yes. We are."

Trish was peeling off a wad of bills and counting them. "A hundred and sixty, right, Maeve?" she asked, putting the money in a stack beside a mixing bowl. "Artun says that the banana bread was dry last week."

"Everyone's a critic," Jo said. "And a word to the wise, Trish: Try to soften the blow before you deliver news like that. This one here," she said, jerking a thumb in Maeve's direction, "will be up all night recalculating the ingredients, and you won't get a moment of peace until she gets it right."

Trish nodded. "Got it."

Maeve put the money in her apron pocket. "Trish, Judy Wilkerson from the high school called and said Taylor wasn't feeling well. She went home."

Trish pulled an apron on over her head. "Home?"

"Yes. Home. I wasn't aware that I was your emergency contact, but Judy said that if I gave my permission, Taylor could go home. She wanted to get some rest because she had a migraine." Maeve grabbed the mixing bowl from the counter and threw that in the sink along with the growing collection of pots and pans.

"She's not there," Trish said. "That's why I'm a few minutes late. I stopped by the house to feed my dog. Taylor's not there."

Maeve looked at the clock. It had been over a half hour since Judy had called. Trish lived within a five-minute walk of the high school; a lot of kids in Farringville did, since the high school was in a central location. "Maybe she stopped to get lunch on the way?"

Trish punched some numbers into her phone. "Straight to voice mail," she said. She tried another number. "There's no one home, either." She looked at Maeve, a look of panic on her face. "She's not there. She's not home."

CHAPTER 4

In Farringville, everyone in the village knew that the lead detective and the bakery owner were dating. Both Maeve and Chris Larsson had tried to keep it under wraps, but now that it was out there, it was a bit of a relief. Still, they attempted to keep it strictly professional and aboveboard when they were in her place of business. Neither ever expected that his business would intersect with hers, though. Maeve sat at the high counter in the kitchen and relayed her conversation with Judy Wilkerson again.

"She said that Taylor had a migraine and would walk home."

Chris wrote a few notes in his little notepad. "And that was what time?"

Thank God for Donna Fitzpatrick and her daily drop-in. Maeve wondered if the disappearance of a high school student might put Donna's icing quandary into some perspective. Probably not. "Twelve twenty-five. Approximately."

"And she was going straight home?"

"As far as I know." Maeve dropped her head to the counter. "How bad is this, Chris?"

His face gave nothing away. In the front of the store, Trish was talking to another officer and trying to figure out potential places that Taylor might go instead of home. Maeve's initial thought was that the girl had lied, that she hadn't had a migraine, that she had gone to meet someone, somewhere, and didn't want anyone to know. Trish's immediate assumption was that she was abducted. Given that their suspicions were on opposite ends of the spectrum, Maeve kept her thoughts to herself.

But Chris wanted to know what she thought. "Ran away? Met someone she wasn't supposed to?" Maeve asked.

Chris closed his notebook and stood, not giving any indication of whether he agreed with Maeve. "I'm going to talk to Trish again," he said, leaving the kitchen.

Maeve stared at the order board across from where she was sitting, just a piece of corkboard nailed to the wall. She had done the wrong thing, letting Judy send Taylor home. She should have waited for Trish to return. She shouldn't have made that decision for the girl or her mother. Guilt for some things—but not others—took hold of her sometimes and wouldn't let go, shaking her to the core. This was one of those things. She could feel it already.

Uniformed cops had already been all over the village and had even gone to the train station to see if anyone had seen a girl buy a ticket, board a train. There wasn't a lot they could do at this point, her disappearance being barely a few hours old, but something had caught the local police's attention, and they seemed determined to bring this girl home, even if she had just cut school to do a side trip to Old Navy.

While she was waiting for Chris to come back in, Cal burst through the back door with his toddler. The jogging stroller that Devon sat in had probably cost more than the engagement ring Cal had given Maeve a long time ago in another life. "What's going on?" he asked, breathless.

"Did you run here?" Maeve asked.

"Yes. I was out for a jog and saw police cars coming in this direction. When I got closer, I saw that they were here." He put the brake on the stroller and tore a hunk of bread off a loaf that Maeve had planned to sell, handing it to the toddler, who took a hearty bite, smiling at Maeve through the crumbs. Cal broke off another piece and shoved it in his own mouth. "What happened?"

"A girl has gone missing," Maeve said.

"A girl? What girl?"

"I just hired someone new, Trish Dvorack. Her daughter is missing."

"Missing?"

"Yes. Missing." Maeve could see Trish's tear-streaked face, hear the terror in her voice. She still wasn't sure why everyone was behaving as they were—as if something truly terrifying and awful had happened—but she was grateful that the police, as inept as they sometimes seemed to be in this village, were being so attentive. "She went home sick from school but never arrived. They are looking for her now."

"Did they check the malls? The train station?" Cal asked. "And how long has she been missing?"

"Couple of hours. I'm sure they are doing all of that," Maeve said.

He peered over her shoulder, trying to get a glimpse into the front of the store. "Dudley Do-Right in there?"

"If you mean Chris Larsson," Maeve said, "then yes."

"God help us," Cal said. "This case, whatever it is, will never be solved."

"Keep your voice down, Cal." She got up and looked through the glass of the kitchen door. She needed him gone before Chris came back to the kitchen and Cal threw off some vibe that raised her boyfriend's hackles. A jealous ex-husband. That was a new one. "They keep asking me the same questions over and over again."

"Why is everyone so upset about a girl who has been missing for a couple of hours?" he asked.

Good question, and one she didn't have an answer to.

"Why don't you go back home? I'll keep you posted." Maeve handed him the loaf of bread that he had desecrated.

"No," he said. "I'll stay. You need company."

What he meant, as he always did, was that he was staying because he thought she needed him. And that wasn't true. He forgot that she had been on her own a long time and didn't need him to protect her, to help her navigate the muddy waters of a messy life. She put her hands on his shoulders and looked him in the eye so that there would be no mistaking her intentions, or the message she wanted to give him. "Leave. Now. You don't need to be here. No one needs a retired corporate lawyer to deal with this right now."

He leaned in so close that their noses were touching. "When will I see you again?"

"You won't," she said. "No more, Cal. We're done."

He smiled, and she pulled away just before he landed a kiss on her dry lips. "No. We're not." He pulled away and angled the stroller toward the back door.

"People are talking, Cal," she said, her voice barely a whisper.

"What people?"

"People in this town. Someone saw something or heard something and . . ." A thought dawned on her, fully formed and a little sickening. "Are you sleeping with other women?" she asked. There was no way that anyone could have known what had happened between the two of them. That was the only answer. She wasn't the only one.

He didn't answer directly. "Keep me posted on this one. If she really is missing, this may be beyond your boyfriend's investigational capabilities. Really. They should call County. The FBI. People who actually know how to solve cases."

Before she could respond, he was gone, getting the last word as he often did.

Kurt Messer, a customer, held the door for Cal as he exited with the stroller. The older man nodded at Cal and smiled at the baby as they walked past. "I know I say this a lot, Maeve," he said, watching Cal push the baby across the parking lot, "but they grow so fast. I hope your ex-husband appreciates that now that he has a little one again."

"I'm not sure, Kurt," Maeve said. "You'd think he would have learned after how fast Rebecca and Heather grew up, but he may need reminding."

Kurt pointed toward the front of the store. "I hope it's okay I came in the back. Seems like there's something going on? Should I leave?"

"The cupcake order, right?" Maeve asked. Fortunately, it was wrapped and on top of the butcher-block counter; she wouldn't have to go into the front of the store and disturb what was going on there to find it. "Here it is."

Kurt took the wrapped package from her and admired it. "Gorgeous, Maeve. Thank you."

"Having a party?"

"Mark's birthday," he said. Kurt's son worked for the DPW—the village's Department of Public Works, where Kurt had recently taken the reins—and came into the store for lunch sometimes. "He's twenty-two."

"That's lovely, Kurt. I hope you enjoy them," she said.

"What do I owe you?" he asked.

"They're on the house." Before the older man could protest, Maeve put up her hand. "I can't tell you how helpful Mark has been to me over the last six months. That March snowstorm nearly pushed me over the edge, but he came and shoveled out the back parking lot for me without my asking."

"He's a good kid," Kurt said.

"Tell him to enjoy his birthday," Maeve said.

"Will you have a table at Founders Day, Maeve?" Kurt asked.

"I will," she said. "The mayor hasn't stopped hounding me since the village council decided to celebrate the hundred and fiftieth anniversary. I hope the weather holds."

"Well, October is usually a good month, so the weather should be good. One can only hope. I'll be doing a little party for my team the day before, but I'll call you closer to the event so I can place my order," Kurt said.

"That sounds great, Kurt," Maeve said, but she was distracted by the events of the afternoon.

Kurt lingered for a moment. "May I ask what's happening in there?"

Maeve hesitated, not sure how much to tell, but the man's kind face, coupled with his obvious concern, loosened her lips. "Trish Dvorak's daughter never came home from school today. Trish is worried that something may have happened to her." By the look on Kurt's face, she could tell he was acquainted with Trish.

Kurt looked at his watch. "It's the middle of the afternoon. What could have happened?" Realization dawned on his face slowly. "Runaway?"

"They don't know," Maeve said, "but keep her in your prayers. I'm really hoping that by dinnertime this is all over and she's being punished for giving her mother such a scare."

He stood for a moment, his face clouding over with concern and something else. Sadness? Maeve couldn't tell.

"These are the tough ones."

"The tough ones?"

"The tough cases," Kurt said. "I'm retired from the police department myself. City. These kinds of cases always got me in the heart."

"Missing persons?"

"Missing girls. Missing children." He looked down at the cupcakes. "I remember every single one." He looked up again, let out a breath to cleanse himself of the memories. "I will keep her in my prayers, Maeve, just like you said." Kurt pointed toward the back parking lot. "I'll send the crew over with some gravel. You've got a major pothole out there."

"I know," she said. "Don't remind me. It nearly swallowed the Prius last week."

"That's not good," he said.

"It's nice to have friends in high places," she said..

"Or low, depending on where we work," the older man said, smiling back. "I'll make sure it's taken care of, Maeve."

She watched him go, calling after him again to wish Mark a happy birthday, and then stood in the quiet, empty kitchen, staring out the window over the sink, hoping against hope that she would see Taylor coming along the sidewalk to the store, looking for her mother, for five dollars maybe, for a ride to the mall.

But there was nothing except the sight of cars driving back and forth along the road that ran adjacent to the river; a tree beyond that; someone else, not Cal, pushing a baby in a stroller.

The people who had been in the front of the store—the chief, Chris, two uniforms, and Trish—exited through the kitchen, Trish's expression inscrutable as she pushed through the back door and into the parking lot. Maeve wasn't listening to Chris as he told her that he'd be back, he'd see her later, he hoped she was okay. She was thinking about that look on her new employee's face. It wasn't as mysterious or inscrutable as Maeve had thought at first. It was very clear, in fact. In it was the one sentiment that Maeve had feared would take hold.

It said: It's all your fault.

CHAPTER 5

That night, after the store closed, Heather, with a disconsolate shrug of her shoulders, acknowledged that she knew Taylor was missing but didn't know what the big deal was. "Maybe she went to visit her boyfriend."

"Does she have a boyfriend?" Maeve asked, slicing some chicken from a roaster for Heather's dinner.

Another shrug. "I don't know."

"Well, do you know her at all? You're in the same class. What is she like?" Maeve asked, putting the knife down and stirring some gravy on the stove. "Potatoes?" she asked.

"Yes." Roast chicken was one of Heather's favorite dinners, and Maeve had hoped that by cooking a bird along with gravy, stuffing, and mashed potatoes, she could ease the vise that seemed to be around Heather's heart and mind where her mother was concerned.

"So, what is she like?" Maeve asked again.

"Plays soccer. Hates her mother. Works at Walmart. What else do you want to know? She's just like everyone else."

Maeve winced, the statement hitting her in her emotional gut. She had once read a book in which the advice from the "expert" had been "Don't take your daughter's barbs personally. Her brain is underdeveloped, and she says things to purposely hurt you." That had been the worst $24.95 Maeve had ever spent. She already knew a lot of what was in that book, but short of becoming a robot there was no way she could listen to the things Heather said to her and not take them personally. Almost every single word she used was meant to wound in one way or another, whether in a passive-aggressive way or just a plain old aggressive way. "She hates her mother?" Maeve asked as innocuously as she could.

"Everyone hates their mothers right now," she said. "Don't you remember hating . . ."

But Heather had the good sense to stop herself short. Maeve's mother had died long before Maeve had had the opportunity to hate her. In Maeve's mind and in death, Claire Conlon was an angel now and had been even before she had been killed in a hit-and-run by a neighbor, a crime for which he had escaped unscathed.

"Sorry, Mom," Heather said, closing down that aspect of the conversation. "Taylor plays soccer. She was on the team for one year with Rebecca, wasn't she?"

"Yes." She didn't remember seeing Trish at a lot of games, but back then, her mind had been on other things. Her divorce. The store. Her father and his deteriorating mind and body. Murder. There hadn't been a lot of room for other things, friendly pursuits. Other friends besides Jo.

"Maybe Rebecca remembers something."

Maeve put Heather's meal in front of her, her daughter bending her head, her hair falling forward, as she took in the scent of the chicken and the gravy. "Thanks, Mom."

"You're welcome." Maeve wanted to lean over and kiss the top of Heather's head, smell the scent that she knew like the back of her hand—sweet, honeylike—but she resisted. Heather had thawed, if only slightly, and Maeve didn't want to do anything that would form that wall of ice again.

Heather pushed some potatoes around on her plate. "She's still missing?"

"As far as I know."

"Her mother must be worried."

"That's probably an understatement." Maeve hadn't meant for it to sound as harsh as it came out. "Yes. She is. More than I can imagine." *And I've worried about you a lot. More than you can ever imagine.*

"She's got to be around here somewhere," Heather said. "Why is everyone losing their shit over this?"

Maeve didn't know. But as soon as she got Chris Larsson alone, she would ask him that very question.

She fingered the brochure for the Mississippi trip, which she had left on the counter, hoping Heather would look at it and have some kind of epiphany. *Yes! Mississippi! That's what I need to do!* But the brochure was right where Maeve had left it, and if Heather had seen it, she hadn't let on. Maeve picked it up. "Heather, I don't know if you saw this . . ."

"I did. Don't bring it up."

"Well, I just thought . . ."

"That what? That I should go build toilets or schools or houses for people in Mississippi? There are people right here, Mom, who need our help."

Like mother, like daughter. It was the same thought Maeve had had.

"So why don't you help them?" Maeve asked, crumbling the brochure in her hand.

"Who?"

"The people here who need help."

Behind Maeve, there was a knock at the door, ending the conversation. The sight of Chris Larsson's face, illuminated by the porch lamp, did nothing to lighten her mood. She plastered a fake smile on her face and walked down the hallway, leaving Heather to finish eating and put the dishes in the dishwasher. The girl's mood darkened considerably when she saw her mother's cop boyfriend at the front door, a bottle of wine in one hand and a pizza box balanced on the other. Heather took one look at him and made a beeline for the basement, professing to have laundry to do. There was only one problem with that excuse: Heather had never done her own laundry, claiming that the new washing machine Maeve had bought the year before was too "complicated" to use. Maeve had to admit that her daughter had a point; it had taken her no fewer than five loads of laundry to figure out exactly how to start the machine on the first try, the front of it blinking furiously as Maeve punched every button on the keypad. She had finally gotten the hang of it, but not without a lot of cursing and swearing at whoever thought that a washing machine needed a computer.

Maeve opened the front door and let him in. "This is a surprise."

"What a day," he said, walking into the kitchen and placing the pizza on the counter. "I need to shake off everything that's happened."

"I'm sure you do," Maeve said, taking two mismatched wine glasses from the cabinet over the sink. One was a red wine glass, the other a white wine glass from a collection that seemed to be dwindling quickly. "Do you want chicken? Or do you want pizza?" Maeve noticed that it was from her favorite place a town over, and although her chicken and gravy was one of his favorites as well, they both opted for the pizza so they could eat outside without making too much of a mess.

They each made a plate and took it outside. Cal had installed a porch swing after they had gotten divorced—some kind of home renovation peace offering, she supposed—and Maeve had put new cushions on it at the beginning of the summer. They had weathered the heat and the rain nicely. She settled into the side of the swing she considered hers and stabilized herself until Chris lowered his much bigger body onto the other side. She gave him a long kiss to let him know just how much she had missed him over the last few days.

"I missed you, too," he said. "I thought we were going to get some time together, but with this girl going missing . . ."

"Yeah, that," Maeve said. "Why was everyone so concerned about her so soon after she didn't show up at home? If that had been Heather, I would have given it a couple of hours, and if nothing bad had happened, she would have shown up eventually. Kids need to eat, after all," Maeve said, attempting a joke that fell flat. "But really. It was an all points bulletin immediately. What's going on?"

Chris took a long sip of wine, a screw-top cabernet that Maeve knew was one of his favorites. "I don't want to say too much."

"Like what?" Maeve asked. She had proven to him already that she could keep a secret or two, that she could be trusted.

"I really don't want to talk about it, Maeve," he said, but he really hadn't said anything at all. He stared straight ahead as he devoured first one piece of pizza and then a second. He paused before getting up to get a third to ask her a question. "Does Heather know this girl?"

"Told me she was a typical teen who hates her mother," Maeve said, trying to make it sound less hurtful than it had felt at the time.

Chris turned and looked at her, not responding. He was careful not to say too much about how Heather treated Maeve, but his eyes told Maeve that he didn't approve. "Another slice?"

She held up her plate. "Still have this one."

She could hear Chris's footfalls in the hallway when she saw Cal pull up in front of the house. She ran down the porch steps and to the curb, where she banged on the passenger-side window until he rolled it down. "What are you doing?" she said, trying to keep her voice at a whisper. The baby was in the backseat, and Cal had a radio station blaring that was playing a reggae version of "The Itsy-Bitsy Spider." She leaned in and blew the baby a kiss; no reason why he should feel the negativity emanating from her every pore. "Go home," she said.

"I need to talk to you," he said, lowering the volume on the radio. This elicited a low moan from the baby, followed by an ear-splitting shriek, and he turned it back up. "He loves this song."

"Go home," Maeve said, turning to see Chris coming from the house, two slices of pizza on his plate, a puzzled look on his face. "We're done." When Cal opened his mouth to protest, she banged her hand on the car door. "So, good night! I'll see you tomorrow!" she said, all fake cheer and happiness. "Thanks for stopping by, but we can work this out tomorrow!"

"We can't be done," Cal said to Maeve's back. She turned and mouthed, "But we are."

On the porch, Chris was eating his pizza and looking at the minivan. "Everything okay?"

"Tuition payment," Maeve said, hoping that the lie falling from her lips sounded better to Chris than to her own ears. "I thought he paid and he thought I paid . . ."

Chris chewed his pizza slowly, looking first at the car, its head-lights twinkling in the distance, and then back to Maeve. "I hate when that happens," he said, but his tone suggested that it was just filler, a way to respond to Maeve until he figured out what he really wanted to ask her.

Never lie to a cop. That was one piece of advice that Jack had given Maeve but she hadn't been able to take, having lied now to more than one cop in her life, her father included.

CHAPTER 6

Jo was waiting for her outside The Comfort Zone, in the parking lot, when Maeve showed up for work the next morning, her bike propped up against the brick building, Jack nowhere in sight.

"Where's the baby?" Maeve asked. "And why are you here?" she added, an alarm bell going off in her head. Jo had never been here this early when she had worked for Maeve; her early-morning appearance was concerning.

"First of all, my mother spent the night and told me to do whatever I wanted to do today."

Maeve narrowed her eyes. There had to be a catch.

"What I want to do, more than anything, is help you at the store again," Jo said, standing up and stretching. "Do you always open this early?" she asked, knowing well that Maeve did; otherwise, she wouldn't be by her friend's side, her work outfit of jeans and white T-shirt on her slim body, Doc Martens on her feet.

"You. Want to help me. At the store," Maeve said, her disbelief halting her speech. "I must be dreaming. You didn't even want to help me at the store when you actually worked here."

"Now, that's not nice," Jo said, but she knew it was true, smiling at the memories of having been Maeve's only real employee for many years. She followed Maeve into the kitchen. "Anything changed since I left? Everything still in the same place?"

"Nothing's changed. Everything's still in its place."

Jo donned an apron. "Still sleeping with your ex-husband?"

Maeve didn't answer immediately, choosing her words carefully. "Technically, no."

"Meaning?"

"Meaning that it happened once and it won't happen again." She pulled the money pouch out of her tote bag and threw it onto the counter. She sat down and started counting the money from the previous day's receipts, coming up short by four hundred dollars after three different attempts at settling the tally. "Jo, do me a favor. Count this?" she said, pushing the stack of bills toward her.

"Eight thirty," Jo said after riffling through the money. "Is that what you've got?"

Maeve nodded, even though she knew the total should have been well over a thousand dollars. She thought back to the day before, to Trish, to Evelyn, to everything that happened. Evelyn had been known to "borrow" the odd head band, or an old nail polish Maeve didn't even know she had. But money? That was a different story. Evelyn had her own money, and Maeve wasn't even sure she knew the value of it. Money held little interest for her. Relationships were her currency, and seeing Maeve and the girls was the thing she craved.

Back-to-school night came into her mind's eye, as did Trish's very short job interview.

Jo pulled some cupcake liners from the shelf in the pantry and set about putting them into a tin. "Just so you know, it's getting around. I don't think anyone knows it's you, but Patsy Morrow overheard Gabriela crying in the bathroom at the gym and telling someone else that she thought Cal was cheating."

"What?" Maeve asked. She looked down at the stack of bills, finally pushing them all into the money pouch and zippering it shut.

"Patsy Morrow. Gabriela. Crying at the gym."

"What's she got?" Maeve asked. She'd worry about the money later. "What does she know? Did they say?"

"Said he stayed out late a few nights, and one night in particular, when he came home, he smelled funny."

"Funny?" Maeve asked, sniffing her hands. They always smelled a bit like nutmeg, a little bit like cinnamon. There was always a smudge of icing under the cuticles. "Funny how?"

"I don't know," Jo said, concentrating on the cupcake tin. "Apparently, Gabriela burst into tears during spin class, jumped off her bike, and ran into the locker room. Of course, that was far too juicy for the rest of the spin class to ignore, so one or two women did reconnaissance and then reported back to the others."

"Good old Patsy," Maeve said, shaking her head. The village had more gossips than it needed, and Patsy was often in The Comfort Zone at one of the café tables, her head bent conspiratorially in the direction of some other disaffected housewife, dishing the dirt on someone who, nine times out of ten, had just left the store.

"You're done with that, right?" Jo asked. "The cheating? I kind of never took you for that kind of girl, Maeve."

"What kind of girl, Jo?" Jo herself had been known to blur the lines of what was right over the years, but Maeve guessed that now she was married and had a baby, her moral compass had recalibrated. "The kind of girl who gives in to something familiar and comforting?"

"Is this about your dad?" Jo asked.

"Oh, God no," Maeve said. Jo blamed every one of Maeve's emotions on her father dying, not realizing that of all the things she had been through, all of the traumas, that one had been the most normal and the easiest to move past. Yes, she missed him, but he had been old and frail and, worst of all, had kept from her for her entire life the reality of a developmentally challenged sister, whom she now knew and loved. No, this had nothing to do with her father and everything to do with an unsettled score between her, her ex, and his second wife.

She wasn't proud to admit that, even though she only admitted it to herself.

"It was one time," Maeve said. "One. So why is this all around town?"

Jo voiced a thought that Maeve had had more than once. "Maybe there are others."

Maeve went to the sink and washed her hands. When had a roll in the hay with your ex become one of the top ten crimes committed against man? She looked down at her hands and scrubbed the icing from around her cuticles, Donna Fitzpatrick's Thulian pink more stubborn than any other color she had created. It was a mistake. It had happened once. Everyone could move on with their lives.

The back door opened, bringing with it the smell of the rain, which had started falling after Jo and Maeve had entered the store. Trish Dvorak came in, her face drawn, looking as if she had lost twenty pounds since the day before, attempting a smile to lighten the mood.

"Trish," Maeve said, her eyes going to the pouch on the counter. "I didn't expect you today."

Jo lifted her head and smiled sadly in greeting, returning to stuffing the cupcake tins with liners, a job that was taking an inordinately long time. The more things change, Maeve thought, the more they stay the same.

"I can't sit around the house, Maeve, so I wanted to come in. To do something normal," Trish said, doing her best not to cry but failing. "I can't not work," she said. "I have to work. I have to make money."

Jo stopped what she was doing. "I'm going to go out front and get ready for the morning rush," she said, picking up the money bag and taking it with her. "Take your time. I can handle whatever we get."

Maeve pulled out a stool and told Trish to sit. She pulled a muffin from the refrigerator and put it in the microwave to warm up before she went into the front to get some coffee. She had one pot that was on a timer so the coffee was ready when she arrived every morning, one of Cal's suggestions that she had employed. Trish picked at the muffin but drank the coffee, silent in the kitchen.

"Nothing on Taylor, Trish?" Maeve said as gently as she could.

"Nothing."

"What's the next step, then?" Maeve asked, thinking that she would have asked Chris, but he didn't seem to want to talk about the case or anything having to do with the girl's disappearance.

"I don't know."

"Do you think maybe she ran away?" Maeve asked.

Trish looked up at her. "Your boyfriend asked me the same thing," she said, her tone sharp. "No. I don't think she ran away."

"Her father? Maybe she went there?" Maeve was assuming there was a father somewhere; maybe the girl had gone to him.

"Taylor never would have gone there."

"A boyfriend?"

Trish gave Maeve a hard look. "What are you a cop now? What's with all of the questions?"

"I'm sorry. I was just wondering . . ."

"What? What were you wondering, Maeve?"

"I was wondering if she had any reason to want to leave Far-ringville," Maeve said. To her, it was a legitimate question. To Trish, obviously, it was as if Maeve had thrown a verbal Molotov cocktail into the conversation.

"What were you wondering? If our home life was so bad that having a mother who can't afford the things everyone else has was enough to make her want to leave? That living in an apartment behind a half-empty strip mall embarrassed her and made her want to run? That not being able to pay for college is the only thing she thinks about because it's the only thing I think about? Is that what you were wondering, Maeve?"

Maeve wasn't wondering that, but she did question how the conversation had taken such a wrong turn, how it had become a conversation on the socioeconomic realities of life as a single mother. She wanted to remind Trish that she was a single mother, too, and practically had to break her back to make ends meet, but the woman didn't seem to want to hear anything. A deep-seated hostility came off Taylor's mother in waves.

"Maybe you should take a few days off, Trish. Focus on finding Taylor. I'll get by here," Maeve said, hoping that she wouldn't have to be more forceful in her suggestion. The woman's hostility coupled with the missing cash was all Maeve needed to convince her that she was doing the right thing after having done the wrong thing in hiring Trish so precipitously. "I'll need help for Founders Day if you want to come back in a few weeks."

Trish looked at her. "Are you firing me?"

"No. I'm not firing you. You have other things to attend to. You have to find your daughter. Coming to work every day may not be the best thing for you right now."

But Trish wasn't buying what Maeve was selling.

"Really. Come back when Taylor comes home," Maeve said.

"And what if she doesn't come home?" Trish asked, clearly without any hope that the situation would change. Maeve just couldn't figure out why. There had to be more to this story than she knew, and by the look on Trish's face, Maeve wasn't sure she wanted to know.

Jo poked her head into the kitchen. "There's a kid here from the high school who says you have something for him. A donation?"

Trish was silent as Maeve rooted around her desk for the envelope with her donation for the Mississippi trip. "Here. Give this to him."

"Bye, Trish," Jo said, making herself scarce, wanting to be part of the drama and eschewing it at the same time.

Maeve turned back to the bereft mother, the woman with the shortest employment in history on record at The Comfort Zone, trying to find some kind of common ground with her. "Trish, you have to have hope. Chris and everyone else in the police department are going to do everything they can to find her." Now she was defending the Farringville police, who, as a group, sometimes needed a little help in the investigation department. They tried, but for something like this, Maeve suspected that they were all in way over their collective head, something she would never articulate to Chris.

Trish stood next to the counter for a few minutes, looking at Maeve for an uncomfortably long time. "Thanks for nothing, Maeve," she said.

"Founders Day, Trish. I'll need help." Maybe in the meantime she would find out that she had lost the money herself, that Trish wasn't to blame. Until then, and only then, she would stand by her decision.

"I don't need help in a few weeks, Maeve, I need help now."

With nowhere else to look, Maeve looked up at the ceiling, thinking. Having Trish in the store didn't seem like the right thing, particularly in light of the missing cash, not to mention her missing daughter. Trish took the silence to mean that Maeve was standing her ground, that she didn't want her back.

"Thanks for nothing," she said again.

She needed someone to blame. Maeve could see that. She remembered the advice of the adolescent-expert author and tried not to take it personally, but Trish's anger was ten times stronger than it had ever been from either of her daughters. Like an altercation with a teen, the ones the author claimed had underdeveloped brains, this conversation had gone south quickly, and there was no getting it back on track. Maeve watched as Trish exited the kitchen and got into her car, the engine roaring to life just before she drove away, leaving a trail of exhaust in her wake.

Jo came back into the kitchen. "She's a mess."

"Understandably so," Maeve said, wrapping her arms around herself. She looked at Jo. "If I give you a three-dollar an hour raise and you only have to work from eleven to close, will you come back?"

Jo smiled. "I thought you'd never ask."

CHAPTER 7

Heather had the late shift at the grocery store that night, something that Cal knew and tried to take advantage of. He showed up at Maeve's a little past eight, and although she wasn't expecting him exactly, she'd had a feeling he'd show up, despite their last conversation.

She didn't open the door. "I wasn't kidding."

"Don't worry. We're safe," Cal said, letting himself in. "Larsson is working the night shift. I saw him at Dunkin' Donuts."

"Maybe he was just getting a coffee."

"Or maybe he was getting a doughnut." Cal shrugged off his sweatshirt and hung it on the newel post. "As cops do."

"I don't know why you don't like him, Cal," Maeve said, picking up the sweatshirt when it fell to the ground. "He's a great guy. I love him, actually."

Cal raised an eyebrow. "Really? You love him? Could you?" He waved a hand in the space between the two of them. "With this going on?" He leaned in and nuzzled her neck. "This is kind of hot, don't you think?"

It had started out innocently enough, a mistake that she wasn't planning on making or repeating. The summer coming to an end, he had come to pick up Heather, forgetting about her job at the grocery store, that on certain nights she worked late. Rather than drive the one mile home to his gorgeous, spacious Tudor, complete with adorable toddler and gorgeous wife, he had elected to stay to wait for his daughter, diving into the bottle of Falanghina that Maeve had opened up for herself and had planned to finish. She was three-quarters of the way through it, her senses pleasantly dulled, when he arrived, telling her things she didn't want to hear. Gabriela didn't love him. It wasn't working. He needed a change. It was all stuff she had heard before, and it bored her, but that night, delicious white wine running through her veins, she felt loose. And he felt familiar. So she had let him kiss her once, and then kiss her again, knowing it was a mistake, understanding that it could never happen again but powerless to stop it. Before she knew it, it was more than she had bargained for, a cry leaving her lungs that she hadn't heard herself utter since her marriage had ended.

She had awoken the next morning with a pounding headache, and had leaned over the sink while filling her palm with water and drinking it down, the thought of what she had done not eliciting the feelings she had expected upon awaking. There was no shame, there was no guilt. There was one strange, unfamiliar feeling, a feeling she shouldn't have had.

Satisfaction.

He had left her so unceremoniously years earlier, and that wound, she had come to find, had never closed. Now, the morning after, the feeling of his chest and his cheek and his mouth all coming back to her, she remembered when it had been good before it had become bad. It wasn't her; it wasn't that she wasn't attractive enough, or adventurous enough, or sexy enough. It was him and what he needed and wanted. And what he wanted right now was her, and that was enough.

She had looked at herself in the mirror the next morning. She looked the same; she smelled the same, with maybe a little more cinnamon about her than a normal woman. She was exactly the same except that now, she was no longer the dowdy ex-wife, the junker that had been traded in for a new model, but the shiny new thing that her ex-husband—him with his self-diagnosed adult-onset ADHD—couldn't get enough of.

"We're done with this, Cal," she said, pushing him away now. "I was just about to have some leftovers, and you're welcome to join me. But if you're not hungry, then you should go home. To your *wife*." She pulled the leftover chicken out of the refrigerator, the containers with the mashed potatoes and gravy, the plastic-covered bowl of string beans. She knew that at his house, carbs were never on the menu and gravy was something of an urban legend, served at the local Greek diner but never in the Tudor. Beside her in the small kitchen, she could practically feel Cal salivating over the feast that she was about to prepare, even though it was two days old.

"Where's Devon?" she asked.

"With Gabriela. She's making an effort to get home earlier so she can spend time with him."

"Really?" Maeve asked. In the child's short life, Maeve had never seen his mother hold him. "Why the change of heart?"

"She doesn't like the baby stage. Now that he's a toddler, she's bonding with him more. He can talk now. Interact. She likes that."

Maeve prepared two plates of leftovers and put one at a time in the microwave. "And where does she think you are tonight, Cal?"

"Bible study at church."

"I don't know whether to laugh or gag."

"You can do both." He came up behind her and put his arms around her waist. "I'm really bad," he whispered. "I probably *should* go to Bible study."

"You probably should. You should throw in a couple of stints in the confessional as well." Maeve pulled his plate out of the microwave and placed it on the table. She was one to talk. "Here. Eat this."

He dived into the food like a man on death row eating his last meal. "I forgot how much I love your gravy."

"It's all about the roux," she said, pouring them both a glass of wine and joining him at the table with her own plate. "Listen, Cal. I'm not kidding. This has to stop."

He looked up from his plate long enough to give her a Bronx cheer. "Says who?"

"Says your wife."

He dropped his fork onto his plate and gave her his undivided attention.

"She had a meltdown during spin class, and someone overheard her telling a friend that she thinks you're cheating."

"Huh," he said.

"We're done. The thought of her crying at the gym is not one I want to carry around."

"You feel sorry for her? After everything?" Cal asked.

"I feel sorry for any woman who is saddled with a lying, cheating asshole for a husband."

He looked, at that moment, as if he felt coming here had been a huge mistake, the delicious gravy notwithstanding.

"Are you sleeping with someone else? Other women?" Maeve asked.

His denial was so vociferous and swift that it had to be a lie; she knew him well, something he failed to take into account. "No!

How could you even imply that?" He pushed his plate away. "You really know how to break a mood, Maeve."

She didn't believe him but that didn't matter. "It's my gift," she said. "More potatoes?"

He crossed his arms over his chest. "No. No more potatoes."

"Lost your appetite?" she asked.

He had the same expression on his face that Heather used to get when Maeve put her in time-out. His plans for the evening changed, he pushed his chair back. "I'm gonna go. Will you bring Heather over later?"

"No."

"No?"

"No," she said. "Cal, I won't bring Heather over later because you're in a snit because I won't sleep with you and you refuse to wait for her. I won't bring Heather over because I'm completely exhausted from work and from lying awake at night wondering where Taylor Dvorak may have gone. I won't bring Heather over because it's your responsibility to make sure she gets to your house when she is supposed to be there." She realized she was yelling. "I won't."

He grabbed his sweatshirt on the way out. "Remember when I said that you had changed?"

Maeve was halfway between the kitchen and the front door, her hands wound up in a dish towel.

"Well, you haven't," he said, pulling the sweatshirt over his head. "You're exactly the same." He slammed the screen door on the way out, not unlike an adolescent being sent to his room.

Maeve watched him drive off in the minivan and, without a second thought, returned to her leftovers, scraping his uneaten food onto her plate and having herself a feast.

CHAPTER 8

Jo found a daycare in town that would take Jack for the hours she needed and came to work the next day complaining that her husband, Doug, was none too happy that the stay-at-home wife and mother he thought he married was really someone who, if she spent another minute pushing the baby's swing at the park and didn't go back to work at least part-time, might go completely insane.

"He's kind of old-fashioned," Jo said, stating the obvious. Maeve had known that from the moment she met the guy, touting Jo's pot roast on her single friend's behalf; that was all he needed to hear to make a beeline for the divorcée, and it wasn't long before they were engaged, getting married, and having the baby Jo always wanted. "But I told him that I would be a better wife if I could get out of the house for a few hours every day."

Maeve turned and looked at her. "Who are you?" Gone was the free spirit that Maeve had become friends with, and in her place was a woman who promised to become a "better wife."

"I know, I know," Jo said, grabbing a bottle of window cleaner and a rag and spraying the glass counter in the front of the store. "I can hardly believe some of the things that come out of my mouth."

She rubbed at a crusted bit of icing. "Hey, this is a nice color. What is it? Is it 'Fitzpatrick pink'?"

"Yes, it's a cross between Thulian pink and salmon," Maeve said. "The Fitzpatrick twins are being christened tomorrow. You have no idea what I've been through with Donna."

"I can only imagine. I run into her at the park occasionally, and it's 'organic' this and 'gluten-free' that." Jo pointed at the smudged icing. "I guess that only counts when cupcakes aren't concerned. I'm surprised she didn't ask you to incorporate the twins' placenta into the batter." Jo opened the drink case and counted the number of iced teas on the right side. She turned to Maeve. "Thirty-six. I think we're good for a while."

Maeve rearranged some cakes in the case, making sure that the tart she had made the day before was front and center, so hopefully it would be gone by the end of the day.

Jo had made a few notations about the drink inventory on a napkin that she handed to Maeve. "Anything on Taylor?" Jo asked. "Someone put a sign in front of our house with her photo and a number to call with information. That was fast. I didn't think you could get signs printed that quickly."

"I only know what I've seen on the news, Jo. And it doesn't sound like there have been any leads."

Jo stopped what she was doing and stood up straight. "I don't know if I would have understood this as well before Jack. But right now, when I think of that girl and where she might be or what could have happened, I get a little sick."

"Me, too."

"A lot sick, actually."

Maeve knew the feeling. "The last two days have been hell, Jo. I can't stop thinking about where she might have gone." Maeve pulled a newspaper from the stack by the front door. On the front page of the local paper, Taylor's photo was large and surrounded by text. Maeve was struck by how at first glance, the photo could have been of Heather; the girls had similar looks. Long brown hair. Brown eyes. A grim set of lips. Similar facial bone structure.

Jo went into the kitchen as Maeve was spreading the paper open to continue reading the story of the investigation past the front page. It didn't seem that a lot had changed or that the police had any leads. One tip said that she had been spotted on a southbound train, heading toward the city, even though the police had been all over the station asking people who had been there. Another said that she was seen walking along the side of the road by the dam. Still another reported that she had been seen in the middle of town, carrying a coffee cup, looking like she didn't have a care in the world.

Chris Larsson came in the front of the store, the pleasant jingle of the bell above the door at odds with his stern face, his serious demeanor. His usual greeting—"Hiya, beautiful"—accompanied by a kiss or a hug, was replaced with a barely audible sigh and a tone that suggested this wasn't a social call. Maeve grabbed a blueberry muffin from under the footed stand and put it on a napkin anyway. The guy was a sucker for her muffins, and she hoped that one bite would change his black mood.

She came around the counter and joined him at a café table by the drink case. "That's a lot of iced tea," he remarked.

"Biggest seller," she said, wondering why things were so uncomfortable. A tingling starting at her toes accompanied the dreaded thought that flashed through her head.

He knows.

But he started with something else. "Tell me again what you said to the school nurse."

Maeve squirmed in her chair. She wasn't used to being on the other end of a line of questioning, and the fact that it was Chris doing the questioning made it more uncomfortable, not less. "I told you everything already, Chris."

"Tell me again."

"Judy called and said that Taylor had a headache that she was afraid was going to turn into a migraine. She said she wanted to go home. I asked if she needed a ride, and she said that Taylor was going to walk home." Maeve looked at him expectantly.

"Is that it?" he asked.

"Is that what?" Maeve asked, unable to keep the annoyance out of her voice. "Yes. That's it."

"A girl is missing, Maeve," Chris said, as if that needed to be repeated.

"I get that."

"So anything else you might remember would be helpful."

"There's nothing else, Chris," Maeve said. "What's going on here?"

Chris pushed the untouched muffin toward her and stood, his face still grim, no evidence of his usually playful demeanor beneath the surface. "Judy Wilkerson said that Taylor was very ill and needed a ride, but that you refused to pick her up."

The sentence was so far from the truth that it nearly took Maeve's breath away.

Chris continued. "She said it was your idea to let her go home alone."

CHAPTER 9

All around town, signs like the one Jo had described had popped up on lampposts, on telephone poles, in front of people's houses.

HAVE YOU SEEN TAYLOR?

A large photo accompanied the query, the same one that Maeve had seen in the newspaper and that was now the official photo of the missing-person case. There wasn't one lawn, or so it seemed, that didn't have a sign, not unlike the kind you would see during village elections, when red signs appeared on some lawns, blue on others.

Maeve was still reeling from Chris's revelation earlier that day about Judy Wilkerson. Maeve hadn't had much to do with the school nurse over the years, but she hadn't thought she was a liar, or someone who would go to great lengths to maneuver the truth into a space that would cast her in a better—more blameless—light. Rebecca was one of those perfect-attendance kids and was loath to miss a school day, or even come home sick in the middle of the day if she had a sore throat or felt nauseous. Heather, despite being a pain in Maeve's ass, had a pretty good attendance record as well, so

Maeve's contact with Judy throughout her girls' high school years had been minimal.

She left Jo to close the store. She parked in the one tiny spot she could find, sandwiched between a sleek convertible and a big SUV. While she waited for the students with cars to drive away and the buses to transport other kids had left the parking lot, she thought about her conversation with the detective. She'd been flabbergasted when Chris told her what Judy said, shocked that the school nurse would tell a lie so blatant to cover her own ass. And even if Maeve had done what Judy said, had said to send Trish home, why did Judy listen to Maeve? That was some faulty logic there that even Chris couldn't make work. He'd looked perplexed, but when he heard what Maeve had to say, that it hadn't been her idea, he had believed her. She thought. Before he left, there was no hug, no kiss, no promise of a late-night drop-in to see her once more before the day ended. It was just him, a trace of incredulity still on his handsome face, professing to believe Maeve. He didn't know, and he never would, that she did keep some secrets from him, but this wasn't one of them. What this was was one school nurse trying to keep her job after making what turned out to be a tragic error in judgment, despite her following protocol. And the law. Let's not forget that, Maeve thought as she watched kids stream out of the school.

When it was clear that the school was down to just the regular staff and a few student stragglers, Maeve got out of her car and walked through the back doors and up to the second floor. The smell of the place brought her right back to her own high school days; the smell of teenage funk and old lunch meat was the odor of every high school in America, or so it seemed.

Judy Wilkerson was sitting behind her desk doing paperwork when Maeve knocked. "Maeve, hi," she said, her eyebrows rising at

Maeve's appearance in her doorway. "What can I do for you? Terrible thing about Taylor, right?"

Maeve closed the door behind her. The office itself was incredibly small, adjacent to the room that held the cots for sick kids and the area for the ones who awaited a pickup by a parent. Maeve poked her head into the room and determined that it was all clear before sitting down in front of Judy. She had thought about how this would go: if she would ask after family first; if she would make small talk, a little chitchat, before getting into the reason for her visit. When she saw Judy's face staring across at her, both of those ideas went out the window. "What you can do for me," Maeve said, "is tell me why you lied about our conversation to Chris Larsson."

Maeve could almost see the wheels turning in the other woman's head, the smoke that her thought process was producing under a copse of dyed-blond tresses, a spiky pixie cut on a woman far too old to be sporting one. Clearly she fancied herself "the cool nurse," one who would be down for a rap session with her high school students. "What do you mean?"

There were a few things Maeve hated. Obtuseness was one of them. She leaned forward and put one hand on Judy's desk. "Let's not play games, Judy. Our conversation was short and sweet. I asked you if it was okay to send Taylor home, and you said that it was fine."

"That was before she disappeared."

"So the conversation changes based on the outcome? If she had arrived home and her mother had raised a fuss, would you have still thrown me under the bus, so to speak? Or would you have handled it like an adult, telling the truth?" Maeve watched Judy's face for any sign that she understood just how angry she was, how angry she could really get. There was none. "You need to tell Chris Larsson that I questioned you before telling you it was okay, that I wondered if it was standard procedure to let the girl go home by herself."

"But that's not what happened, Maeve," Judy said. "That's not what you said."

Maeve felt as if she were having an out-of-body experience. She remembered the conversation word for word. "So which is it, Judy? That you lied after you found out that Taylor disappeared or that you remember an entirely different conversation, one that, if you indeed heard it that way, speaks to an inability on your part to do your job?" Maeve said, losing her breath midsentence. "Because if that's what you heard, then you are either deaf or have dementia." She leaned back in her chair, afraid of what she might do to this school nurse, someone for whom pushing paper around on her desk came so naturally, it seemed to be her calling.

Judy stared at her for so long that Maeve feared she had gone into a trance. Her blue eyes, unblinking, held Maeve's gaze, the silence in the room finally broken by the principal's voice coming over the PA system, asking that Judy come to his office as soon as possible. Judy stood. "I know what I heard, Maeve."

Maeve stood in front of the door. "Well, you heard wrong."

"What? You're going to trap me in my office?"

Maeve realized that as much as she wanted to trap Judy Wilkerson in her office, keep her there until she admitted that she lied, it was a faulty gambit and one that would only result in Maeve finding herself in the local paper's police blotter. That was the last thing she needed, particularly if she was now not getting the Emergency Contact of the Year award for "refusing," as Judy had told Chris, to pick Taylor up. "If I hear anyone repeat what Chris Larsson told me yesterday or see it reflected in any news account of Taylor's disappearance, Judy, I will—" Maeve stopped herself, straightening when she saw the look on Judy's face. Great. Now she was Maeve Conlon,

Crazy Baker. It would be all over the school, then the village, and reported to the police if she didn't back down, let this go. "Thank you for your time, Judy," she said, the buzzing in her head alerting her to the fact that at any moment, she was prone to losing it completely. She smoothed her hair back and squared her shoulders, righting her emotional compass.

She backed away from the door and let Judy through. After counting to ten and getting her breathing back to normal, she left the office and walked down the hall, her clogs making a squeaking noise in her wake, sounding like *it's your fault, it's your fault, it's your fault,* following her all the way to the asphalt of the parking lot.

Maeve drove through town, up and down village streets, not sure what she was looking for, not sure what she was hoping to find. She drove past Cal's, where she saw an unfamiliar car parked out front, no sign of Gabriela's little red sports car, a completely impractical Audi TT that fit Gabriela, her giant purse, and nothing else. It was a weekday; she was at work. Cal was alone during the week, sometimes until late into the evening when Gabriela had a photo shoot to oversee or a magazine layout to finalize before she went home. As Cal often said, "That damned magazine doesn't print itself."

No, but it kept them in that gorgeous Tudor and him as a stay-at-home dad with far too much time on his hands. Maeve noticed that he, too, had a sign on his front lawn beseeching someone, anyone, to call the police with a tip regarding Taylor's whereabouts, where she had last been seen. She pulled over to the curb a few feet down from his house and kept an eye on the front door in the sideview mirror, wondering just who Cal Callahan was entertaining at a little after three in the afternoon. The car wasn't a minivan, and a quick glance as she had driven by indicated that there was no car seat in the back of the beat-up Honda Accord, so her curiosity was piqued.

She would put nothing past him, but prayed, nonetheless, that whoever was in the house was giving him an estimate on new tile for the front foyer or fixing a wonky toilet, one that had been running at all hours of the night, disturbing the beauty sleep of Mrs. Callahan #2, a woman far more likely than she had ever been to take him to task for falling down on the job of crossing off chores on the honey-do list.

Maeve scrolled through her phone, looking for something besides an online order to occupy her time. A sexy text from Chris. A funny joke from Jo. But there was nothing except Donna Fitzpatrick's plea for an extra dozen cupcakes, same color frosting, please, and an e-mail from Maeve's heating company informing her that this winter, her oil bill was going to go up considerably.

She put her phone away and watched Cal's front door for movement. Finally, after fifteen minutes, a quarter hour in which Maeve wasn't sure if she had fallen asleep or not, the door opened and a woman came out.

Maeve wondered what business Trish Dvorak might have with Cal.

CHAPTER 10

"I couldn't stay away," he said, as they lay together on the sofa in her living room. Maeve had made sure that Heather was at the library before allowing things to go as far as they had.

"I missed you." She wriggled out from under him, grabbing her wine glass from the coffee table. "I have to be honest: I don't really like Detective Chris Larsson."

"Sometimes, I don't like him either," he said. "He's kind of serious."

"And sort of scary."

"Really? Scary?" He seemed proud of that. "How so?"

She wasn't kidding. "Do you really want to go there?" They were having a nice time; did he really want to hear that she was disappointed in the way he had handled Judy's lie, even if he didn't immediately know that it wasn't the truth? Did he want to know that what she expected in a partner was complete trust in what she said, a lone sexual encounter with her ex-husband notwithstanding?

He touched his lips to hers. "I'm sorry. I sometimes forget that not everyone has deep, dark secrets."

She tried to hold his gaze, but she closed her eyes and kissed him instead so that she didn't have to see herself reflected in his irises, telling herself that she was a liar, plain and simple, and he was the nicest guy any woman could ask for or even dream up.

Outside, a car drove past, slowing and then stopping in front of her house. She didn't need a crystal ball to tell her that it was Cal, checking up on her, letting her know that he was there but smart enough to know he would be unwelcome. She had her own part-time stalker, someone not industrious enough to put a lot of work into the task, using his baby's bedtime as an excuse to get the little lad to sleep while finding out if his ex-wife was being visited by her boyfriend. She was sure she'd hear about that the next time they saw each other, which would be their meeting with Heather's guidance counselor about college applications.

"I'm hungry," Chris said.

In the kitchen, Maeve threw together a chicken salad, toasting some leftover bread that she had brought home from the store. After a few minutes, she plated two sandwiches and refilled their wine, the two of them sitting at her small kitchen table and eating in silence.

"This is a tough one," Chris said finally.

"I can only imagine."

"Not a lot goes on in this town, and that's why I like it here."

"Me, too," she said. "Another sandwich?"

"No," he said, patting his stomach. "I've gained seven pounds since we started dating."

"Then my work here is done," she said. "And by the way, I hadn't noticed."

"Well, the guys at the station did. All I hear is how I'm getting fat since dating Maeve Conlon, the best baker this side of the Hudson."

"Is that what they call me?" she asked, blushing.

"That's what *I* call you." He pushed his plate away. "I'm amazed I can eat with this case. It's horrible."

Maeve knew there were other details that she wasn't privy to, and she wasn't sure she wanted to know what they were. She also knew that seeing Trish Dvorak coming out of Cal's house was not a good thing and was something she was going to keep to herself. "Anything? Any tips?"

"We get tips every day. She was here. She was there. 'I saw her at the mall.' 'She was at the Bronx Zoo.'" He rubbed his big hands over his face. "Cases like this bring out the crazy."

Maeve took his plate and scraped it into the garbage can. "So what do you do?"

"You run them down," he said. "And you call in County. Maybe the FBI. I don't know. We can't handle this, Maeve. As much as I'd like to think that the Farringville PD is capable of finding a missing girl, we're not. We bag business owners selling booze to minors and chase speeders. We try to keep kids off the streets and off drugs."

Heather's face flashed in front of Maeve's eyes. "And do business owners sell booze to minors?"

He chuckled. "Oh, yeah. There's not a kid in this town who can't get a six-pack when they want it. A lot of the shopkeepers around here have what I call loose standards when it comes to selling booze."

"Good to know," Maeve said. She pulled a piece of cake from the refrigerator. "Chocolate cake? It's your favorite."

He thought for a minute. "What the heck. I'm already turning into a fat slob. Will probably have a heart attack. Might as well go happy."

"Don't say that, Chris. About the heart attack." She sliced off a piece of her chocolate cake and put it on a plate, handing it to him. "Milk?"

"No, thanks," he said, taking a big bite. "Actually, yes, please," he said around a mouthful of chocolate.

"So there's nothing on Taylor's disappearance? Nothing at all?" Maeve asked.

He put his fork down, his appetite gone. "Nothing." He poked at the crumbs with his finger. "County says there's a missing person from a few towns up that they wonder about. A connection."

"Same kind of thing?" she asked.

"Yes."

"Did I hear about it?"

"I don't know. Maybe? It was last year." He picked his fork up again. "Sounds like a runaway to me and everyone else. Girls leave small towns and then . . ."

"Then what?" she asked when he didn't elaborate.

"They disappear. They never come back."

"That's horrible," she said.

He ate his cake in silence. She could see a sliver of a love handle pushing out the side of his shirt. He was right; he was putting on weight, but for some reason, it made her happy.

"You'll find her, right?" Maeve asked.

"That's my job."

But he didn't sound certain, and Maeve wasn't sure either of them believed he would get the job done. After he left, she turned on her computer and poked around, looking for the story about the case of the other missing girl.

Caroline Jerman, seventeen years old. Worked at the Rite Aid on Route 3, disappeared after work one night. No leads, no sightings.

It was as if she had vanished into thin air.

No mention of a father. Her mother had worked at Farringville Stone and Granite until it had shut down several years earlier. The former owner, Charles Connors, had offered a ten-thousand-dollar reward for any information leading to Caroline being reunited with her mother and sister.

Charles Connors. The name rang a bell. Maeve searched for him and found him, realizing that he had been at back-to-school night and had thanked her for her interest in his son's mission in Mississippi. He had been the sole owner of Farringville Stone and Granite and had incurred the wrath of its workers when he closed it down and sold the land to a developer. Maeve had been aware vaguely of this happening years before but hadn't paid too much attention, her focus on the girls and realizing her dream of becoming a business owner in her own right. The former stone yard was now home to a neighborhood of multimillion-dollar homes, contributing little in terms of taxes, ambience or respect for the town's historical roots.

Cal had accused her of being "checked out" to what happened in the village, and if this story was any indication, he was right. She didn't pay attention to local politics, and anyway, Farringville Stone and Granite wasn't technically in Farringville, being on the far edge of town, so what did it have to do with her? Not much. The people who had moved into the homes were mostly the type who didn't eat cupcakes or brownies or quiches, spending their time at the gym and at the waterfront, running and biking and trying to elude the inevitabilities of aging.

Of death.

Maeve smiled. If she was going to go, she was going to go happy, a little flesh on her bones, a glass of wine by her side. If not, what was the point?

She turned her attention back to Taylor. Although Maeve had deleted her fake Facebook profile six months earlier—too risky, a little too dangerous, even for her, to pretend to be a teenager—she still had the one associated with the store, so she could poke around the pages of various kids who she knew didn't have privacy settings on their own profiles. She went to Taylor's and saw that it hadn't been updated for almost a year. And of the kids whose profiles she viewed, kids that were in the same class as Heather and Taylor and should have been friends with the girl, they all had one thing in common: Not one of them seemed to care that a girl their age had disappeared, their lives carrying on with regularity. There were parties to attend and Homecoming dresses to get. Not one questioned the disappearance of her classmate, wondered where she had gone. No drama, no virtual gnashing of teeth. Not a prayer offered for her return.

It was as if no one really cared about Taylor Dvorak and didn't miss her, now that she was gone.

CHAPTER 11

Donna Fitzpatrick came in to pick up her cupcakes on Saturday morning, dressed for the babies' christening in a pale blue silk suit, three-inch pumps on her feet. She was either Spanxed to the max or had done an excellent job of losing the baby weight that she had accrued while carrying twins; Maeve subconsciously put her hands on her own fleshy hips and wondered why, almost eighteen years after giving birth, she still felt vaguely postpartum, still a little dumpy, always a lot tired.

Maeve hadn't sealed the cupcakes box, as she wanted Donna to see her handiwork before she covered them up. "See? On the spectrum between Thulian pink and salmon," she said.

Donna studied the cupcakes as if she were about to begin open-heart surgery on an anesthetized patient. "Okay," she said, the length of the two syllables leading Maeve to believe she wasn't happy.

"It's exactly what we discussed, Donna. Are you happy with the outcome?" Maeve asked. She heard Heather come through the door of the kitchen and then quickly retreat; the girl had heard enough about the Fitzpatrick twins and their special cupcakes to last a lifetime.

"I guess they will have to do, Maeve," she said, digging into her expensive handbag for her wallet.

If you weren't a new mother, you'd be on my hit list, Maeve thought. Don't think I have one? Guess again.

Maeve smiled. "I think they're gorgeous." She did. She had worked hard to get them just right, and so what if Donna was less than overwhelmed? That couldn't take away the fact that once her guests bit into one of Maeve's cupcakes, they would be overcome with gustatory delight.

"The gold leaf is a nice touch," Donna said, unconvinced, turning the box to get a look at the cupcakes from all angles. Finally, somewhat satisfied, she pulled out a platinum Amex and handed it to Maeve. "I'll take three quiches, too," she said. "I don't think we have enough food."

Maeve took three quiches from the refrigerated case and started wrapping them.

"Terrible thing about that girl, isn't it?" Donna asked while looking into the cake case.

"It's awful," Maeve said. "I can't imagine what Trish is going through." That was a lie. She could imagine it, and it was the worst feeling in the world.

Donna didn't meet her eye. "I want my babies to stay babies forever. At least I know where they are all the time, even if they are just crying and driving me crazy."

"Little children, little problems," Maeve said, reciting something she had heard a thousand times when the girls were small.

Donna lingered by the cookies. "I heard that you were the one who said she should go home alone. That you wouldn't go get her."

Maeve froze. Now I really have to kill someone, Maeve thought. The list was long, but she thought she might move Judy Wilkerson to the top of it, and if Donna didn't show a little sympathy toward

Maeve—believe what she had to say about the situation—babies or not, she was on the list, too. "That's not true, Donna. Taylor's almost eighteen and Judy though it was okay for her to go home on her own."

Donna focused on a giant red velvet cake, pointing at it with one lacquered nail. "How much?"

"Thirty-eight dollars," Maeve said. "Listen, I'd appreciate it if you could dispel the rumor that I said I was too busy to go over there." She laughed, hoping to offset her tense tone with some levity. "Everyone who shops here knows that I close the store at the drop of a hat."

Donna put her hands up. "I don't want to get involved. I don't know what happened."

"But you were here, Donna," Maeve said. "You heard the whole conversation. Remember? My sister was here that day?"

"Can I get my cupcakes?" Donna said.

Maeve closed the box and sealed it with a Comfort Zone sticker. She pushed the box across the counter along with the three quiches and rang up the order. "Do you need help getting these to the car?" Maeve asked.

"I've only got two hands!" Donna said, giving a mirthless chuckle and moving herself from low on Maeve's hit list to the number one spot. Sure, the kids would be motherless, but did Donna really bring any joy to anyone in this world? Maeve mulled that over as she walked into the back of the store to ask Heather to cover for her while she helped Mrs. Fitzpatrick to her car. She had pressed Heather into service today, giving Jo a "much-needed" day off, according to her returning employee, hoping that she and her daughter could have a little fun at work, catch up on everything in each other's lives. Instead, she got stony silence and one-word answers.

The more things change, she thought.

Donna's tiny sports car, short on cargo room, was packed to the gills, and Maeve had a hard time finding a place for the extra boxes in the order. Donna looked at her. "You'll have to deliver the rest of it." She saw Maeve eyeing the low-slung car. "My husband has the minivan," she said. "You have my address, right?"

Maeve did, but it was in the store, along with all of the other orders she needed to complete, and the to-do list that seemed to get longer every time she stepped out of the kitchen. "Remind me?"

"Fourteen Mockingbird Lane. Will you remember that?" Donna asked, putting on a pair of aviator-framed sunglasses.

"Mockingbird Lane? Like the street where the Munsters lived?" Maeve asked, thinking back to one of her favorite television shows from childhood.

"I don't know the Munsters, but if they lived on Mockingbird Lane, then yes, that's the street," Donna said.

Maeve didn't have the energy to get into it with Donna, to let her know that if the Munsters lived on her street, she'd know it. There would be no missing a guy with bolts in his neck and a wife who was a vampire. "Okay. See you in a few," Maeve said, then muttered, "You're welcome," under her breath as she watched Donna drive away in her impractical car.

She went through the store, her arms laden with boxes, and let Heather know that she'd be back as soon as she could.

She pulled into Donna's circular drive about fifteen minutes after having begun her trek. This was why she didn't know about the stone yard, the houses here, the people who lived in the gigantic homes: It was way out of the way, and Maeve was hard-pressed to remember a time she had last been here. Neither of the girls had had play dates out here, and Maeve certainly didn't have any friends for whom she would have made this schlep on a regular basis. She opened her trunk as a white-coated chef hurried out to relieve her of her haul and send her on her way. The "help" weren't seen here; that was clear.

Maeve pulled out onto the street and parked the car, taking a minute to meander through the neighborhood, wondering if she should have been more upset about the yard closing, the sudden development of homes cropping up out of a gorgeous landscape that sat high on a hill and overlooked a body of water that was also unknown to her. Metal canoes dotted its shore, leading her to believe that it fed into the reservoir, a place where only county-sanctioned watercraft could be launched. The view from above was spectacular; Charles Connors had been sitting on a prime piece of real estate and had sold the land for a small fortune, she guessed, incurring the wrath of the local environmentalists and longtime locals who would have preferred the jobs and the industry to the development of large, impressive homes.

Farringville was a place that appreciated its history and wanted to preserve it. The upcoming Founders Day celebration was a testament to that.

After she returned to the store, having been gone longer than she should have, Maeve had one of those off days, the kind where every fondant turned to cement, every sauce broke, every batter was wrong. She started over on the fondant, taking care to add water when necessary, just a little bit, so that it didn't tear when she tried to form a nice ball to wrap in plastic, thinking that with time and care, anything could change for the better. She just had to have patience, take her time, take things into her own hands. It had been in the back of her mind, she realized, the thought of a missing young girl. It wasn't about clearing her name. It was a new mission, a new reason to engage. She had done it the year before when she had found Evelyn, missing to her for many years, but whose whereabouts had been no secret to her father and his best friend; it would have been a hell of a lot easier if they had both been honest with her, but that was water under the bridge. The fact remained that she knew she had the chops to do what the Farringville Police Department couldn't, and she started thinking, as she stared at the plastic-wrapped fondant, about what those steps would be.

She would find her.

Using whatever means necessary.

In the front of the store, Maeve could hear a male voice extolling the virtues of her cupcakes, how his birthday had been "the best ever" because his father had brought him some of Maeve's treats. Maeve heard something unusual, something almost foreign, as well and realized it was the sound of Heather laughing. She peeked through the window in the kitchen door and saw Mark Messer, Kurt's son and one of her regular DPW customers, leaning on the counter, talking to Heather, making the girl laugh at whatever he was saying. In front of him was a large cup of coffee and half a doughnut, the other half of which he offered to Maeve's daughter, who took it and nibbled at it while they chatted.

Things could change with time. The relaxed girl eating the doughnut at the counter was evidence of that.

CHAPTER 12

"It's always a nice day when I get to see my old friend," he said, strolling into the coffee shop on Broadway later that afternoon.

Rodney Poole always characterized their relationship as one of friendship; Maeve thought it might be a bit more complicated than that. But there was something about his easy nature—the one that hid the dark truth about who he was and what he was capable of— that made it easy for her to pretend that what they were doing was what old friends did. Meet for coffee. Catch up on their lives. Talk about their kids.

He knew that Maeve didn't do casual meet-ups with him, though. Two years earlier, he had investigated her cousin's death. His murder, really, if Maeve wanted to be specific, a loss that she considered just and necessary. What had come from that was unexpected and strange but had grown into a comfortable relationship, one built on a secret that they both knew the other would keep. After they covered the usual topics, he looked across the table at her. "What's going on, my warrior queen?" he asked, using his nickname for her.

"I don't know if you've seen the news, but a girl went missing in Farringville."

"Yes. Saw that."

"She's the same age as Heather. Looks like her a bit, too, which is a little disconcerting," Maeve said, adding a creamer to her coffee.

"Friends with your daughter?"

"No. I don't get the sense Taylor had a lot of friends, really, but I could be making that up," Maeve admitted. In her mind, she had cast Taylor as an outcast, a loner. But she wasn't sure.

"Why are you involved?" he asked. "Was the girl abused? I know you can't abide that."

Maeve shook her head. "Not that I'm aware of." She recounted her phone call with Judy Wilkerson, the lies going around town. "People think that I wouldn't go get her, that somehow I am implicated in all of this."

"That's ridiculous," Poole said. "Anyone who knows you knows that's just ridiculous."

She sighed, relieved. No one understood her like Poole, someone she had only seen in person a handful of times. Life was complicated, and their relationship more so. She couldn't explain to anyone why that was, but they both understood, and that was the most important thing. "It's all over town." She looked out at the traffic going up and down the busy avenue, thinking that although she was a native of this borough, she was more content in sleepy Farringville, something she never would have imagined when she was growing up. "There was another girl, too. Last year."

"So what do you want to do, Maeve Conlon?" he asked.

"Tell me what you do," she said. "Tell me how you find someone."

He stared across the table at her as if he knew that trying to talk her out of it was an exercise in futility. "You start at the beginning,

where she was last seen. You pound the pavement. You talk to everyone who knew her, could have possibly seen her. You talk to her
friends. Her family. And you look at what you've got, every single
night, until one puzzle piece, usually the one that seems the most
innocuous, becomes the one that tells you 'This kid is a pawn in a
domestic dispute, a bad divorce.' Or 'This teenager is a runaway.'"
He paused. "'This person is dead.'"

She was silent. She had considered that Taylor might be dead—
everyone must have, without giving the notion voice—but she tried
not to think about it.

"So you want to find her because you're tangentially implicated
in her disappearance?" he asked. "Or something else?"

"It's always something else, Poole," she said, pushing her coffee
to the side, unable to drink it. It, or something else, was leaving a
bitter taste in her throat. "It's always about making sure that everyone is safe. Where they need to be."

He nodded. "I understand."

Their shared history—the abuse, the fear, the terror—made
them kindred spirits. That and the fact that he had once let her get
away with murder.

"How's your sister?" he asked.

"She's great," Maeve said, and that was the truth. There was no
one happier or healthier or more positive than Evelyn Rose Conlon.
Maeve felt a twinge of guilt at the mention of her sister. Evelyn
wanted to see her more often, but she would never understand how
many directions Maeve was pulled in, nor should she have to, in
Maeve's opinion. "I'm glad you asked about her."

"Why?"

"I've been thinking about something, about an unanswered
question."

"You hate those," he said.

She smiled. "I do. You're right about that."

"So what is it?"

"Right before he died, my father made me a DVD and told me that he wasn't my sister's father." She looked him in the eye as she said it, matter-of-fact, even though it was less matter-of-fact, more emotional, than she would ever let on. He knew, though. He always did. "It still is hard to say out loud."

Poole wisely didn't respond.

"He took care of her and made sure she was safe, but he wasn't her biological father."

Poole knew her well. "And you want to know who is."

"Exactly."

Poole pursed his lips. "Not exactly my forte, Maeve Conlon." He thought for a moment. "Who's on the birth certificate?"

"My father."

"So they had some help there, maybe. Someone to fudge the paternity." He shrugged. "I don't know. Just a guess."

The same thought had crossed Maeve's mind.

"Let me see what I can do," he said.

He helped her, time and time again, and she didn't know why. There was no romantic love between them, just a shared hurt transcending that. There was an inexplicable, unholy bond between them, and in that, she only found comfort. Nothing else.

He finished his coffee, asked the waitress for one to go. "I'm getting divorced."

Since they were sharing, she confessed, too. "I slept with my ex-husband."

He chuckled. "Well, he's a good-looking guy."

"True. But he's kind of an idiot, too. I had forgotten about that part."

He let that go. "You ever think we'll be like normal people, Maeve Conlon?"

"I try so hard, Poole, but I'm not sure I've got it in me."

The waitress delivered his coffee, and he threw a couple of singles onto the table. "Let's go," he said, holding the door for Maeve. Out on the street, he pulled back the tab on his coffee and blew into the little hole in the lid. "So what do you need? What are you going to do?"

"I'm going to do what you said," she said, a little woman looking up into the sad, knowing eyes of the taller man. "That's it, right? There's nothing else I should think about?"

"You still got the gun?" he asked.

She shook her head. "I don't have the gun," she said, whispering.

He laughed. "No one around here cares, Maeve Conlon. You could be wearing a holster with two six-shooters and no one, except maybe some of my more conscientious colleagues, would give a damn." He shook his head. "Too many freaking guns on the street." He looked up at the train on the elevated track overhead, pulling into the station. "Where'd it go? Why'd you get rid of it?"

"My sister. I can't do this anymore, not with her around. She's inquisitive, Poole, goes through my things. There was nowhere to put it." She smiled. "Takes every tube of lip gloss that comes into my house. I couldn't run the risk of keeping the gun."

"Girls love the gloss."

"And don't worry about where it went. The gun. It will never come back."

"Okay. I understand."

"I feel as if that part of my life is over. Does that make sense?" she asked.

He did understand. Sometimes she felt he was the only person who did.

"Let me know what else I can do." He took a sip of the coffee. "Swill," he pronounced it. "Name is Taylor? Dvorak? Like the composer?"

Maeve shrugged. "I guess." She spelled it for him.

"I'll keep an eye out. An ear to the ground."

Before he walked away, she touched his arm. "Your decision or hers? The divorce?"

He laughed again, the most mirth she had ever seen him show. "Oh, definitely hers. You might be surprised to hear this, but I'm not exactly what you'd call marriage material."

"But you've been married a long time," Maeve said.

"I have."

"So why now? Your kids are older. You're close to retirement, right? Shouldn't this be the good part?"

He put a paternal hand on her shoulder. "It should be. You're right about that."

"So? What happened?"

"You know. This and that," he said, before walking away. "Plus, there's no good part with me."

CHAPTER 13

It hadn't been that long ago that she had been back here, her old street, driving up and down and reliving memories both good and bad. Today, in the neighborhood after her coffee with Poole, she tried to focus on the good, thinking about riding her bike until the sun had set, the streetlights coming on and attracting all sorts of bugs. Lightning bugs had been her favorite, magical in their own way. She remembered catching them in her hands and watching their lights flicker on and off in her palm. Jack would tell her to keep them in a jar so she could watch them flicker on and off all night but she always set them free.

Jack would lean out the front door, and his voice, loud and distinctive, would call her home. "Mavy! Dinner!" Dinner was some kind of well-done meat—a London broil or a pork chop that could never be revived from its desiccated state, even with a helping of ketchup—mashed potatoes if he had had time, and string beans or peas from a can. Everything was salty and, after a day in the sun and playing outside, would taste delicious in a way that she could never understand now, her tastes having become more sophisticated and cultivated over time. He would have a beer, and she would have a giant glass of milk, and they would sit across the Formica table from each other, Jack quizzing Maeve on her times tables, even in the summer, and Maeve regaling Jack with what had happened on the block while he was at work.

"Mary Lou Donaldson got stitches in her foot."

Or "I hit the ball the farthest in stickball."

And him, reporting, "I caught another bad guy today, Mavy!" in a way that made her laugh, as if bad guys were like butterflies that he caught in a net and put in a jar somewhere like the ones he told her to put her lightning bugs in, not how they really were.

They would exchange the news of the day. She would leave out certain things, though, and she suspected he did, too, and that created a space between them that neither knew existed.

Now she parked a few houses down from the one in which she had grown up, counting off the numbers, remembering the names of the people who lived inside their four walls in what seemed like a completely different and forgotten time. The Bresnahans. The O'Rourkes. The Haggertys. The McGills. The McSweeneys.

She stopped. In front of the McSweeneys' house, she noticed that it still bore their surname on the door, that an *S* still adorned what had to be the original screen door that had fronted the house from the beginning. She sat up straighter in her seat and wondered if Mrs. McSweeney—Colette, if she recalled correctly—was still here, probably one of the last holdovers from her youth.

Maeve opened the wrought-iron fence and walked up the tidy flagstone path to the front door. Mrs. McSweeney had been a large woman with a full head of jet-black hair that contrasted nicely with her nurse's cap. Maeve remembered Jack telling her that when Mrs. McSweeney's husband died, she had gone back to school, walking a few blocks to the all-female Catholic college on the avenue that specialized in nursing, her crisp white uniform and cap generating awe in young Maeve, a girl without a mother. Of all the neighbors, Mrs. McSweeney kept to herself the most, not inserting herself into other people's business or affairs, not concerned that Maeve was a little "sassy," according to more than one good Christian mother, or that her father didn't dress her like a little girl should be dressed, that it wasn't an accomplishment to hit the ball in stickball farther than any boy on the street. Mrs. McSweeney kept a tidy house, probably to avoid the gossip that a messy yard would generate, and Maeve would pass her every Saturday, as she herself made her way to the deli to buy Jack his paper, out front, weeding or even mowing the grass herself. The woman wore pants all the time when she wasn't wearing her nurse's uniform, and sometimes, when it was dark and Maeve was supposed to be asleep, she would look out her back window and see the glow of a cigarette in the night, the woman sitting atop the picnic bench in her backyard, silently putting the day to rest.

The woman who answered the door didn't have black hair anymore, but she was still turned out in a blousy white shirt and slim jeans, a miraculous medal around her neck. "Can I help you?" she said when she saw Maeve.

"Hello, Mrs. McSweeney. It's Maeve. Maeve Conlon," she said, feeling like a young girl again in this imposing woman's presence.

It took a moment for the realization to dawn on the woman's face that the small woman before her had once been a little girl. Mrs. McSweeney was old now, as old as Jack had been when he died, but still sharp, still living life, unlike her late former neighbor, Maeve's father. "Maeve Conlon?" she said. "It must be . . ." She searched her brain for the number of years.

"Almost thirty probably," Maeve said.

The woman opened the screen door. "Nothing like seeing a grown-up you knew as a child to make you feel old," she said, letting Maeve in.

In the narrow hallway, pictures hung on a wallpapered wall. Although it had been a long time ago, Maeve remembered the day Jamie McSweeney—his picture hanging in the center of all of the other family photos—had died, two uniformed military men showing up on Mrs. McSweeney's stoop to let her know that he had served honorably and well.

Mrs. McSweeney stood in back of Maeve, reaching over her shoulder to touch the large photo. "Phuoc Long sounds like a very exotic place, and today, probably is. For all I know, it's got fancy hotels and spas. Back then, it was hell."

"I'm sorry," Maeve said, though it sounded empty. Her recollections of Jamie McSweeney were few, but she did remember seeing him once in his uniform and thinking that he looked old, older than she would ever be. Little had she known that that was as old as he would get. "I remember Jamie."

"Great boy," the woman said. "Come."

They walked into a living room that seemed frozen in time, an overstuffed, chintz-covered sofa against another wallpapered wall, a large mahogany coffee table in front of it. Mrs. McSweeney lived in a house almost identical in layout to the one in which Maeve had grown up, the difference being that the orientation was opposite. Her living room had been on the other side of the house, the stairs going up on the north side instead of the south. She took a seat in a Queen Anne armchair, sitting near the edge, not wanting to get comfortable or give the impression that she was staying for long.

"Something to drink?" Mrs. McSweeney asked.

"No, thank you," Maeve said. "I'm sorry to barge in like this, but I wanted to ask you a few questions."

Mrs. McSweeney sat across from Maeve in an identical chair, the whole living room suite one matched set of old but cared-for furniture. She rested her arm on the doily-covered rest. "Questions?"

"I guess I should start by saying that my father passed late last year."

Mrs. McSweeney clutched her chest. "I'm so sorry, Maeve. He was a lovely, lovely man."

"He was." Maeve looked down at her shoes. Just what was she doing here anyway, going down memory lane with a woman who didn't know her intentions? She decided to blurt it out, not wait any longer, waste any more of the old woman's time. "I have a sister I never knew about. Her name is Evelyn."

Maeve studied the woman's face and saw an almost imperceptible cloud pass across it. She had already known, Maeve guessed. But she remained silent, not giving anything away.

"She has been living in a group home in Rye for many years. She's well taken care of. We're still getting to know each other, but I'm just so glad to have the family, you know?" Maeve said, realizing, too late, that she was talking to someone who had no immediate family of her own. "I'm sorry."

Mrs. McSweeney raised a hand and waved the apology away. "It's fine, Maeve. I've become rather good on my own," she said, chuckling sadly. "A sister?"

"Yes. My father never told me. Didn't want to burden me." She pulled a loose thread on the doily on her armrest. "Do you remember her?"

"No, I don't." Maybe she was telling the truth.

"But you were here then?"

"Yes. Probably. Maybe. But I don't remember her."

"Really?" Maeve asked. "Not even a little bit?"

Mrs. McSweeney shook her head. "Not even a little bit."

Maeve pushed a little harder. "See, the reason I want to know is that my father was not her father."

The woman's face went slack, but Maeve couldn't tell if it was the shock of hearing that or the knowing; it was hard to tell.

"He adopted her, and she was his own in his heart, but he definitely wasn't her biological father. He told me so on a video he made for me."

"Well, that's quite a story, Maeve," Mrs. McSweeney said. "So you're not just stopping by for a visit, then? Revisiting the past?"

"No. I'm not," Maeve said.

"I imagine that those days would be hard for you to relive. Your mother's death."

Maeve swallowed. "Yes. My mother's death," Maeve said, even though the truth was much worse. She was murdered, left to die in the street, the victim of profound recklessness.

Mrs. McSweeney clucked sympathetically, in a way that let Maeve know she really didn't understand the gravity of what had happened.

"It was Marty Haggerty. Drunk driving," Maeve said. "He ran her down and left her there, and my life was never the same."

The old woman sank back in her chair and rested her head in her hand. "And you found that out how?"

"The police," she said, leaving out that it was Poole, the one person she trusted completely and with her life.

"The police." Mrs. McSweeney crossed one leg over the other, trying to affect a posture of nonchalance, of not caring. But she cared, and she was troubled; those two things were written on her lined face. "Maeve, I can't help you. I'm so sorry for everything you've been through, but I can't help you."

"Please, Mrs. McSweeney. Anything. If you know anything about my sister or who her father was, please tell me. I remember this street well. There were always secrets and more than a few lies, but someone always knew the truth." Maeve sighed. "Maybe everyone. I think maybe everyone knew the truth. And it can't hurt anyone anymore."

The old woman shook her head sadly. "But not this time, Maeve. It was a long time ago, and I really don't remember."

Maeve dug around in her pocketbook for a business card from The Comfort Zone. She held it out, but the other woman didn't take it. Maeve dropped it on the coffee table. "If you happen to remember anything, will you call me?" When Mrs. McSweeney didn't respond, Maeve pleaded with her. "Please? I have to know."

Finally, the woman spoke, staring at the card. "Yes. If I remember anything, I'll let you know."

Maeve let herself out, pausing briefly at the large photo of Jamie McSweeney. *She knows loss,* Maeve thought. *Maybe that will push her to tell me everything she knows.*

Because I'm betting she knows a lot.

CHAPTER 14

Maeve took Rodney's advice, starting at the beginning the next day, thinking about those days, not so long ago, when she spent time at the soccer field. Taylor played soccer. That was all she knew about her, beyond the fact that her mother was encouraging her to go to a state university in the hope that she could afford it. That made Maeve wonder: If they were as destitute as Trish claimed, surely financial aid would be of assistance? Cal had navigated that entire process for Rebecca, and Maeve knew that they hadn't qualified for one penny of assistance, but Trish's situation was different. Maeve wondered about the delinquent father that Trish referred to and how well off, or not, he was.

After the store closed, she drove over to the high school. She remembered that when Rebecca was on the team, the team practiced constantly when they weren't playing games. So, a Sunday practice was not out of the realm of possibility. She parked in the same spot in which she had parked when she had visited Judy Wilkerson.

The girls' soccer team exited through the back door a few minutes after she arrived, ready to take the short walk over to the soccer field to start practice. Rebecca had been off the team for two years, so Maeve didn't recognize a lot of the girls. If they had been freshmen when Rebecca had been a senior, then they had changed into young women Maeve wouldn't know. Gone would be the knobby knees and angles of ninth grade, and in their place would be more weight, a bit more heft, and a change in their features. Every one of them, or so it seemed, was long and lithe, jogging effortlessly from the back of the school building and down the hill to the soccer field, a place where Maeve had spent many an afternoon, watching Rebecca run up and down the length without losing her breath or really breaking a sweat. Maeve marveled at her older daughter's athletic ability. Sure, Maeve had played CYO basketball and youth softball, but she was small and not wiry and really, when she thought about it, not all that coordinated. Her body, like the bodies of her female ancestors, was more suited to long hours in a field, low to the ground, nimbly picking the day's harvest. The Irish peasant body, she called it. Rebecca's prowess must have been inherited from the Callahan side of the family, but Maeve had never considered Cal that much of an athlete either, something with which he probably would take issue. The way he saw himself was often at odds with the way the world viewed him, which as of now was middle-aged, trying to be hip, too old to be the father of a toddler.

She got out of the car and followed the team down the hill, walking past the playground where the girls used to play and where now, younger siblings of varsity soccer players spent hours while their sisters were on the field. There was the porta-potty that she had used more than she cared to admit, her bladder control having taken a hit after she gave birth to Heather and never recovering, that little bit of wetness every time she sneezed reminding her that as hard as she tried not to think it, Heather provided challenges both great and small as a daughter.

She took a seat on the hill overlooking the field. The last year Rebecca had played, a new coach had joined the coaching staff, a young guy—too young as far as Maeve was concerned, a little too close in age to her almost-eighteen-year-old—who ran the girls ragged at practice and demanded nothing less than perfection, both on the field and off. There had been curfews and grade minimums, uniform checks—more than one of which Rebecca failed because Maeve was incapable of getting grass stains out of white shorts, no matter how hard she tried—and a host of other requirements. Team dinners. Big buddies. Study partners. Running drills. Maeve could never keep track of what was required and what was optional, and apparently neither could Rebecca, because she did everything he asked and more, going so far as being the equipment manager in her senior year, long after she should have been saddled with that responsibility.

She had to say this for the guy: He was good-looking. Running around in his baggy soccer shorts, a loose Arsenal jersey on his thin frame, David Barnham was the all-American boy type that every woman found attractive, even Maeve, even though she was dating a meaty Germanic type who looked like he would be just as comfortable behind the counter of a butcher shop wearing a white apron as in the sport coat and dress slacks he wore to his actual job. Barnham ran up and down the field with the girls, blowing a whistle every now and again to stop the play, to instruct the girls on the field.

Maeve pulled out her phone. It was the rare occurrence when she called one of her girls and she answered the phone; today, she was in luck. Hell must be freezing over, she thought as Rebecca answered, breathless and on her way somewhere, the sound of cars in the background.

"Can you talk for a minute?" Maeve asked.

"That's exactly what I have," Rebecca said. "I'm almost to the library. I'm behind on a paper."

"Okay, I'll make it brief. I don't know if you saw the news, but—"

"Yes. Taylor."

"Right. You played soccer together, didn't you?"

"She was a midfielder."

"Anything else you remember?"

"I've gotta go, Mom. What are you asking?"

"Anything else? Happy? Sad? Popular? Unpopular?"

"Not sure 'popular' is the right word," Rebecca said, but there was a hint of sarcasm in her voice. "And one of Mr. Barnham's favorites."

Maeve detected a subtext. "What do you mean?"

"He had parties. Invitation only. She was on the list."

Maeve felt that familiar tingle in her gut, her mouth going dry. "Parties?" She wondered why this was the first time she was hearing about this, and then wasn't surprised that it was. That last year Rebecca had played soccer, Maeve had been preoccupied a lot of the time, her father the lead suspect in a murder investigation despite his failing faculties, her attempts to keep him out of jail alternately ham-fisted and brilliant. "Did you go to these parties?" Maeve asked, her eyes zeroing in on Mr. Barnham, her mind whirling with thoughts of just how she would kill him, how she could isolate him and remove him as a threat once and for all.

"No!" Rebecca said. "Even if I had been invited, I wouldn't have gone."

"What happened at the parties?" Maeve asked, not sure she wanted to know.

"Nothing that I heard of."

"Tell me the truth."

"I am telling the truth," Rebecca said. "I would have heard. I would have known. But I still thought it was weird. He's single. No wife. Just weird that he would have girls over."

"No assistant coach?" Maeve asked.

"Nope." Rebecca had reached her destination. "I've gotta go, Mom. I'll call you later."

But Maeve knew she wouldn't and she would have to track Rebecca down again. She had a whole new life at school, one that didn't include or involve her mother or her sister, and she was happy there. Maeve wondered if she would come home after she graduated, if they would ever live together again, and the thought of that made her sad. The thought that her girls would go their separate ways and maybe not be close was something that she thought about frequently, wondering, again, if that would be her fault.

Things were changing. Life was different. People moved on.

She wondered where she would fit in once all of the pieces were shuffled and reassembled.

She stood and stretched, her eyes still on the field below. From the street side of the field, a car pulled into the parking apron and came to a stop. The Farringville police weren't great at hiding the fact that their one unmarked car was a Dodge Charger that anyone with one good eye could tell was a cop car. Chris got out of the passenger side as his chief, a taut and thin brunette named Suzanne Carstairs, got out of the driver's side. Maeve had seen her photo in the local paper a few times. They approached the field with purpose, standing to the side until Barnham made his way over, commanding the girls to keep drilling until he returned, something Maeve gleaned from his hand gestures and the fact that the girls kept running without breaking stride.

In the distance, Chris put a hand over his eyes to shield them from the sun, looking around the area, his eyes landing on Maeve, high on the hill above the field. Maeve couldn't see his expression—time for progressive lenses, which her ophthalmologist had recommended the year before and which she had never gotten around to getting—but if she had to guess, she would say that he was con-fused, wondering why she was there, if he could even tell it was her in the distance.

She wasn't so big a soccer fan that she could profess to wanting to see the girls practice, so she got up and started for her car, think-ing that she'd have to come up with a reasonable explanation for why she was watching soccer practice.

Whether he believed her or not would be the question.

She took one last look down at the field, watching the girls con-gregate midfield, running some kind of drill that looked like it would be painful in execution. She didn't recognize any of the girls any-more, or so she thought. Because suddenly she did recognize one.

Heather.

CHAPTER 15

The next day, the store was closed but Maeve decided to go in and bake, asking Jo if she would come in and help with any potential customers who might see the lights on and decide that it was the perfect day for a cupcake. She was far behind on her baking and although she had told Trish that it was a six-day-a-week routine, it was really seven and always had been. After making two batches of scones and cleaning out the refrigerated case, Jo took a seat at one of the café tables, a break being "just what the doctor ordered," according to her. She had tired of reading the local news to Maeve and turned to national stories, unfolding the *Times* with a snap of her wrist and starting her recitation.

"Dateline, Miami, Florida. U.S. Marshals are hot on the trail of the international drug lord known as El Gato, Mexico's most wanted criminal." She looked over at Maeve. "El Gato? The Cat?" She thought on that for a moment. "If I were an international drug lord, I think I'd have a better nickname."

Maeve surveyed her quiche inventory, half listening. "Like what?"

"The Jaguar. The Cougar," she said, shaking her head. "Okay, maybe not the Cougar, because that implies something completely

different. The Shark? It would have to have a kick-ass Spanish trans-
lation, though."

The phone rang, but it wasn't until Maeve raised an eyebrow at
Jo indicating that she should pick it up that her assistant moved
from the bar stool. Jo blanched at the number on the caller ID.

"The daycare," she said. She listened intently. "One hundred?"
She looked at Maeve and mouthed "Is that high?" Since Maeve had
no idea what she was talking about, she shrugged in response, continuing her review of the items in the refrigerated case. "I'll be right
there," she said, slamming the phone down on the counter and
stripping off her apron. "I've gotta go. Baby's got a fever."

"A hundred?" Maeve said. "He'll be fine, Jo. Don't worry. Is this
his first fever?" Judging from Jo's reaction to the news, it had to be.

"Yes," Jo said, grabbing her knapsack from under the counter.
"Do you think it's because I put him in daycare?" she asked.

"Babies get sick, Jo. You've been lucky so far." But as she watched
her friend race out the door, she acknowledged that the child, who
up until this point had only been with his mother, had probably
gotten sick from being in daycare. It was inevitable. She hoped that
this didn't bring an issue that existed between Jo and Doug to a
head and would leave her without a trusted employee at the store.
Outside, a large clap of thunder telegraphed an inevitable downpour
of rain, one that Jo just missed before she jumped into her car and
sped off.

Maeve looked at the clock; school was almost out for the day.
She texted Heather. *SOS. I need you at the store. Can you help?*

As was usually the case, the text was met with virtual stony silence, but fifteen minutes later, Heather walked through the back
door, surly, sullen, and more than a little wet, and threw her backpack on the counter. "Where's Jo?" she asked.

Maeve handed her a cupcake. "Baby's sick."

That softened the girl's demeanor, but only slightly. "Will he be okay?"

"Just a fever," Maeve said.

Heather donned the apron that Jo had left on the counter. "Devon had a fever once and Dad took him to the emergency room."

"I'm sure it's fine, Heather. Babies get fevers all the time."

"Did I ever get fevers?" she asked, standing behind the counter and watching her mother rearrange items in the case.

"All the time. You got a lot of ear infections."

"And what did you do?" Heather asked.

Maeve got up from her crouch; her legs were achy. She continued to look into the case, making sure that everything was as she wanted it, arranged so that it would sell. "I'd hold you and rock you until you fell asleep." Memories of Heather's sweaty head, her dark hair matted to her forehead, her breath coming out in yeasty gasps, were what she remembered of that time. Rebecca had been hale and hearty and her younger daughter a little more illness-prone, chronic ear infections the bane of Maeve's existence until a kindly nurse practitioner at the pediatrician's office suggested garlic oil drops as a homeopathic cure for what ailed the little girl. They had worked like a charm. "I used to put garlic oil in your ears."

Heather approximated a smile. "I remember that. Smelled nasty."

"Yeah, but it worked." Maeve pulled a cake past its sell date from the case and put it in a box to take home. "Hey, I have a question for you."

"What?" Heather asked, standing at the far end of the counter, her back stiff and straight, preparing herself for whatever it was. Her mother never asked innocuous questions.

"You're playing soccer?"

"What do you mean?"

Maeve laughed. "What do you mean, what do I mean? I saw you at the field yesterday. You don't play sports."

"I do now."

"Really? Why?" Maeve was suspicious. Heather had lasted two days in soccer back in the first grade, just long enough for Maeve to pay for her membership and uniform, walking off the field after some overzealous coach had yelled at her for letting in a goal. Maeve was happy she had quit because otherwise, she probably would have killed the guy; the sight of Heather's humiliated face walking off the field and toward the car made her heart hurt even now.

"I need extracurriculars for my college applications."

"Huh," Maeve said. "And soccer? You've never really played soccer."

"Have you seen the team since Rebecca graduated? They aren't exactly what I'd call all-stars."

"And you can just join midyear? Just like that?"

"They stink. And they're short-handed. It didn't take much to get on the team. Coach Barnham didn't even care that I haven't played in ten years."

Rebecca's words about the coach rang in Maeve's ears. "You like it?" she asked, not looking at Heather, trying to make her line of questioning seem innocent, just small talk.

"Not really," she said.

"So?"

"Extracurriculars," Heather said and brushed past Maeve on her way to the kitchen, the conversation over.

"You could go to Mississippi. That would be a great extracurricular."

"Trip's too late. I'll already be in college somewhere by the time it happens." She frowned. "Hopefully."

"Yeah, but interviews. You could mention that you're going."

Heather turned and looked at her. On her face was a look that Maeve recognized because it was the same look she got on her own face when she didn't want to do something, when the discussion was ended. "I'm not going to Mississippi." She closed her mouth and then opened it again. "Plus, I hate—"

"What?" Maeve said, cutting her off. "Mississippi?"

"No, not Mississippi."

"Then what?"

Heather walked toward the kitchen, letting the door swing shut behind her. She muttered something before the door closed, something that sounded to Maeve like "Not what. Who."

Maeve followed her into the kitchen, getting the message and letting the conversation go for now. "Can you dust the cases and handle anyone who might come in? We'll close up at four like usual."

"Sure," Heather said and, without being asked, grabbed some glass cleaner and a paper towel and started wiping away the smudged fingerprints left by the preschool class who had come in earlier that day to meet "Miss Maeve, the Cupcake Lady." Her daughter was adopting a work ethic that Maeve recognized as being second only to her own. She wondered how she could get Heather to train Jo in the finer points of executing closing tasks prior to the end of the day.

Maeve stayed in the kitchen and planned the rest of her day, watching the clock for the stroke of four, when she could close up and do what was next on her to-do list. She had been without a mission for a while, and it felt good to have one again.

"Mom, go," Heather said at ten minutes to four. "I've got it covered."

And she did. So Maeve hung up her apron and prepared to leave, Heather confirming she knew what the security code was and how to make sure the store was closed up tight.

In the kitchen, going through her bag to make sure she had

everything she needed, she heard the bell over the front door ring, a final customer arriving before close. Maeve peered through the round window in the swinging door that separated the kitchen from the retail area and spotted Mark Messer, his DPW shift done for the day. Heather was still behind the counter, and if Maeve wasn't seeing things, she could swear that Heather smiled at the guy, her face tinting pink at his entrance. He leaned on the counter and ordered a coffee and a cupcake, the two of them chatting amiably. Mark looked up and spied Maeve in the window, waving at her to come into the front of the store.

"Hey, Maeve," Mark said as he ingested the cupcake in two bites, "your chocolate cupcakes are the best. What's your secret?"

"Butter! Lots of butter!" Maeve said as she exited the front of the store, hearing his hearty laugh behind her. She didn't know what made her happier: his compliment for her cupcakes or his ability to make her daughter smile.

She didn't tell Heather where she was going; it was better that way. The kid already thought her mother was insane and paranoid; why give her the evidence to back that contention up? Maeve went back to the high school and parked a few spaces down from a pickup truck. The day she had been to the field there had been one parked on the grass and since cars, most cars anyway, weren't allowed to drive past the gate at the top of the hill, she assumed it was Barnham's.

She looked out the window of the Prius and watched as Coach Barnham sauntered out of the school building, a big bag of balls slung over his shoulder, his lips puckered as he whistled. He was alone, and Maeve was relieved. Nothing would have set her off more than seeing a gaggle of devoted acolytes following their coach, one or more maybe jumping into his red pickup truck, the kayak in the back a fitting accessory.

Maeve waited until he was in the car and had driven around the bend before she left her spot. She trailed behind him, only losing sight of the pickup once, until they had traveled about a mile and he turned into a driveway that Maeve knew led to a house tucked back in the woods off a hiking trail. If Maeve had had to choose a house for the guy after having seen his truck and his kayak, this would have been it. She couldn't follow him down the driveway without revealing herself, so she parked the car on the side of the road and walked along the edge of the driveway until she got closer to the house.

At times like this, she was happy she had a silent hybrid and was a small person. And middle-aged. She was coming to that age where she was invisible to most everyone, especially younger men, and for her darker pursuits, that served her well. That's not to say that he wouldn't notice her if she was out in the open, as she was now, walking along his driveway, the look on her face suggesting that this wasn't a social call. She forced herself to smile. Her nonsmiling face, she had been told by the girls, was not friendly, and the last thing she needed was for him to get his hackles up at her arrival. She crept forward, stopping a hundred feet or so in, noticing that in addition to the pickup truck, kayak, and house in the woods, Barnham had another obvious accoutrement of the young, single jock—a giant dog, who spotted Maeve lurking in the trees and sounded the alarm that there was an unknown person in his master's midst. The dog, playing in a giant puddle that had formed from the earlier downpour, ran toward her. The coach saw her among the pines and followed close behind the dog. By the time he reached her, he was smiling.

"Mrs. Callahan, right?" he said. "Rebecca and Heather's mom?"

Maeve came out from behind the copse of trees and tried to affect a nonchalant stance. "Yes, hi, Coach."

"I got my mother's birthday cake from you," he said. "She's still talking about it."

Maeve didn't remember ever having seen him in the store, so either he was as adept at lying as she was or, as she feared on a regular basis, her mind was going just like her father's had prior to his death. "Great!" she said, smiling so wide that all of her teeth showed. *See? I'm not dangerous at all. I'm not following you. I'm just a doddering middle-aged woman with saggy jeans and an icing-covered T-shirt under a zipped Farringville High School hoodie.*

He waited for her to reveal why she was on his driveway, hidden in the trees that fronted his property. The dog sat at his side, nothing interesting to him about the lady talking to his master. "Are you lost?"

"I guess I am, a little bit," she said. "Uphill Terrace. I can never remember where that is off of this street."

"Well, the reason you can't remember is that it's not off this street," he said, pointing to a spot over her shoulder.

No wedding ring, she noticed, but then again, she didn't expect one. Everything about him said "single," from the small log cabin in front of her to the free and easy way he carried himself. This was a guy with few responsibilities and no one else on his mind. She could tell.

"It's off of Shady Lane," he said.

"Oh, right!" she said, laying it on thick. "You'd think after all the time I've lived here, I would remember." She stood for a moment, wondering how far to take this, but given that she wouldn't have much of an excuse to talk to the soccer coach again without it seeming odd or suspicious, she brought up Taylor and her disappearance. "The girls on the team must be really upset about Taylor Dvorak."

She studied his face for some kind of sign, but there was none. All she saw was concern and nothing else. "Terrible. I've already spoken to the police at length," he said.

"Really? Did they question you?" she asked, adding just the right amount of righteous indignation to indicate that she was appalled at the idea of it.

"I volunteered," he said. "Offered to tell them what I knew about her."

"She seemed . . . ," Maeve said, trailing off. She didn't know the girl from a hole in the wall but hoped he would insert the proper adjective.

"Sad?"

"Maybe," Maeve said.

"Depressed?"

"I guess."

"It was hard to say what it was exactly," he said, offering up more information than Maeve could have hoped for. "But she was troubled. Soccer was a way for her to be free, to let herself forget about whatever it was that was bothering her."

Maeve wondered if he'd heard about her part in the story. "Well, let's just pray that she's found."

"Yes. Let's do that," he said. "I'm glad Heather has decided to try soccer."

"Me, too," Maeve said, wondering if he had picked up her hesitation about Heather as an athlete. She felt off-kilter about seeing Heather on the field, wondering if the story about needing extracurriculars was true or if there was some other reason that her daughter had joined the team but she couldn't think of what that might be. She studied the coach's face for a clue to his intentions toward her daughter, or any girl for that matter, but all she saw was an open and honest expression, nothing seeming to lurk beneath the surface.

Either he was telling the truth or he was a complete sociopath.

Takes one to know one, she thought. Would she still know one or had she lost her touch?

The dog had lain by Barnham's side throughout the entire conversation but perked up as a bird flew low overhead. "Ready to go, Cosmo?" the coach asked, the dog jumping up. "I'm sorry. I should have introduced you. This is Cosmo."

"Hello, Cosmo," Maeve said, keeping her distance. She hadn't been raised with dogs, and her first memory of canines was of the Doberman who lived next door who had tried to take a bite out of her ass as she rode her bike down the street. Cosmo did what came naturally to all dogs and planted his nose right in her crotch. She pushed him away as gently as she could, his persistent nuzzling making a wet spot on her right thigh. Barnham did nothing to help her. "Well, thank you for pointing me in the right direction, Mr. Barnham."

"Please. Call me David."

"David, then. Thank you. I guess I'll be seeing you at some games," Maeve said as she turned and walked back down the driveway. When she got to the end, she turned around to wave, but he was gone, as if he had vanished into thin air.

As if the day couldn't get any weirder, when she got home, Heather had made a meat loaf, and it was the first thing Maeve smelled when she walked into the house. Heather was at the kitchen table typing on her laptop, which she slammed shut when her mother walked in.

Maeve peered into the oven. "Looks good. Smells even better," she said. "What possessed you to make a meat loaf?"

"Ground meat was on sale at the store, so I brought some home last night. But it was the last sell date," Heather said, knowing even more about sell dates than Maeve did. "Aunt Evelyn called," she added.

"What did she have to say?" Maeve asked, smiling. Evelyn's conversations ran the gamut from the last movie she had seen to remembrances of Maeve's father, the man who had secretly taken good care of her until he died, something that Maeve was trying to forget, trying to forgive.

"She said she saw The Comfort Zone on television," Heather said.

Maeve turned so quickly that she got a pain in her side from the exertion. "What?"

"The store. She said she saw it on News 12."

News 12 was Evelyn's favorite station, showing county news, weather, and sports all day and all night. "News 12?" Maeve went into the living room and turned on the television, knowing that the station rebroadcast the top stories throughout the day.

Heather joined her on the couch. "What's the matter?"

"I'm wondering why the store would be on television." Maeve suffered through high school sports scores, the weather, and a story about a bedbug infestation at a local hotel before the top story, the disappearance of Taylor Dvorak, was run again. The details were the same as the ones Maeve knew. A shot of The Comfort Zone flashed on the screen, as did an old photo of her from the Farringville Chamber of Commerce dinner from two years earlier—yes, she had put on weight since then, thank you for noticing—where she was smiling while standing next to the mayor.

The blonde doing the report sounded a little judgmental to Maeve's ears. "A new development in this case . . . we have just learned that the girl had an emergency contact, a woman named Maeve Conlon, owner of The Comfort Zone. Conlon gave the school nurse permission to send Taylor Dvorak home. Where she is now is anyone's guess, but the Farringville Police Department assures the citizens of Farringville that they are doing everything in their power, including bringing in the county police, to find the girl. If anyone has any information on Taylor's disappearance, please call—"

Maeve turned off the television and looked at Heather, hoping her teenager would have something to say that would make it better, that would let her know that although she felt responsible, she wasn't. The entire viewing population of the local news was now privy to her role in the teen's disappearance, and she felt hopeless, trying not to let it show.

Heather stared at her, wondering how her mother was going to react. "It's not your fault."

"I think it is," she thought to herself, realizing when she saw Heather's face that she had said it out loud. She had done a lot of things in her life—some of them not the right thing—but this felt like the worst thing of all.

CHAPTER 16

Cal showed up just as Chris Larsson was leaving later that night, the memory of Heather's meat loaf writ large on the cop's friendly face; he was pale and a little shaky. Maeve wondered if the sale meat was really a good idea. She hadn't touched her own helping of meat loaf, her appetite gone after seeing the store and her photo on the news report. Heather's appetite seemed to disappear as well. She wondered how long it would be until the story was picked up by the metro news, until it was the lead story for the networks. She shuddered at the thought.

Evelyn called every time the story ran, which turned out to be more times than Maeve could count. "I see your store!" she would say when Maeve picked up, not getting that it wasn't really the kind of publicity that Maeve wanted.

Chris has been tight-lipped during dinner, but it was clear to Maeve that they still had no leads on Taylor's disappearance. She wondered if the awful meat loaf, in conjunction with the sickness that he felt in his gut every day that the girl was missing, was the reason that he had left so quickly, if seeing Heather, so reminiscent of the missing girl, had started to make him physically ill.

Cal stood in the hallway, pointing over his shoulder as Chris ran down the front porch steps to his car. "He has time for dinner?" Cal asked. "Shouldn't he be pulling double duty looking for that girl?"

Maeve didn't have time for Cal's sarcasm, nor his implication that Chris was doing anything but looking for Taylor. "Why are you here?" she asked, her mind flashing on the sight of Trish leaving Cal's house a few days before.

Cal looked up the long flight of stairs to the second floor of the house to make sure that Heather was in her room and that the door was closed. "She knows."

"Who knows?" Maeve asked, too exhausted for the guessing game that he wanted to play.

"Gabriela," he said. "She knows."

"Knows what?" Maeve asked. "There's nothing to know. We've been done for a while." There was nothing to know except what had happened that one time, and that was between them—but clearly the cat was out of the bag if Jo's intelligence on what had come out of Gabriela's spin class was any good.

Payback's a bitch, huh? Maeve wanted to ask but wisely kept her mouth shut.

"Well, she knows that something happened between us specifically."

Interesting choice of words. Clearly there had been others. "How?"

"Trish." When Maeve looked at him for more information, he came clean. "She heard you talking to Jo."

"Shouldn't she be worried about finding her daughter?" Maeve asked.

"Oh, she is," Cal said. "But she's also holding you responsible."

"Okay, now you're just being ridiculous," Maeve said, trying to sound calm, the high-pitched timbre of her voice belying that. "Responsible?"

"She came to me and told me she'd be quiet. Not make a bigger deal out of you and what you did. For money."

"Why didn't she ask me for money?" Maeve asked, thinking back to the missing money from the short time Trish had worked for her. Oh, right, she preferred to just steal it, Maeve thought. Now she had the reason for Trish's car being in front of Cal's house. She was almost relieved that the reason was blackmail and not something more salacious and for that, she wasn't proud.

Cal raised an eyebrow, implying that everyone knew the truth: Maeve didn't have any money. For once, she was grateful for that fact.

"Did you give her any?"

"No!" he said. "That's why Gabriela knows. Trish told her what she overheard in the store."

Maeve thought back to the day when Jo came in and figured out that she had slept with Cal. She hadn't seen Trish but that wasn't to say that the woman hadn't heard every last sordid detail. Just Maeve's luck.

"And Gabriela confronted you?"

"Yes," he said. "I denied everything."

"And I'm sure you were really convincing," Maeve said. What was that thing her father always said? No good deed goes unpunished? The missing money would have been enough to make her change her mind, but extortion was another thing entirely. Desperate people do desperate things; she knew that. But what she hadn't known was exactly how desperate Trish Dvorak was. "We never should have done it, Cal. You're married. You have a child."

He didn't respond to that, preferring to focus on Trish's shaky moral code. "What kind of woman has the time to blackmail someone when her daughter is missing?" Cal asked, shaking his head.

"Did you tell the police?" Maeve asked.

He nodded. "Yes. Chief Carstairs." He smiled. "Have you met her? She's kind of hot."

Maeve ignored the remark. He was a like a walking, talking cauldron of testosterone. Or a sixteen-year-old boy. Maybe both.

Behind him, Heather charged down the stairs. "I'm going out," she said as she breezed by them, running down the front steps and jumping into a car that was unfamiliar to Maeve.

"Wait!" Maeve called after her, but it was too late. "Be home by curfew," she said to the ceiling.

Cal waited a beat. "So what are we going to do?" he asked.

"I don't know, Cal," Maeve said. "Right now, I need you to leave. That's as far as I can get in my thinking."

"Thanks for nothing," he said.

She opened the front door, holding it for him. "You're very welcome."

After he left and she had cleaned up the dinner dishes, she went over to Chris Larsson's, just to see if he was still alive. He was, but barely, from the sound of things. She could hear him moaning as she stepped up on the porch. Giving the doorbell a quick push to announce her presence, she let herself in with the key he'd given her.

"Chris?" she called.

He responded by retching loudly from behind the door to the bathroom off the front hall.

She knocked on it lightly. "Chris? Do you think you have something besides food poisoning?"

"Maeve? Please go away," he said as gently as he could before resuming his activities behind the door.

Maeve went into the kitchen, where it was clear that the minute he had walked through the door, he had divested himself as quickly as possible of his clothes and the things he had been carrying.

His gun was next to a bowl of apples; Maeve traced her fingers lightly over the metal. His belt. His tie.

His notebook.

He had thrown it so quickly and carelessly onto the table that it had flipped open to the page where he had written notes about his conversation with Maeve. Nothing mind-blowing, just the facts. She picked up a pencil and flipped through the notebook, landing on a page with several names that were familiar to her for some unknown reason. She committed them to memory anyway, thinking that they might come in handy at a future date.

Tim Morehead.

Jesse Connors.

Steven Donnell.

Maeve searched her mind, finally arriving at how she knew them. At one time, in what she considered her more paranoid days, she had had a fake Facebook page, a teenager's profile, filled with "friends" who went to the high school, all the better to keep tabs on Heather—who she was seeing, where she was going, what she was doing. She had since deactivated the page, thinking that dating Chris Larsson might be the prime time for her to stop her more illicit pursuits. But she recognized the names as ones she had seen on that friend list.

She also realized that two of them—Morehead and Connors— were the two solid citizens she had met while they were raising money for the Mississippi trip. "Not what. Who" was something Heather had muttered when they had last had a conversation about the trip. Maeve would have to find out exactly who Heather meant.

And why.

She closed the notebook, hearing water running in the bathroom. Chris emerged a few seconds later looking wan and exhausted.

"Meat loaf, huh?" he asked, falling onto the couch. "More like a serving of *E. coli*."

"I'm so sorry, Chris."

"How come you're not sick?" he asked.

"First, I didn't eat any of the meat loaf, and second, even if I had, I have an iron constitution," she said. "Remember, my dad did most of the cooking when I was growing up, and suffice it to say, that wasn't really his forte." She smiled at him, but he didn't have the energy to return the gesture. "What can I get you?"

"Nothing," he said. "I think I need to sleep."

"Sure?"

"I'm sure. This is not the sort of thing you want anyone else to witness. I know we're close, but we're not that close," he said. "Thanks for checking on me."

"Ginger ale? Gatorade?" she asked.

"Just go," he said. "Kid hates me. She's trying to kill me."

Maeve laughed in spite of the situation and the gastric pain written on his face. "Not true, Chris," she said, and while she wanted to wrap her arms around his strong chest, the thought of catching what he had made her stop. "Call me if you need anything."

She let herself out into the cool night air and took a deep breath. She loved him, she did, and because of that, she had tried to mend her ways, but sometimes she thought that maybe something was wrong with her, that she didn't have the capacity to be normal. Happy. Content.

With three names filed in her brain, she started for home, wondering what she would do with this new information.

CHAPTER 17

Watching the early news the next morning, Maeve couldn't help getting the sense that Trish Dvorak was enjoying the attention having a missing daughter could bring. And then she felt a stab of guilt for feeling that way as she watched the woman burst into tears, a photo of her daughter clutched against her thin chest.

"I just want my daughter to come home," she said, and Maeve felt her own eyes fill with tears. "Please come home, Taylor. This never should have happened," she continued, and with that, Maeve felt the words creeping into her brain, the same ones that populated her thoughts when she least expected them.

It's all your fault.

The logical side of her brain knew that it wasn't, but the illogical side, the one that sometimes overtook her thoughts and made her think dark things, had a hold on her. She continued watching, hoping that there would be some mention of a father. She was in luck. Although he didn't say anything to the reporter camped out in front of his house, she recognized him from back-to-school night as the man whose son, Jesse Connors, was raising money for the

Mississippi trip. His house, a shot of which appeared on the television, was on the other side of town, the last part of Farringville before you entered Prideville. The houses were big and imposing, some, like his, with iron gates fronting them. She made a mental note to find the house.

Maeve thought back to her conversation with Trish at back-to-school night, the woman's antipathy toward her daughter's father, his reluctance to accept her as his own. He had been there that night, too, in the same building, out in the open. Someone had located him, and there he was, right in the same village, something Trish had never mentioned.

The reporter identified the man in the video footage. Maeve wondered if just saying the name—Charles Connors—made Trish sick. Because to her, the thought that Taylor's delinquent father lived in the same village, in comfort and wealth if the house they showed was any indication, made her want to throw up. Her heart went out to Trish again, thoughts about their short, troubled history being replaced with another, stronger emotion.

Anger.

They were from opposite sides of the proverbial tracks, Trish and Connors, and he had left her to raise a girl on her own while his own son grew up without a care in the world, at least financially. Cal had his faults, but he was there for the girls. What kind of man could do what Taylor's father had done?

Maeve finished dressing, turning off the television, and spent the day at the store in deep consternation. Even Jo noticed.

"What's going on?" her friend asked as she rearranged a tray of quiches in the refrigerated case.

"This town has a lot of secrets," Maeve said, the best way she could articulate what she was feeling.

"You're telling me," Jo said. She leaned over the counter, looked around, and whispered, "From what I gather, the local baker had hot and heavy monkey sex with her ex-husband."

Maeve took a roll of paper towels from atop the refrigerated case and threw it at Jo's head, missing her and knocking the wall phone to the ground. "We are never to talk about that again," she said.

"But it's so great! And juicy!" Jo said. "I can't help it."

"And what, exactly, is monkey sex?" Maeve asked.

Jo shrugged. "Not sure. It just sounded as dirty as sex could get, and when I imagine you and Cal together, I imagine dirty," she said.

Maeve waved a hand over her body. "This? Dirty? Not so much, Jo."

Jo pulled a quiche from the case. "Can I take this home? I've got nothing for dinner."

"Go ahead."

"And secrets? What kinds of secrets in this village?"

Jo had an ear to the ground at all times, and now that she had a baby and hung around the local playgrounds, there was so much more to hear. And to share. Maeve told her what she knew; maybe Jo would be able to fill in the blanks. "Charles Connors is Taylor's father, from what the news reports say."

"Who's he?" Jo asked.

"He used to own Farringville Stone," Maeve said, "and he has a kid in the high school."

"Taylor has a half brother?" Jo asked.

"Seems that way. And Trish hinted that Connors certainly doesn't support the girl."

"All that's coming out now?"

Maeve went behind the counter and picked up the paper towels. "Yes. It makes me wonder."

"About what?"

"Trish was trying to extort money from Cal to keep her mouth shut about what had happened between Cal and me."

Jo turned around, her mouth hanging open, her eyes wide. "And maybe she was doing the same to the father?"

Maeve touched her finger to her nose. "Bingo."

"So he kidnapped her?" Jo asked. "Is that where you're going with this? That seems a little far-fetched even for me to cook up, don't you think?"

Maeve shrugged. "Secrets. Lots of secrets." She stuck her head into the cookie case and grabbed one that had fallen between the shelves, popping it into her mouth. "Nothing in this town would surprise me anymore."

"I'll see what I can find out," Jo said. "I have playgroup at the church next week."

"Playgroup? Church?" Maeve asked. Neither jibed with what she knew about her friend.

"Yeah, bunch of women come together in the church basement for an hour or so. Some nice people there. Kids are kind of horrifying, though," Jo said. "But that's where I get my best info."

The idea came to Maeve while she was washing a hotel pan in the kitchen sink a few minutes later, her hands red and raw from being submerged in hot, soapy water. When Jo came in, she turned around, wiping her hands on a dry towel. "I miss Rebecca. Can you believe I'm saying that?"

"Of course I can," Jo said. "She's always been your favorite."

"Oh, don't say that!" Maeve said, although there was a hint of truth there. If being her favorite meant never giving her a day's worth of *tsuris,* as Jo called it, then, yes, trouble-free Rebecca was her favorite. There had been one time when she had let Maeve down, but it was in protecting her sister, so Maeve couldn't really blame her. She loved Heather, certainly, but a part of her wondered just how much of her mother the girl had inherited, and that worried her. "I love my daughters equally."

Jo smirked. "Sure you do," she said, exiting the kitchen.

Maeve called Rebecca from the phone in the front of the store, not expecting to reach her but happy when her daughter answered. "Hey!" she said, sounding a little more eager than she intended, but these little mercies—the answering of a phone, the hearing of her girl's voice—were few and far between with work, the house, Heather, and life in general. "Can I take you to dinner tonight?"

Rebecca sounded suspicious. "What's the occasion?"

"No occasion," Maeve said, hearing the jingle of the bell over the door behind her. She turned to find Chris standing there, still a little gray, but none the worse for wear. She held one finger up. "I figured it was about time you had a good meal."

"Bring me a quiche?" Rebecca said, her agreement to the dinner implied.

"Sure. Anything else?"

"Bread? Cupcakes? A couple of mini pies?"

"You've got it. See you at six."

Chris took a seat at one of the tables, his big frame sagging. "Going up to Poughkeepsie tonight?" he asked as she came around the counter.

She hugged him from behind, wrapping her arms around his chest and leaning her head against his back. "Yes. I miss my girl." She put her hand on his forehead to check for a temperature. "How are you feeling?" she asked, his brow warm to her touch.

"Not great," he said. "But there's a lot going on in this case, and I can't afford to be sick."

"You're sick," she said. "Not poisoned, right?"

"I think that's correct," he said. "Tell Heather I forgive her for day-old meat loaf."

She went over to the refrigerator and pulled out an iced tea, his favorite. "Drink this. I don't want you to get dehydrated."

"Too late," he said. "But thanks."

She pulled up a chair. "So what's going on? Any new leads?"

His face clouded over, whether from the sensation of the cold liquid hitting his stomach or something else, she wasn't sure. "Maybe. It's been too long. The trail is getting cold. I feel like I'm racing against the clock and the clock is winning."

"County any help?"

"A bit," he said. "What did you know about Trish before you hired her?"

"Not much," Maeve admitted. "We reconnected at back-to-school night. I used to see her a lot when the kids were small. Class trips, recitals, things like that. She came into the store occasionally. I liked her," Maeve said. "She was frank about Taylor's aspirations and her own financial limitations at back-to-school night. I appreciated her honesty."

"And that was enough to hire her on the spot?"

Maeve looked down at her hands, rubbing at a spot of blue frosting in the crease of her palm. "She's a single mother. So am I. She needed a job. I wanted to help."

He tried to smile, but the effort was almost too much. "You're a good person, Maeve."

"Thanks for saying that." She reached across and took his hand. "You need to go home. You are as sick as a dog."

"In a couple of hours," he said, getting up. "Thanks for the drink." He started for the door. "When this is over," he said, and she wasn't sure if he meant his illness or the case, or both, "I'm taking you out. And then I'm taking you home."

"It's a plan."

"Limber up," he said, attempting a laugh. He clutched his stomach. "That hurts."

"Go home!" she said, pushing him out the door. After he left, she grabbed a spray bottle of cleaner and went over every square inch of every place she could remember him touching.

After Jo left for the day, Maeve puttered around the store, killing time until she had to leave for Poughkeepsie. Vassar had been Rebecca's first choice, and it suited her as a school, the academic embodiment of her own personality. Maeve wondered if Heather would find the same thing in the school where she ended up or if, as she did with everything else in her life, she would chafe at the things that made it unique or charming or a place of contentment for everyone else.

Maeve received no response to the text asking Heather to join her, so she sent her another text letting her know what she would find in the refrigerator for dinner, not receiving a response. She made it up north in good time and texted Rebecca from the circular drive in front of her dorm. It had been several weeks since they had last seen each other, and Maeve felt as she always did when she visited her daughter at school: happy with a sense of dread. It was all different now, her little girl not little anymore, her daughter more of a woman in her own right than someone dependent on her mother for anything other than the payment of tuition or advice on how to handle the flu, whether or not to precook the noodles for lasagna, how to make chocolate chip cookies. These were little things that didn't require much of Maeve but that she held on to, knowing that motherhood as a concept and a job was slipping away from her in drips and drabs. Every call brought her joy, even if it was filled with complaint, because she knew that soon she would be completely alone, and all she would have would be the intermittent phone calls, the requests for an extra twenty, the questions about how to do their own laundry while at school.

Rebecca came out, and Maeve tried to temper her response so that she didn't appear as needy and excited as she felt. She played it cool; nothing scared the girls off more than when she descended upon them, wanting to hug and kiss them the way she used to—and they loved—when they were small. "Hi, honey," she said, accepting Rebecca's kiss on her cheek. "How are you?"

"Exhausted," Rebecca said. "And starving. Where are we going?"

"Your choice," Maeve said.

Rebecca chose an Italian place not far from campus. The smell of garlic swept over them as they walked in, and not in an entirely unpleasant way. Maeve realized that she, too, was starving and didn't need a lot of time with the menu before settling on the pasta special of the day.

Rebecca regaled her with stories of her professors, what she was doing in her classes, a party she had been to the Friday before and left early because the "music was too loud." At twenty, she was turning into a chip off the old block, going to bed as early as possible because of her laserlike focus on doing as well as she could in school. Maeve had been the same way.

"How are Heather's applications coming?" Rebecca asked and then, seeing her mother's face, laughed. "Or should I not ask?"

"Your guess is as good as mine," Maeve said. "What do you know?"

"She's got her heart set on Washington."

"D.C.?" Maeve asked.

"State. University of Washington," Rebecca said.

"What? As in across-the-country Washington?" So Maeve's lie

on back-to-school night hadn't actually been a lie. "Out west" was what she read. "Out west" it appeared to be.

Rebecca laughed. "Maybe Heather being so far away would be a good thing?"

Maeve wondered about that. Maybe it would be. Probably not. Maybe so. She couldn't decide. All she knew was that while she was looking forward to the upcoming year and Heather taking the next step in her life, she was not looking forward to the empty house at the end of the day, something she would have to figure out how to handle.

"She's playing soccer," Maeve said.

"Who?"

"Your sister. Heather."

Rebecca dropped her fork onto her plate with a loud clatter. "What? 'Soccer is for losers.' 'Only girls who can't play anything else play soccer.'" She looked across at Maeve. "You know that's what she used to say to me, right?"

Maeve didn't, but she wasn't shocked to hear that Heather had taunted Rebecca. "I'm as surprised as you are."

"Why the sudden interest?" Rebecca asked.

"You've got me. One day she wasn't playing soccer and the next day she was. Something about extracurricular activities looking good on her college applications."

"It's a little late for that," Rebecca said, leaning over and slurping up the rest of her soda through the straw. "She should have been doing extracurriculars all along."

"Well, maybe this will help her feel a part of something. Be a nice hobby for her," Maeve said. Hadn't Cal said those same words to Maeve once, hoping she would find something other than baking and motherhood to keep her occupied? He hadn't banked on the fact—and would never know—that her hobby had turned out to have a murderous bent.

"Such a weirdo," Rebecca said under her breath.

"Rebecca," Maeve cautioned.

"Well, she is. I don't know what's up with her half the time. Sometimes we get along great, and other times—"

Maeve held up a hand to stop her. "Say no more. I feel the same way."

"She's. . . ." Rebecca started, searching for the right word. "Mercurial."

"Sounds good. Your English classes are paying off. Now, if I knew what it meant . . ."

Rebecca smiled. "You're smarter than you think, Mom. I know you know what that means."

It was after they had placed their dessert order that Maeve mentioned the three boys whose names she had seen in Chris's notebook.

Rebecca had never been good at hiding her emotions. "Yuck," she said, her face clouding over. "Why do you want to know about them?"

"Yuck?" Maeve asked, making room on the table for the giant plate of tiramisu that arrived. She took a bite. The one she sold in the store was better by a lot.

"You know the type. Rich. Has a BMW or a Mercedes. Thinks his shit doesn't smell."

"You have quite the vocabulary," Maeve said, raising an eyebrow.

"You know what I mean. They think they run the town."

"Run the town?"

"They decide who's cool, who's not. They throw the parties."

"Did you go to the parties?"

Rebecca took a bite of the dessert, grimaced, and put her fork down. "Yours is so much better." She answered around a mouthful of pastry. "I did not go to the parties."

"Your sister?"

"Probably." Rebecca put her napkin over the dessert plate. "Bunch of assholes."

"Rebecca!"

"I'm sorry, but they are." She looked at a spot over Maeve's head.

"I met Morehead. The Connors kid. They were raising money for a trip to Mississippi." And may be suspects in this disappearance, she thought but did not add.

Rebecca smirked. "Sounds like them. Kissing up to parents and looking like they wouldn't harm a fly. They're not good, Mom. Don't get sucked in."

"I'm not getting sucked in," Maeve said, but her mind flashed on the fifty-dollar bill she had tucked into the envelope for the trip funds. She had gotten sucked in but good.

"The Donnell kid moved, I think. Ask Heather." She looked intently at her mother. "Why do you want to know about them?"

Maeve shrugged, not wanting to say how she found out their names. "I heard something."

Rebecca nodded, not believing her. "You heard something."

"That's all I can say, Rebecca."

"Jo?" Rebecca asked.

Maeve laughed. "No. Not Jo. All Jo talks about is the baby. When he poops, how often he smiles, why he is the smartest baby who was ever born."

Around them, the restaurant was a beehive of activity, families filling the red vinyl booths, pizzas flying out of the brick oven at the back of the space. Waiters carried carafes of mediocre red wine and pitchers of soda to the tables around them, the little kids slurping up red-sauce-covered spaghetti, the adults drinking the red wine and chatting amiably. What people saw was a middle-aged mother having dinner with her college-aged daughter, not imagining that the turn their conversation would take was something Maeve hoped they would never have to discuss with their own children.

Rebecca looked down at the table. "I don't know if I should say this, but it may help."

"What?"

"I've been debating whether or not to say this because it's only something I heard and not something I know for sure." She sighed. "I heard that they drugged a girl at a party and something may have happened. I heard it might have been Taylor."

Maeve felt sick to her stomach and asked for the check so that they could get out of the restaurant as soon as possible and into the fresh air. She chose her words carefully, not wanting to reveal that there must have been a link, their names in Chris's notes on the investigation. "Who knows this?"

Rebecca made a face that indicated almost everyone. "There was a rumor that something was said on social media. This generation's version of the town crier."

"When?"

"I don't know. A year ago?"

That explained why Maeve hadn't heard a word about this; she'd had her own troubles to contend with, namely finding her sister, a sister she hadn't known she had and now, whose paternity was still a mystery.

"And did Taylor go to the police?" Maeve asked.

"I don't know," Rebecca said, a look of fear passing across her face. "Do I need to? You know, go to the police?"

Maeve thought about that. "I don't know," she said, knowing that Chris had these kids' names already. That and his circumspect response to why everyone had upped the investigation so quickly after the girl disappeared confirmed what Maeve thought: Something else was going on. Whether it was something to do with child support or abuse or something else, she didn't know, but Chris and the rest of the Farringville Police Department did, and maybe this was it. "Just don't say anything. It's hearsay, right?"

Rebecca nodded. "I guess."

"How did you hear this? When?"

"Facebook. Maybe a year ago?" Rebecca said. "I don't remember exactly. There was something on someone's page right after it happened, and then it was gone. Everyone knows."

"Like a post?" Maeve asked. "A video?"

"One of the guys posted some kind of gross status update, and from the comments, you could tell what it meant," Rebecca said. "I feel sick."

"That makes two of us," Maeve said.

"He took it down. I don't know why."

"Which guy?" Maeve asked.

"Morehead. He's the worst of the bunch." She bunched up her napkin and threw it on the table. "Yet I heard he's going to Harvard." She shook her head. "Life is just not fair."

No, it's not, honey, Maeve wanted to say. "What about Taylor's father?"

"What about him?" Rebecca asked.

"According to the news reports, Taylor and Jesse Connors have the same father."

Rebecca's mouth hung open. "Are you kidding me?"

Maeve shook her head. "Nope. Hard to believe, right?"

"I have never heard that before," Rebecca said. "And you know how everyone in the town gossips. How did that remain a secret?"

"Not a clue." Maeve's one dalliance with her ex was practically reported in the local paper, but the paternity of a young girl had remained a secret to most everyone for almost eighteen years.

"I never saw him, not at a game or anything. Right? You didn't either, I bet. But that's the way it is in Farringville."

"What way?"

"You see the moms but not the dads."

"I guess we haven't gotten very far as a community in terms of gender roles."

"Farringville is a traditional place, Mom. As much as it likes to pretend it's not."

The check arrived, and Maeve glanced at it, then extracted enough cash to cover the bill plus a generous tip and laid it on the table. She picked up her purse. "Let's get out of here."

Out on the street, Rebecca threaded her arm through her mother's and pulled her close. "I will never admit this under oath, but I missed you, Mom," she said. "I'm glad you came up."

"Don't worry," Maeve said. "I won't tell anybody."

They got to the Prius, and Maeve took out her wallet. She pressed five twenties into Rebecca's hand, the girl starting to voice a complaint but stopping when Maeve put her other hand over the girl's mouth. "Here. There will come a time when I either won't be able to give you cash or you won't want or need to accept money from your dear old mom, but for right now, take the money and run."

Rebecca pretended to sprint down the street. "Okay."

"Listen to your mother," Maeve said. "And if I'm not around, channel what I would do. What I would say." Just not how I might act, she thought.

"Like WWMD?" Rebecca asked. Maeve looked confused. "What would Maeve do?" Rebecca explained.

"Exactly," Maeve said, accepting a hug from her much taller daughter.

They drove back to campus, Maeve pulling into the same spot in which she had picked Rebecca up. "Have a good night, honey."

"Thanks, Mom," Rebecca said, leaning in for another hug. "Oh, and hey. Sounds like Heather's in love, huh?"

But she was out of the car, the paper bag of goodies Maeve had brought in her arms, before Maeve could ask her with whom, leaving her mother to wonder just what her second-born was up to when Maeve wasn't around.

CHAPTER 18

There were a lot of different directions to go in, but Maeve thought she'd start with the easiest one. David Barnham was an easy target. After she left Rebecca, she buzzed past his place to make sure he was home and that he was alone with his beloved Cosmo, but he was on his way out just as Maeve turned onto his street. Before she really knew what she was doing, she had followed him to the grocery store, keeping a safe distance as he meandered through the aisles, buying more kale than any one person should need. When he was done, she tailed him to the local Episcopal church and noted, from what was posted on the sign outside, that there was a meeting of the volunteers for the upcoming Founders Day celebration, at which the church would have a booth.

Guy was a regular altar boy.

The appearance of being perfect—and into health—didn't deter Maeve. If what she had heard through the grapevine was true, he would slip up eventually, and she would spot something that would let her know who David Barnham really was, not the guy that he was presenting to the rest of the world, the guy with a million ways to cook kale.

She knew better than to ask Heather to confirm what Rebecca had said about the boys whose names she had seen in Chris's notebook. Kid wouldn't even tell her what she had had for lunch, never mind whether she knew the trio or if she had been at the party where, according to what Rebecca had heard, something terrible had happened, something Maeve could only guess at. She also knew better than to ask Heather who this new love of her life was; with the exception of that last night when Cal had been over and she had raced out the door, she had stayed close to home, her trips to the library confirmed by the village librarian, a loose-lipped lover of Maeve's brownies who was a regular customer.

She went to bed that night, restless and slightly queasy, wondering how two boys who had the whole world at their fingertips could possibly be involved in something so horrible that if it truly was pinned on them, could ruin their lives.

The next night, Maeve had a date with Chris, but she built enough time into her afternoon schedule to take a ride to a tony part of town that she rarely visited. It was close to the reservoir, wooded, and, like many developments with multimillion-dollar homes, quiet and serene. Maeve cruised up and down the street, spying Taylor Dvorak's father's home, the last house on the right, the gate closed, a camera mounted to the brick pillar on the right side. He lived below the former location of the stone yard, where the bigger and newer houses had been built. She stayed inside the car but noted a late-model Mercedes in the circular drive as well as a brand-spanking-new BMW SUV. The house itself was understated—something that couldn't be said for the rest of the houses on the block—but it certainly spoke to the owner having money and a lot of it.

The gates swung open, and a low-slung sports car shot out of the driveway. Maeve sank down in her seat and watched as it drove off, kicking up gravel and dust in its wake. The gates swung closed slowly, and the house went back to being just another silent architectural monstrosity set in a beautiful landscape, cold and quiet and dark.

She was tapping the steering wheel, thinking about what she might want to do next, when a late-model sedan pulled up to the gates, the driver speaking into the microphone and gaining access to the house. She scrolled through her phone, checking the local news station app for any new developments in the case, and hit the jackpot as a headline popped up saying that Charles Connors was in the process of preparing a statement to the media about Taylor Dvorak.

As she drove away, she passed a news van on its way toward the house, the people inside the vehicle, she suspected, readying themselves for any additional coverage that might be needed.

Maeve had an hour before she was to meet Chris for a drink at a local restaurant, one not unlike the Italian place she had taken Rebecca three nights earlier. She went home and put on the television, pouring herself a glass of wine while she waited for the meteorologist to finish talking about the impending thunderstorm. She settled in on the couch to watch the report on Charles Connors's statement.

The reporter, now standing in front of the Connors home, read the short statement. Yes, Charles Connors was Taylor Dvorak's father, something that he hadn't admitted publicly up until this point. A brief affair with his former housecleaner, Trish Dvorak, had transpired many years prior, and a settlement had been reached upon Taylor's birth for her care. He appreciated the village granting his family privacy during this difficult time and said it would be the last he spoke on the subject.

Maeve put the glass on the coffee table and stared at the television. The phone rang and she picked it up, still stunned.

"Can you believe that?" Jo asked.

"You saw the news?"

"You'd better believe it. You weren't kidding when you said this village had secrets." Maeve heard Jo soothing the baby. "'Grant the family privacy'? There's a girl missing. You've got no privacy anymore, buddy."

"Something tells me this only scratches the surface of the secrets here," Maeve said.

"Well, ask your buddy Larsson when you go out tonight. See what you can get out of him. This is the most exciting thing that's happened since Jack's umbilical cord fell off," Jo said before hanging up.

Chris was already at the bar when she arrived a half hour later, a glass of wine waiting for her. She touched it to his pint glass, even though he didn't look like he was in the mood to celebrate.

"This whole thing is getting weird," she said.

"You can say that again."

She thought she'd have to press him to get him to talk about it, but he was particularly chatty that night. "He came to us early on. Didn't want to appear that he was hiding anything from us. He doesn't know anything."

Maeve wondered why he had come to that conclusion so quickly. In her experience, people knew more than they let on. She thought about the list she had seen at Chris's. Jesse Connors. "His kid is in Heather's class. Like Taylor."

"He's the uncle. Adopted the kid after his father and mother died in a car accident. Raised him like he was his own son," Chris said.

"Any other kids?"

Chris looked at her, leaning in close so that no one else could hear them. He dropped his voice to a whisper. "No. He and his wife don't have biological children." He stopped her before she could ask. "I don't know why and I don't care why."

"And still, he never acknowledged his own daughter?" Maeve asked.

"How easy it would be," Chris said, turning back around to look out at the bar and not at Maeve, "if we could just either demonize or canonize." He signaled the waitress for another beer. "But it's not that easy because people are complicated. Life is complicated. Sometimes good people do bad things and vice versa."

"You're feeling pretty philosophical tonight," she said.

"You know what I mean. Heck, with what I've been seeing since this case started, I wouldn't be surprised if there were things I didn't know about my closest friends," he said, finishing his beer just as the second one arrived. "About you, even."

Inside, her stomach gurgled slightly, acid trickling into her digestive tract. "There's nothing, Chris. You know it all."

"I don't know, Maeve. You have seemed kind of preoccupied lately."

She took a deep breath, knowing she had gone pale, hoping that the guilt she felt about how she had lied to him would be mistaken for something else, something that would throw him off the scent of her betrayal. "It's this," she said, waving a hand between them. "This missing girl. How I've been implicated. How I feel."

That softened him a bit, and it seemed as if he realized he had come on too strong. He turned on his bar stool and pulled her close, putting his nose into her hair and inhaling deeply. "I was only kidding. Bad joke."

"Good," she said into his shirt, putting a hand to his chest, feeling his heart beat beneath it.

He inhaled again. "I can't get enough of the way you smell."

There it was again. Her smell. The same thing that Gabriela

had mentioned about Cal, how he had "smelled funny" when he returned home that night that seemed like a thousand years and a minute ago. She had an expensive bottle of body wash—a gift from a grateful customer—way at the back of her linen closet, just waiting to be opened. She had decided to save it for a special occasion. Nothing like two people commenting on the scent you emitted to get her to break it open the minute she got home.

"What have you been up to?" he asked. "Besides making my favorite blueberry muffins?"

Nothing really, she thought. Just following a guy that you should have on your radar. "This and that. I saw Rebecca last night and had dinner with her."

"How is she?" he asked.

She thought about their conversation, sorry now that she'd brought the visit up to him. She put on her best poker face. "She's good," she said, a little too brightly to her own ears, but he didn't notice. "We had Italian food."

"Great," he said, checking his phone, distracted until the bartender came back with the drinks. He rubbed his hands over his face, the mood suddenly changing.

"Chris, what's wrong?" she asked. "You seem . . ."

"We had a lead, but it's nothing."

"I'm sorry."

"God, Maeve," he said. "Do you know what it's like to be a detective in this village when something like this happens? What it's like to have every single person you run into ask you about a missing teenage girl and what you're doing to find her? This," he said, running his hand along the bar, "is not what I signed up for."

She watched a few minutes of the baseball game on the television above the bar. "What *did* you sign up for?"

"Being a small-town cop. Busting DUIs. Chasing speeders. Investigating drug buys. Teaching the odd DARE class. Not this," he said. "Not a guy jumping to his death from the dam a couple of years ago and not a girl vanishing into thin air on her way home from school. Not having to look at the guy's remains and tell his wife that we had found him and that he was dead. Not facing Trish Dvorak every day and saying, 'We've got nothing. I'm sorry.'"

Maeve wanted to tell him that he shouldn't worry about the guy from the dam and telling his wife. She was happy that he was gone and could now live her life knowing that she was safe because he was dead. As for Trish Dvorak, she didn't know what to say.

He hadn't signed up for this.

She wondered about that. Was he really so naïve as to think that being a cop in the little village would never bring him a case that he found repulsive, that he probably couldn't solve? She had misjudged him, then. She thought he had a stronger constitution than that, that *he* was stronger. She thought of her own father and what he had seen in the city all those years ago when he wore the badge. Never once had she heard him cry or complain about what he encountered in a day's work. He never brought it home. His job was to try to keep her safe, and keeping her safe meant shielding her from that unpleasantness. Maeve looked at Chris, the attraction dulling just a little bit at the thought that he couldn't handle this. "I'm sorry," she said.

He was quiet.

There was nothing else to say. He had fallen into a horrible mood, and it was obvious to her that their date, if it could be called that, was over.

"I think I'll go," she said, when it was clear he was done talking. He seemed slightly embarrassed at what he had said but didn't stop her from leaving. Out in the parking lot, she looked back at the restaurant and saw that he was on his phone again, punching at the face of it, his own face a mask of pain. Whatever had appeared on his phone between his drinking in the smell of her and his sudden blackness, it had thrown him off completely, another dead end in a series of dead ends.

The house was quiet when she got home, Heather at the library again according to the note she had left for her mother, the kitchen clean, the leftovers put away. Maeve stood in the kitchen, her hands on her hips, looking around, wondering how she got here, alone after what she had hoped would be a night with the guy she loved.

Behind her, there was a short rap at the front door; she turned and walked down the hall. She had locked the screen door after coming in, which was why, when she returned to the door, Cal stood on the other side, wondering why he was locked out. He said as much.

"Because you don't live here anymore?" Maeve said, unlatching the door.

He walked in and looked around. "Heather?"

"Library," Maeve said, returning to the kitchen. "What's going on?"

"She left me," he said. "Gabriella."

She leaned against the counter and crossed her arms. "Really. Where did she go?"

"No idea!" he said. "And she took Devon."

"Really?" Maeve said again. She wasn't sure Gabriela even knew she had a child, let alone would take him when she left. She'd always figured that if the marriage broke up, the baby would stay with Cal.

"Yes," Cal said. "I'm devastated."

"I don't think you have the right to be devastated, Cal," Maeve said. "You've been making a mess of things for a long time, and as a result, a lot of us now have really messy lives."

"Like who?" he asked, defiant.

"Me. The girls. Devon. Gabriela, even." She looked at him, rumpled and distressed, but only felt exhaustion at the thought of still being with him, still having to deal with his immaturity and inability to cope. "I wish I could feel bad for you, but if there ever was a classic case of reaping what you've sown, this is it." She, too, could be defiant.

Still, the minute he started crying, loud, terrible gasps that emanated from deep in his chest, she melted just a little bit and took him in her arms and let him stay there for a long time, her shoulder becoming soaked with his tears.

"You've got to make this right," she said into his ear. "This is on you."

She wasn't sure if he heard her. In the hallway, the sound of footsteps made him bolt upright and turn around, his tear-stained face and her surprised one what greeted Chris Larsson, who looked like he was in a worse mood than the one she had left him in at the restaurant.

"I didn't know you were busy," Chris said.

"I'm not," Maeve said. "We're not."

He looked back and forth, from her to Cal, and back again to her.

He knows, she thought.

"I thought you might be interested to know that there's been a development. I stopped here first because you were so worried."

"A development?" she asked. "Taylor?"

"Yes. We found her car."

CHAPTER 19

An older couple who lived on the other side of town, the Rathmuns spent the better part of the year in Maine but fled before the snow hit, driving down to their house on the outskirts of Farringville in mid-October, hopefully timing it before the first flake flew. They had arrived home that afternoon after their long drive, wondering why there was an unfamiliar car parked in their driveway, one tire flat. As anyone in a small village would do, they called the police department before doing anything else, not knowing that what they thought was an abandoned car had belonged to a missing teenage girl, someone everyone was looking for. Her backpack lay on the front seat, her cell phone on the passenger-side floor.

Chris described where they lived, and to Maeve, it sounded like it was very close to David Barnham's house. She filed that away.

"I didn't even know she had a car. Judy Wilkerson," Maeve said, practically spitting out the woman's name, her anger growing with each passing day that Taylor didn't come home, "specifically said she was walking home."

"She walked to school that day and most days," Chris said. "Her car was at the apartment."

"Parking has always been an issue at that school," Cal said, an indictment evident in his voice of someone or something that offended his delicate sensibilities about teenagers unable to park their rides.

She didn't know why Chris had come to her house rather than texting her this development; she suspected it had something to do with the way they had parted, but she didn't ask.

Maeve rolled her eyes in Cal's direction, hoping that he would busy himself with blowing his runny nose and not get within punching distance of Chris, who was becoming, clearly, as tired of Cal's insinuations into Maeve's life as Maeve was.

Chris didn't stay long after giving Maeve that news, and watching him go, she wondered if she would ever see him again. He had become depressed over the last several days and now seemed angry, a side effect of his inability to solve the case, or of seeing the woman with whom he had spent so much time comforting her sobbing ex-husband.

Maeve took Cal's hand and led him to the door. "As much I would like to help you, I need you to leave."

"Now? With everything that's going on with me?" he asked.

"Yes. Particularly now." She opened the screen. "I'm not your friend. I'm the woman you left with two children for another woman. I am not your confidante." You're lucky you're still alive, she thought. Do you know how easy it would have been to kill you? Hide your body so that it would never be found? But for some reason, the girls still adore you, despite your breaking their hearts as well, and I couldn't do that to them. "Despite my complete lapse in judgment, Cal, I need you to go and not come back unless it has something to do with the girls."

Under the porch light, he looked younger than when she had first met him, vulnerable in a way that she would have found heartbreaking if she were swayed by vulnerability. But all she felt was numb. She closed the door and leaned back against it, waiting to hear the sound of the minivan leaving the front of the house, her street, and then the neighborhood.

Upstairs, alone in her room, a thought went through her head, chilling her to the bone: This girl is not getting found. She wondered how badly Charles Connors had wanted to keep his paternity a secret from the world, if he could have done something to harm his own flesh and blood.

She texted Poole. *They found her car.*

I know, he texted back. She wondered how that could be and decided she didn't want to know; Poole's reach was beyond her comprehension. *What do you need, Maeve Conlon?*

Not sure, she texted. *Can I get back to you?*

You can, he wrote back.

She texted him some sketchy details about her meeting with Mrs. McSweeney, asking if he had had any luck locating information about Evelyn's biological father. In addition to thinking about Taylor, she thought about Evelyn, about who her father might have been. It wasn't lost on her that paternity had become a dominant theme the last few days, starting the year before when she found out about Evelyn for the first time. The text Poole returned took a few seconds longer than she was used to, and she stared at her phone, willing a positive response.

No was his one-word answer.

She turned off her phone, and it was only when she woke up at four in the morning that she realized she had fallen asleep with her clothes on, the phone clutched in her hand. She bounced up quickly, knowing that she had a mission, had found that hobby that Cal always bugged her about. Some women played tennis. Others were in book clubs. She did other things, things she couldn't talk about over a glass of wine with the girls, things she would never tell Chris Larsson.

She showered and dressed in no time flat, figuring she could do what she needed to while it was still dark and before she had to open the store. On her way to the car, she opened the coat closet and grabbed the headlamp that Jo inexplicably had given her a few years earlier for Christmas. She'd thought about tossing it during her last de-cluttering phase; now she was glad she hadn't. That and the shovel her friend had bestowed upon her on another holiday made Maeve wonder about her friend's gift-giving tendencies.

The Prius made its way silently through the quiet streets to her destination. She pulled into the same spot where she'd parked a few days earlier when she had spoken with David Barnham. This time, instead of walking straight ahead, she put on her headlamp and walked to the left and found the Rathmuns' house easily, yellow police tape ringing the trees at the front of the house, a depression in the soft mud where the car had been, the tracks visible in the beam of light that the headlamp provided.

She wasn't sure why she needed a visual, but she did. If this was the last place Taylor had been, surely it held some kind of clue as to where she had gone, maybe even a hint toward with whom. Maeve walked the dark road first one way and then the other, back toward the car, not seeing anything that would lead her in the right direction, the direction that would help her find Taylor.

She passed one long driveway and then another, the houses out here farther apart than in the old part of town where she lived. A car drove up behind her, and she broke into a jog, trying to give the impression that she was an intrepid and determined runner, hoping that the jiggling above the waistband of her yoga pants wasn't visible to the driver. The car slowed and then pulled around her, a fancy foreign job with vanity license plates: HOTT #.

Classy, Maeve thought, as she stopped jogging at the bottom of one driveway, bending over at the waist to catch her breath. She didn't feel very hott right now; the short jog had her wanting to throw up on the street. She looked up at the big houses that sat at the top of the ridge overlooking this bucolic neighborhood, wondering how long it had taken, how much banging and sawing and hammering had gone on before the houses had been built. Had it been a blessing to these older homes below to know that the noise of the stone yard would be gone, only to be replaced by the sound of people splashing in pools and having large parties on their expansive lawns?

A noise not unfamiliar to anyone with a garbage can on wheels got her attention—someone coming down the long driveway. Instinct told her to turn, the light from the headlamp catching the owner of the garbage can by surprise. The man, bathed in the white light, let out a startled cry at the sight of her.

"Maeve?" he said. "Is that you?"

She aimed the headlamp at the street and tried to figure out who it was. The voice was familiar but not one she heard often enough to identify.

"It's Kurt. Kurt Messer," he said. "Are you okay?"

"Oh, Kurt," she said, relieved. "Just out for a jog."

"In clogs?" he said, pointing at her footwear with his free hand.

"These?" she said, lifting one foot. She had to think fast. "You've caught me! It's really more of a walk than a jog." She kept talking. "Garbage day? Ours gets picked up on Monday."

"Yes. Forgot to put the can out last night."

"That's what kids are for, right?" she said. "Although mine aren't very good at remembering, either."

"Mark moved out last year. Got a place in the village," Kurt said. "So it's just me here."

"Well, at least you've got in an 'in' at the DPW," she said. "That ought to help if you get overrun with garbage." She was babbling, and she knew it. She closed her mouth and then smiled insipidly. *See, old man? It's just the crazy baker from down in the main village.*

"Be careful out here, Maeve," Kurt said. "They found that poor girl's car last night." He shook his head. "She went right past my house, but I didn't see a thing."

"It's awful," Maeve said. When it was clear that they had nothing else to say to each other, Maeve started down the street.

"Mark loved the cupcakes!" Kurt called after her.

"Thanks, Kurt," she said, and in order to keep up appearances— and support her lie—she jogged down the street toward her car, where one more visual sweep confirmed that Mr. Barnham was at home, the red truck in the driveway, and no one else seemed to be around.

Maeve stood and looked around. The dam was to her right, the woods to her left. "Where did you go, Taylor?" she whispered in the morning air. But all she heard was the rustling as the wind whipped through the trees, their leaves changing from the vibrant green of summer to the even more vibrant hues of autumn.

CHAPTER 20

"I owe you an apology."

Maeve looked across the counter at Chris, Jo having practically fled at his arrival in the store. Maeve had filled her in on what had happened the night before, and by the contrite look on his face, it was clear that he had a few things he wanted to get off his chest, things that Jo had no interest in hearing but would surely want to know about after he left. That's how their friendship worked. Jo gave her privacy when she needed it but relentlessly peppered her with questions about the details later on.

"Is there somewhere we could go to talk?" he asked.

Maeve swept a hand in front of her. "This, my friend, is all I've got."

Jo had been listening at the kitchen door. "Go! I can handle it!" she called from the other side.

"There's your answer," Maeve said, stripping off her apron. They walked out to the front parking lot; she saw that he had come in a police car. "Should I get in the back?" she asked.

He looked at her across the hood. "Have you committed any

crimes? Anything you'd like me to know? Something to get off your chest?"

If he hadn't smiled at the end, she would have thought he knew something, but it was clear he was teasing. "Do you want to push my head down so I can get in the backseat?" she asked.

"Just get in," he said, laughing.

The inside of the car smelled like old gym socks with a layer of nicotine on top. "Who smokes?" she asked.

"Chief Carstairs," he said. "But she's a closet smoker. She doesn't think we know, but as you can see, or smell, it's not a secret." He headed toward the river.

She didn't wait until he pulled into the parking lot to ask him the question that had been troubling her since the night before. "I have to ask you something."

"Shoot," he said. "No pun intended."

"So you became a cop but you didn't think you'd ever have to do anything as unpleasant as find a teenage girl? You aren't that naïve, Chris. I know you aren't." She folded her hands in her lap. She didn't want to touch anything in this mess of a car; a grease-covered bag from a local takeout place lay on the floor at her feet.

He pulled into a spot that offered them a great view of the river and turned to her. "I was exhausted. I was . . ."

"Scared?"

"Yes. Scared," he said. "What if we don't find her, Maeve? What does that mean?"

"Well," Maeve said, choosing her words carefully, "it means that a family will never be whole again." By the look on his face, she could tell that she hadn't chosen her words carefully enough. "I don't know what you want me to say, Chris. It's the truth." She looked away, out her window. "I know how I felt knowing that my sister was out there somewhere but not knowing where, and I didn't even know I had a sister until last year." She turned and faced him again, grabbing his hand. "This is someone's child."

He put his head on the steering wheel and sighed for so long that Maeve was afraid he was going to cry. She couldn't handle comforting two crying men in as many days. But when he looked back at her, he looked composed, less stressed. More determined. She took the opportunity to find out more.

"So what do you have?" she asked.

"We think she was taken. The father was contacted. For ransom."

"And Trish? Anyone contact her?"

Chris raised an eyebrow.

"Right," Maeve said. "Not likely she could raise the ransom."

"Exactly. Connors made a ton of money."

"Right. The stone yard. The sale."

"Didn't make a lot of friends with that one, but it was his to do with what he wanted, right?"

"I guess." She looked out the window at the water. "You're a local. How did you feel about it?"

"Lots of jobs just vanished. That wasn't a good thing."

"Anybody with an ax to grind?" she asked.

"How much time do you have?" he asked. "Tons of people with an ax to grind. That old trailer park out at the edge of town?"

"Yeah?"

"I'd say that there are about fifty suspects right there," Chris said, immediately regretting that he had gone there; he grimaced before shutting his mouth and looking out his window. "Guys who lost their jobs and never recovered financially from that. Their wives and girlfriends. Their kids, even."

"What was in the car?" Maeve asked. She wanted to know more;

changing the subject to what he had discovered actually seemed the best way to go.

He didn't hesitate, telling her everything without the caveat that it was confidential. He trusted her. "Blood on the steering wheel. A fingernail."

"A struggle. She didn't go willingly."

"You either know a lot about kidnapping or you watch a lot of police shows," he said.

"Police shows." It was clear to Maeve what had happened. "She was taken."

"That's what it seems like."

"Anything else?" she said, his willingness to talk her entrée into finding out everything he knew.

"Backpack was still in the car. On the front seat. Nothing in her school notebooks to indicate that she was thinking of leaving or that she felt like she was in danger."

She went for broke. "The boys. Donnell. Morehead. Connors. What do they have to do with this?"

He was stunned. "What do you know? How do you know?"

"I saw their names. In your notebook." He opened his mouth, but she stopped him. "I'm sorry. I wasn't snooping." Rebecca had told her more, but he didn't have to know that. This was her purview, her mystery. The girls were to stay out of it at all costs.

"It's an angle we're looking at. What do you know?"

"I hear things. I know what you know, probably. They throw parties. I know that they are sometimes up to no good." She watched a young mother push a baby in a stroller, avoiding a goose that stubbornly sat in her path. "That they're rich. That maybe they hurt Taylor."

"You know a lot."

"I hear a lot." She took a deep breath. "And what about that other missing girl? Is there a connection? Her mother used to work for Charles Connors."

He shrugged. It wasn't a casual gesture but more a gesture of defeat. Resignation. "I don't know."

Through the windshield, she could see the playground where she used to take the girls, long before she owned the bakery, a time when she was still married, happily, or so she thought. She would push them on the swings, and Heather would scream "Higher!," her mother's love for just a little bit of danger running through her veins. Rebecca would stand at the top of the slide, and Maeve would try to coax her down, Heather squirming on her hip, anxious to get her turn. They would eat little sandwiches under one of the oldest trees in Farringville, and she would tell them stories about growing up in the Bronx, about riding her bike down the hill toward Broadway. How Jack said he was the strongest man in the world and how he called her his "perfect girl." How her mother had been beautiful and kind and loved by everyone in the neighborhood. How Jack had been a policeman who had a lot of friends. How she learned to cook at a young age and how her father pretended to like every single thing she served him, even if it was a culinary misstep, and how she pretended to like his gustatory mistakes as much as the meals he didn't screw up. She left out that she had lied to keep him safe and had held horrible secrets in her heart for the whole time he had been alive and she had been his daughter.

After finding out about Evelyn, Maeve had realized that the same was true of him.

"It's like she's disappeared into thin air," Chris said, shaking his head.

"And the county police? Nothing there?"

"No one has seen anything or said anything that has been useful to any of us," Chris said.

"You're smart, Chris. Keep thinking." She flashed on Poole's words. "Start at the beginning and go from there."

He looked surprised. "That's actually good advice."

"Something I heard once." She thought about bringing up Trish and her visit to Cal but thought better of it. His mood had improved and she didn't want to break the spell.

"Hey, do I tell you how to make baba ghanoush? Stay out of police work," he said, but there was a lightness to his tone that suggested he was trying to get off the topic by joking with her.

"I don't make baba ghanoush."

"You know, that chocolate cake with the swirls in it. The one I like."

"Babka. Not baba ghanoush," she said, smiling. They had fallen into their old pattern, their conversation coming easily now, the romantic ship righted again.

"You say babka, I say ghanoush," he said.

"And by the way, you haven't met a cake you don't like."

He grabbed a chunk of flesh above his belt. "True enough." He leaned in and gave her a kiss. "Can you make me a babka?"

"At your service," she said, running her hands over his arms, up to his neck. "I also know how to make baba ghanoush if you want a batch."

"A batch?"

"It's a dip. A spread. Made from eggplant."

"A vegetable?" he said. "No, thank you."

He dropped her off at the store, pulling into the back parking lot, driving straight through the giant pothole that had appeared the winter before. "Jesus!" he said, his car swerving to the left.

"Be careful," she said, too late.

He pulled up next to the kitchen door. "Listen," he said, turning to face her. "Don't tell Jo what we talked about, okay?"

"I would never," she said. "No one knows more than I do how big Jo's mouth is."

"She actually said that she heard my ex-wife left me to join a cult."

Maeve burst out laughing. "She didn't?"

"She told you that, too?" Chris asked, looking chagrined.

"No," Maeve said, wrapping her arms around her neck. "But to make me feel better, she told me that she was patently unattractive and that I was way better-looking."

"That's true. And you're not a liar, either," Chris said. "And you don't cheat. And then lie about it."

Maeve held the smile on her face, the one that told him that he was right on both accounts. "Hey, let me go inside and start on the babka," she said. Before she got out of the car, she took both of his hands in hers. "Start at the beginning," she said again, thinking that just by being with her, he had. Maeve felt as if she were ground zero for the Taylor investigation, the person who had set the whole thing in motion. She got out of the car and watched him drive away, hoping that he didn't let his lack of confidence stand in the way of doing the most important thing he would ever do: finding that girl.

CHAPTER 21

After he drove away, she stood in the parking lot for a lot longer than was necessary, staring out at the traffic going by, thinking about the ingredients of a good babka and the things she knew about Taylor Dvorak.

She knew a lot about one but not about the other.

Jo was having a heated discussion on the phone when Maeve went back inside. "He's fine, Doug. You said so yourself. And I can't be there all day with a baby. I'm losing my mind." She turned at the sound of Maeve's footfalls in the kitchen. "I've gotta go."

"Please don't leave me," Maeve said, trying to sound light-hearted, trying to keep the desperation at bay.

"I won't," Jo said, resolute. "I won't leave you."

The "yet" hung, unspoken, in the air.

It was implied in her tone, written all over her face. One more fever or one ear infection and the baby was out of daycare and Jo was back at the house, taking care of Jack and doing nothing else, leaving Maeve to pick up the pieces again.

She was a great baker but a terrible manager and even worse at hiring employees. That was why she valued Jo so much. Sure, Jo wasn't great at her job and would probably be considered lazy by other people's standards, but she knew Maeve and anticipated her needs—both in the store and out—and that kind of sensitivity couldn't be replaced.

In the kitchen, Maeve turned on the tiny television that she kept on the stainless steel counter and put on the local news. There wasn't a lot to report besides Taylor's disappearance: the nuclear power plant was being evaluated for safety (again), the weather would soon turn cooler, there would be repair work on Route 8.

And Trish Dvorak had made another statement.

There she was, in front of a group of photographers and reporters, the sound of cameras clicking and people shouting questions, a huge, framed portrait of Taylor in her small hands. Maeve couldn't tell where she was, but she had an imposing-looking lawyer by her side, his big hand on her tiny shoulder. Maeve moved closer to the television.

"Taylor," Trish said, her voice cracking, "you can come home now."

The lawyer held up his free hand. "Ms. Dvorak won't be taking any more questions. Thank you."

Maeve leaned back against the counter and turned the television off. Odd choice of words, she thought.

You can come home now.

If she could come home, wouldn't she?

Maeve knew that the parents of taken children sometimes appealed to their kidnappers' emotional side, trying to make the captor see that the person they held was a living, breathing human being with a family. Someone had coached Trish to do just that, it seemed. Still, her choice of words haunted Maeve.

Alone with her thoughts for the rest of the day, the hum of the refrigerator unaccompanied by Jo's constant chatter, mindlessly cleaning the same piece of glass for over a minute, Trish's words still in her head—*You can come home now*—Maeve decided that tailing Barnham was leading nowhere and that it was time to take another tack.

After she left work, she drove back out to the other side of town and sat in her car on the side of the road, not too far from the Rathmuns' house, and thought about her options. Maybe, along this lonely stretch of road, where the houses were set back and no one would know whether you were home or not on any given day, she'd start that exercise regimen she never had time for, always wanted to start. She put the Prius in drive and headed into town again.

Exercise. It was as good a cover as any.

There was the gym where the muscle heads and high school boys lifted weights, and then there was the gym where the ladies who lunched, as Maeve thought of them, went to work out, usually following that activity with a scone and a coffee at The Comfort Zone. It was a combination gym and social scene, complete with a state-of-the-art weight room, a mirrored room with a barre for the middle-aged new-to-ballet crowd, and a full-service spa. Maeve touched her neck as she passed it, feeling jowly at the thought of lying back on a table and having someone use lasers or blow-dryers or whatever they used to help her skin become more taut, youthful again. There was also a store that sold high-end yoga pants, T-shirts, and fancy workout clothes, as well as a raft of very expensive "sneakers," as Maeve thought of them, "athletic footwear" to the rest of the world. She wandered into the store, wondering if she could afford one athletic shoe, never mind a pair. It was worth a shot.

She headed straight to the sale area, where a pair of hot pink shoes caught her eye, not because they were anything she would ever wear, but because they were listed as half off—of a hundred and fifty dollars, she came to find out. She held them in her hands, noticing that the sample size, the last pair in the store, would fit her tiny feet. She looked around the display and didn't see anything cheaper, so she took them to the register, where a bored and vaguely hostile woman—the latter trait coming off her like a scent in the air—regarded Maeve, her look saying, "I don't know what you're doing here, but you look lost. You don't belong."

Maeve put the shoes on the counter. "How are you today?" she asked, eyeing a package of socks; her right toe was going through the sock she was wearing. Maybe it was time to upgrade that fleet as well; she took the package and placed it on top of the sneakers. She dug around in her bag for her wallet, her fingers grazing something sticky and not entirely pleasant to the touch. "I can use my debit card, right?" she asked, and it was only after a few moments that she realized that the salesclerk wasn't engaging with her at all. Maeve looked up from her purse, wondering if, in the time it had taken her to put the sneakers on the counter and locate her wallet, the woman—Tammy from her name tag—had had a massive coronary, an aneurysm, or some other life-threatening event that had rendered her speechless and inert.

Tammy looked as if she were struggling to come up with just the right thing to say, the words that would level Maeve emotionally, that she would recount later at book club—which really should have been called "wine club," in Maeve's estimation. "And then I said . . . !" she would tell the ladies, and they would all look at her with admiration, because she had told the bitch in the wrinkled The Comfort Zone T-shirt, the one with the stretched-out neckline and icing-covered sleeve, just where to go. Because that's how she was looking at Maeve: like Maeve was a bitch who needed to be taken down. It was all there, visible all over her Botoxed face, parts of which she couldn't move.

"You're Maeve Conlon, right?" Tammy asked, pushing the sneakers to the side, the package of socks falling onto the floor behind the counter.

"I am," Maeve said, grabbing another package of socks, trying to ignore the woman's hostility. Bad day at the gym? Who knew. Something told Maeve that Tammy wasn't going to start extolling the virtues of her cupcakes. Maeve wanted to buy her overpriced items and beat a hasty getaway, far away from a place in which she normally wouldn't be seen, a place where people went after they had eaten her muffins and scones and cupcakes, cursing her with every footfall on the treadmill, every step on the stair climber.

Tammy went in for the kill. "I'm Gabriela's best friend."

And there it was. Maeve's first reaction was to back away from the counter but in the back of her mind, she knew that that would be an admission of guilt. She stood her ground, her credit card under her hand on the granite-topped counter, and held the woman's steely gaze. "You take Visa, right?" she asked, her debit card lost to the miasma that was the interior of her purse.

"Your money isn't welcome here," the woman hissed back. "And neither are you."

"Well, technically, it's not money. It's credit," Maeve said, pushing the card closer. "Yes or no?"

Tammy might not have known it at first, but the realization was dawning on her slowly: She had picked the wrong woman with whom to get into a pissing match. Maeve looked at her, dispassionate in a way that was almost more frightening than if she had gotten angry. Tammy got the message and took the card.

"You've got some nerve," Tammy said under her breath.

"Really?" Maeve asked. "Wait until you see my Yelp review." She studied the credit card receipt before signing it. "You forgot my socks."

Tammy started another transaction, swiping the card with such force that Maeve was surprised the machine didn't come flying across the counter. She handed Maeve the second receipt, this one for seven bucks.

Maeve signed it with a flourish. "You don't happen to know where she went, do you?" she asked. "Gabriela? Being her best friend and all, I'd think you'd know where she took off to with her son."

"Even if I knew, I wouldn't tell you," she said. "Home wrecker."

Maeve sighed, knowing what it felt like to be the one cheated on. Although Jo had done her best to hate Cal as much as Maeve had during that time, she had been preoccupied with her own life. What would it have been like to have a woman like Tammy on her side? "I'm so sorry you feel that way, Tammy," she said. Then, trying to get her back on the subject at hand—Gabriela—she asked, "So you don't know where she is?"

Tammy attempted to cry, but the Botox wouldn't let her; all she could muster was some bulging forehead veins and two quivering lips. "She's my best friend!"

Yes, Maeve knew that. "Well, I hope she comes back. For your sake," she said. She wasn't sure her coming back was in Cal's best interest, though he was too dumb to realize that. She started for the door, the sneaker box and package of socks in her hands; Tammy had failed to put the items in a bag.

"New York," Tammy said. "The city."

Maeve turned. "What?"

"She's in the city. At a hotel. I don't know which one," Tammy said. "I'm only telling you for Cal. No other reason."

"I wouldn't expect you to have another reason," Maeve said. "But thank you."

"You did a horrible thing," Tammy said, her final volley. "I hope you know that."

Maeve did know that, and she also knew that a moment's gratification wasn't worth the grief she was getting—the guilt that she was going to feel for a long, long time—from this very upset woman.

"You broke the girl code," Tammy hissed, getting in a final dig.

"Girl code?" Maeve asked.

"Yes. Girl code."

I have left this earth, Maeve thought, and am now residing in an alternate universe, a place where grown people use terms like "girl code" and fail to see the hypocrisy of lambasting a woman who had a one-night stand with her ex-husband who was only her ex because his current wife had lured him away. "I am very sorry, Tammy, about the girl-code breaking," Maeve said. "Thank you for the sneakers. And the socks."

In the parking lot, Maeve didn't know whether to laugh or cry. The town had secrets, but it was also filled with lunacy, she was coming to find. She opened the trunk of the Prius and flung her purchases inside, then slammed the lid and turned around.

A man stood in front of her. "You're Maeve Conlon. I've been wanting to talk to you."

In the fading sunlight, Maeve recognized him. "And you're Charles Connors."

"Can we go back inside and talk?" he asked, much larger than Maeve, imposing in a way that he hadn't seemed on television.

"I'm kind of in a hurry," she said, thinking about a glass of wine and nothing else. She had nowhere to be and no one to see, but he didn't have to know that. "What can I help you with?" she asked, steeling herself for the accusations that were coming her way about her role in Taylor's disappearance. What else could it be? A cake order? Unlikely.

"You made a cake for my wife's Junior League brunch a few years ago. Best thing I ever ate. There were leftovers, as you would expect," he said.

Maeve didn't know how she would expect that, but she nodded anyway.

"You know. That crowd. Nary a carb touches their lips," he said.

"Right. Carbs," Maeve said.

In his right hand were his keys; in his left, a large gym bag that he placed on the macadam. "They loved what they did eat, the one bite or two."

"Well, thank you for that," Maeve said, turning toward the Prius again.

"Did you refuse to go get Taylor?" he asked.

She shook her head. "I didn't."

"Because if you did—" he started.

"I didn't. That's a lie that's been going around town," she said.

"Then we have something in common," he said, turning to look at a group of teenage girls coming out of the gym, all long limbs and flowing hair, loud voices and energy.

"What's that?" Maeve asked.

"The lies," he said. "A lot of lies are going around about me, too," he said.

"People believe what they want to believe," Maeve said. "We can't help that." She wondered why she sounded so composed when the thought of people thinking badly of her made her want to scream.

"I saw you sitting in front of my house."

"Oh, that," she said. "I couldn't find a house that I was making a delivery to." The lies came so easily to her that she scared herself.

"You were there for a while," he said.

"Mr. Connors, what is it that I can do for you?" Maeve asked. "What do you want?"

He reached into his pocket. "Well, first, this," he said and peeled off a wad of bills, handing them to Maeve.

"What's this?" she asked.

"That's the money that Trish stole from you." Taking in Maeve's shocked face, he continued. "She told me. When she tried to get more money out of me. She told me that she took money from you to pay for Taylor's SAT tutoring. Tried to make me feel bad."

"She must have been pretty desperate," Maeve said. *And there you were, in your fancy house, driving your expensive car, while your baby mama stole money from a little bakery with an exhausted owner.* She tried hard to conceal it, but the disgust registered on her face; she could see it reflected in his eyes. She took the money and shoved it into the pocket of her jeans.

"No one will tell you this, because no one knows, Ms. Conlon, but Trish Dvorak should have been set for life," he said.

"Clearly she's not," Maeve said, wondering how in the space of two minutes, he could have made her pity Trish for reasons that went beyond the fact that her daughter was missing. "She's worried about college and maybe just living day to day." You used her and threw her away, Maeve thought. You thought your money would be the end of it. She was good enough for you until she wasn't. Maeve wasn't sure why she came to that conclusion so easily or why she was siding with Trish. Girl code, maybe?

"She shouldn't be. Bad decisions on her part, all of them. She's a troubled woman, Ms. Conlon. More troubled than you know," he said, picking up his gym bag. "You were right to fire her."

"But I didn't fire her," Maeve said.

"See?" he asked, smiling sadly. "Lots of misconceptions, lots of lies going around. You of all people should understand how that feels."

"What am I misunderstanding, Mr. Connors?" she asked.

He didn't have anything to say on that subject. "I know you're in a hurry," he said. "I'll let you go." He turned and started for a car three away from Maeve's.

"What does your nephew know about this, Mr. Connors?" Maeve asked, going for broke.

"Jesse?" he asked, turning.

"Yes."

"He's my son. And he doesn't know anything." He pointed his key fob at the car, and the lights flashed. "Leave that one alone, Ms. Conlon."

Maeve stood at the back of her car and watched him drive away. She knew there was a reason she had never joined a gym.

CHAPTER 22

Her new sneakers hurt like hell, but it was only after trudging up a hill that she hadn't remembered existing on Crooked Hill Lane that Maeve discovered this. It was the next morning, the memory of Tammy's outburst and the weird conversation with Charles Connors still weighing on her. She walked past the Rathmuns' house, the trees still glittering with police tape that shimmered in the wind, and sat on a big rock at the side of the road to take off the right shoe first, and then the left, to find out just how big the blisters on her heels were.

Pretty big, as it turned out.

Start at the beginning, Poole had said. Well, the beginning was over, and now there was a new beginning where a car had been found but not Taylor. That new beginning inspired Maeve to renew her silent vow to herself and the girl to start again. To start at the new beginning.

Her car was a quarter mile away, but there was no way she was putting her new shoes back on, so she started for the car in a pair of her brand-new socks, glad that they had been on sale and that she could dispose of them later without feeling guilty about wasting money.

It was dark and it was cold and, as it turned out, a little wet. By the time she reached Kurt Messer's house, her feet were soaking wet and she felt a chill that she wasn't sure she would be able to shake, even once she could get to the store and turn on the oven at full blast. She got into the car and turned it on, using the bi-directional setting on the defroster to send warm air toward her toes, which were starting to get numb.

She was never prepared. She always had cold feet, or an extra layer on when one wasn't needed, or only broken hair ties at her disposal when her hair came loose and was flying around her head.

She wiggled her toes. They were starting to complain, a deep ache that set her nerve endings ablaze. She held them closer to the fan under the dash and waited a few more seconds, sliding down in her seat as she saw headlights approaching from behind her on the road, a vehicle making its way with a loud roar of an engine far bigger than the Prius's.

As it passed, Maeve got a look at it before it disappeared into the darkness and was pretty sure that it was Coach Barnham's truck.

She sat up straighter. He was heading away from the main village, away from the high school where he taught and coached, down a long, dark road that brought its travelers to the far end of the village limits and ultimately to a dead end. Maeve took off after him at a safe distance.

She loved her silent Prius. It made hardly a sound in the still air of the morning, and although it was white, it was dirty enough that it didn't gleam in the darkness like a shiny jetliner cutting through an inky sky. Satisfied with the likely forty calories she had burned while trudging along the deserted road earlier, she bit into a half of a stale muffin that sat on the seat next to her, marveling at how good it still tasted, two days later, and wondering if she was making a mistake by throwing out some of her unsold baked goods at the end of the day. She watched the truck take one bend after another, easily navigating the part of the road that went to dirt and gravel, where pavement hadn't been laid as there were no houses at that end. The truck reached the dead end and came to a stop right at the edge of a copse of trees. She held back, pulling into the last driveway on the road, backing in so that she could stay in the car and peek out at the coach and see what he was up to.

He pulled his kayak out of the bed of the truck and hoisted it overhead; Maeve was amazed that anyone would have the strength to lift a boat that had to be at least twelve feet long and sixty pounds over his head and walk, without stumbling, along a rutted path to the water. She lifted a lot of stuff during the day—bags of flour, tubs of sugar, unwieldy trays of cookies—but she couldn't lift something like that over her head and keep it there without wiping out, caus-ing grave damage to the boat and her body. She watched him walk along a narrow path, disappearing from sight as he got closer to the water.

She looked balefully at the sneakers on the passenger seat next to her, sitting beside the crumbly muffin in its waxed paper bag, and picked them up, putting them back on her feet.

She stepped gingerly from the car. Yep, still painful. She walked to the edge of the bank that fronted the little body of water, an off-shoot from the reservoir that circled Farringville and provided water for the village and its neighboring towns, looking in the murk for the boat or any sign of the coach paddling around. It took her a while in the gloom of the early morning, but she caught sight of him a few seconds later, making his way through the fog rolling up over the water, his back to her. In his hand was a long stick, which he put into the water, gauging its depth. He buried the stick and his arm up to the wrist, then, after a few seconds, pulled the stick out.

Maeve didn't know a lot about tides, high or low, and even less about kayaking, but she did know that putting a kayak in the water and then testing to see if it would float seemed like something an experienced kayaker wouldn't do. There had to be a tide chart on-line that could tell you that, right? What he was measuring for was a mystery.

Beneath her sore feet, the ground gave way with each step she took, the rains that had characterized the end of September and the beginning of October making it hard to gain purchase on the slip-pery terrain. Above her, trees, sporting the spectacular colors of a wet autumn, dripped droplets of dew onto her head as she traversed the slope that led down to the water's edge. She grabbed low-hanging branches to keep her balance, finally making it as close to the little lake as she wanted to, taking cover behind a tree, staying hidden, gripping a branch overhead to steady herself as the ground eroded under her fancy athletic shoes.

She scanned the lake, having lost sight of Barnham, the sound of paddling replaced by the sound of ducks splashing about. The kayak was gone, as was any sign that it had been out there, the water as smooth as glass. Beneath her feet, the ground crumbled a bit more, and her arms, which had moments earlier been bent at the elbows, were now straight up over her head, hanging on to the branch for dear life. Behind her, there was a noise not unlike the sound of rice being poured into a jar: the rocks on the steep incline shifting into new forms, making new rivulets in the dirt.

How had Barnham made his way so easily to the water? Why had he been measuring its depth? How had he disappeared so quickly?

The situation beneath her feet was getting more fraught and

frantic with every passing moment. A sinkhole had developed, and as she clung to the tree branches, she looked around, noticing the smooth, paved path a hundred feet away that Barnham had used to get to the water. There was nothing to do but laugh, and she felt the hilarity bubbling up inside of her, her father's voice in her head: *You've really done it this time, Mavy.*

She thought about what she looked like, a tiny woman hanging from a tree, the ground beneath her gone, a large hole in its place, a hole that she'd have trouble crawling out of on her own. There had been trees in the Bronx, but growing up, she hadn't invested a lot of time in tree climbing as a hobby. She was small enough to have been a gymnast but was short on athletic ability, and as she hung there, her arms now matching the numbness of her feet, she wondered how this would end, how Chris Larsson would feel when his fellow officers told him that a woman had been found, her neck broken, in a hole by a deserted lake. How he would react when he realized that the woman was Maeve Conlon. How he would wonder why she had been at the lake and how she had afforded such expensive sneakers on a baker's salary.

"But I loved her!" he would cry, and they would circle him and offer support, and by Christmas he would have a new girlfriend; a guy that good, not to mention handsome, wouldn't stay on the open market very long.

Her laughing soon turned to crying, and right before she let go, hitting her head on a protruding branch on the way down, she thought, This is not the way I thought I'd go.

CHAPTER 23

Her bed felt soft and moist, and at first she wondered if she had spilled a cup of water overnight. Then water poured down from above, and she sat up with a start, wondering how much rain had to have fallen to cave in her roof. Her hands sank into deep mud on either side of her body, and as her eyes focused on the world around her, they landed on her new pink sneakers, now wet and dirt-splattered, their laces black.

I'm outside, she thought.

She was at the lake, in a hole that had formed beneath her feet. She looked at her hands, red, raw, and streaked with chafing, and felt the lump at the back of her head that had formed after she had hit the tree branch. The lake. Barnham and his kayak. She felt around in the light jacket she was wearing and found her phone.

"Chris?" she said when he picked up. "Can you come get me?"

By the time he arrived, she had crawled out of the hole with considerable difficulty, made her way to the road, taking a seat on a big rock and hanging her head between her knees, waiting for the nausea to pass. Lack of food, the damp, and the headache that pounded behind her eyes combined for a woozy, hungover feeling that she doubted would go away with an ibuprofen and caffeine intervention.

It was six thirty, and the bakery was supposed to have opened a half hour earlier. While she waited for Chris to come, she sent several frantic texts to Jo, letting her know that she would be late and asking her to please get to work as soon as possible. To give every customer a free cup of coffee. She had described to Chris as best she could where she was and told him, not entirely convincingly, that she had embarked on a new fitness regimen, one that had her running before work began and that was started with the goal of making her the hard-bodied woman that she had never been and hoped to become. Lies, all of it. Fortunately, her head hurt too much to let her feel any guilt at the untruth.

Besides, the minute Chris got there, she was going to spill the rest of it. Barnham. The kayak. Testing for the water's depth. That gave her some measure of contrition, that her lies would lead to the discovery of Taylor Dvorak's body, down at the bottom of this little lake that it was getting harder and harder to get to.

She turned and looked at the water, peaceful and placid in the dawning day. She alternately hoped and feared that the girl would be there, because if she was, she was dead, not off on a great adventure that no one really believed she'd embarked on. But at least she'd be found, and then everyone would know, and the investigation could start anew, the police finding out if she had taken her own life or been taken by someone else.

Maeve's clothes were wet, but the urge to fold herself up as small as possible was still there, and she brought her knees to her chest and wrapped her arms around them, wondering what was taking Chris so long to get there. She felt confident that she had gone undetected, but who knew? Out there in the rain, everything was

upended, a morning run turning mysterious, her questions growing
by the minute.

She pulled her phone out; its screen was black. Dead. That explained why she hadn't heard back from Jo, why strong protesta-
tions of Jo's annoyance over having to run the store herself hadn't
come in, fast and furious. She shook in the cold, happy when she
saw headlights crest over the hill that she had trudged up hours
earlier, the sound of Chris's Jeep and crunching gravel marking his
arrival, his appearance the most welcome sight she had seen in a
long time.

He pulled the Jeep over to the side of the road and got out, looking a little disheveled, bags under his eyes. "Maeve?"

She stood up and waved, the motion bringing the nausea into
sharp relief. "Over here!" she called, walking toward him.

They met each other halfway, he a short distance from his car,
she a hundred steps from the rock on which she had sat to wait for
him.

"Are you okay?" he asked. "What are you doing out here? Who's
at the store? Why are you out in the rain?" The questions came at a
rapid clip. He took off his windbreaker and wrapped it around her;
it was so big that it went around her two times, like a straitjacket,
something she was starting to think she might need.

"Is that your normal interrogation style?" she asked. "Do you
pepper all people with ten questions in a row?"

"It was only four, and no, that's not my normal interrogation
style. Glad you still have your sense of humor," he said, looking a
little sour. She wasn't sure if it was the early-morning call or the
sight of her that made him that way.

Under normal circumstances, the setting and the sentiments
would have been romantic, a guy finding his love shivering and
cold, his arms and jacket around her, him whispering into her hair,

kissing her forehead, but she was Maeve, and nothing was ever normal or right or romantic when it was supposed to be, and what she had seen, that morning in particular, colored everything.

This is crazy, she thought, but I have to say it. She looked up at Chris, the cop who didn't have a stomach for the macabre and grotesque, the mysterious and the unsolved, and said what she was sure was the last thing he wanted to hear.

"You have to drag the lake."

CHAPTER 24

Maeve told Chris everything she knew and remembered.

"Here's the thing, Maeve," Chris said. "He's denying everything."

They were in her kitchen now, a few hours after arriving home, and she was in dry clothes, a scalding cup of tea on the table. Farringville didn't have divers or any of the equipment necessary to search or drag a lake, so they would have to call in County; Chris had completed his phone calls up the chain and was awaiting word. Maeve didn't have a lot of faith in the county police; they hadn't turned up anything related to Taylor's disappearance and hadn't been a tremendous amount of help to the Farringville detectives as far as she could tell.

"I saw him, Chris. He was there. Does he have an alibi?"

"As good as anyone else's at five in the morning," Chris said. "He was sleeping."

"Alone?"

"No," he said, and that made Maeve wonder who the coach might be involved with, who would vouch for his whereabouts. Someone stupid, obviously. Someone willing to get caught in a lie.

Chris shrugged. "I think I would have been happier if you had been with me and not running around the backwoods of Farringville, alone with an almost dead phone." He leaned over and brushed some damp hair from her forehead. "What were you thinking?"

What was she thinking? She didn't know. "Hey," she said, trying to make a joke of it. "I have a hot boyfriend. I also have love handles. I was thinking I should make one of those things go away. I chose the love handles."

"Lucky me," he said.

They both turned at the sound of a knock at the front door, and Chris let in his boss, Suzanne Carstairs, who came in trailed by the smell of cigarette smoke.

"Hiya, Maeve," she said, her aging, former-prom-queen good looks at odds with the job she held. "Do you have another one of those?" she asked, pointing at the tea. "An errant scone lying around?"

Maeve made her a cup of tea and found a frozen scone in the freezer; she put it in the microwave while the chief asked her a series of questions, all of them similar to the ones that Chris had asked her already.

Suzanne raised an eyebrow. "Out for a run, you say?"

Maeve placed the tea and scone in front of the other woman. "Why does everyone find that so hard to believe?"

Suzanne shrugged. "I don't know. You run a business that opens at the crack of dawn and closes ten hours later. Doesn't seem like it would leave a lot of time for a regular exercise routine." She patted her own stomach. "I should know."

Maeve stayed quiet. The less said, the better.

The chief picked at her scone. "You're a better woman than me, Maeve. I can barely find time to eat during the day, never mind exercise."

Chris shot Maeve a look that said her statement wasn't entirely accurate. The takeout wrappers that Maeve had seen in the police car were another indication that the chief didn't miss many meals, despite her lithe frame. She was probably one of those people who could eat anything and not gain an ounce. Maeve wanted to hate her for that, but she couldn't. Suzanne seemed plainspoken and warm, but Maeve could also tell that she was canny and sharp underneath the choppy brunette bob and behind her dark eyes. She had been appointed chief only recently, no doubt because of her ability to see through the lies as well as navigate the political, shark-infested waters of a small-town department.

"Laurel Lake, you say?" Suzanne asked, pulling a little notebook out of her blazer pocket, a blazer that matched her slacks. Slacks, that was the only thing you could call them. Practical, functional, and perfectly suited to the woman's line of work but stylish nonetheless. Maeve wouldn't be caught dead in a pantsuit, but Suzanne managed to pull it off, particularly because what her clothing lacked in style, she made up for with a pair of very expensive leather boots.

"Is that what it's called?" Maeve asked. "I didn't know it had a name."

"Yep. Laurel Lake. Story goes that someone named Laurel drowned there," the chief said, sipping her tea. "Hence the name." She wrote a few words in her notebook; Maeve couldn't read them upside down and wasn't sure she wanted to know what they said anyway. "So, Barnham? The coach? He was down there in a kayak?" she asked.

"All true," Maeve said.

"And you sustained a head injury upon falling from a tree branch?"

Chris leaned against the counter, his arms crossed over his chest. Maeve looked at him. Clearly he knew where this was going, but he kept his mouth shut.

"I know what I saw," Maeve said.

Suzanne pursed her lips. "I'm just concerned that you may be misremembering," she said. "And by the way, is your head okay?"

"My head's fine."

"Need to get checked out?"

"No."

"Okay," the chief said, returning to her scone. "The problem we have is that Barnham has an alibi. So who was it that you saw?"

Maeve put her head in her hands and thought back to the events of a few hours earlier. It had been Barnham; she was sure of that. "I know what I saw. It was him."

"I'm just not sure I can call in County divers to search a lake based on this story, Maeve."

"I'm just not sure you shouldn't be doing everything in your power, including listening to me, even if you think my story is cockamamie, to find Taylor Dvorak."

Suzanne smiled sadly. "Here's what I've got, Maeve: I've got a woman who took up running, God knows why, who saw someone doing something in a little lake, but who hit her head and may not be our most reliable witness, accusing a guy with an airtight alibi, and a pillar of the community to boot, of kayaking in the wee hours of the morning. You see my problem?"

Maeve looked at Chris and then back at his boss. To her ears now, it was a completely ridiculous story. "And why is his alibi airtight?"

"Well, he's sleeping with someone on my force, Maeve," Suzanne said. "Is that airtight enough for you?"

CHAPTER 25

It wasn't until she was in bed that night that it occurred to her to call Poole. Unlike her daughters, he always answered the phone when she called, no matter the day, no matter the time. Tonight was no exception.

"So, I've had a bit of a day," she said, touching the back of her head. This was her second bump on the head this year, and she wondered if getting hit on the head twice in a short amount of time would lead her down the same road her father had been on prior to his death. Confusion. Anger. Disorientation. Moments of resignation, but not many. She pushed those thoughts aside and focused on the task at hand. "I'm looking for background on someone named David Barnham."

"Spell it."

When she was finished, she added, "I don't know, Poole. Something isn't right about this guy."

"Just because he kayaks before dawn?"

"That and he seems to get involved with the girls on his team."

"What do you mean 'get involved'?"

She realized she didn't know. "I don't know. Has parties. Invites the girls."

"How do you know this?"

"I hear things," she said.

"Good sources?"

"Maybe?"

He let that go. "Anything else?"

"I don't know."

"That's not a lot to go on, Maeve. Lots of coaches have parties."

"Single men with teenage girls?"

"It's not unheard of," Poole said. "Listen. We're different, you and me. We've been changed in a way that we don't even understand. If this guy has an alibi, and the alibi is a cop, I'm not sure you saw who you think you saw."

She ignored that. When Poole turned against her, didn't believe what she was telling him, that was the time she knew she was starting to lose it. "What about the fact that he was testing the water's depth from his kayak this morning?"

"They gonna drag the lake?"

"I don't know. The chief and Chris weren't too forthcoming with the next steps in the investigation."

"Chris the boyfriend?"

"Chris the boyfriend."

Poole paused. "Maybe they don't want you to know what's happening next. Ever think of that, Maeve Conlon?"

"Maybe. Hey, I was just giving them my opinion. Telling them what I saw."

"Police don't like amateur sleuths," Poole said. "Messes up our game."

"The Farringville PD has zero game, Poole. Trust me."

"Even the boyfriend?"

Especially the boyfriend, she thought. But she didn't answer. "So, can you help me? Find out about this Barnham guy?"

"I can try." In the background was the noise of the city—cabs honking, pedestrians talking, a train going by overhead. He was close to his precinct, still at work. "I'll see if I can find him the usual ways. Find out what he may have been up to before he became coach. Will that help?"

"Thanks, Poole."

"You get yourself into a lot of messes, Maeve Conlon. But this is a new one on me." He chuckled. "Running at dawn? Following a kayaker? If I didn't know you so well, I'd say that you were a little loco."

But you don't know me that well, she thought, as she listened to silence on the other end. You only know my secrets.

"Hey," she started, before realizing she was talking to a dead connection. "Anything on my sister? Her paternity?" But he wasn't there any longer, and knowing him the way she did, she knew that if he had something to tell, he would have told it. Poole was a man of few words, and the words he used always counted.

She got out of bed, having already made the decision to close the store the next day, her head still aching to the touch when she reached back.

Downstairs, sitting on the bottom step of the long staircase that led to the second floor of the old Colonial, she laced up a different pair of shoes, old hiking boots that she found in the hall closet, left over from the days when she and Cal were dating and his idea of a fun date was a picnic at the top of Bear Mountain. Her ideas had been much different; sipping a Châteauneuf-du-Pape in the cozy confines of a dark-paneled bar, a plate of paté or oysters in front of the two of them. But he had had no money and she even less, so sandwiches that she prepared and an eight-dollar bottle of Char-donnay had been their reward for reaching their destination.

Maeve stood and wiggled her toes in the boots; they were defi-nitely more comfortable than the sneakers and would serve her well on her latest excursion. She leaned on the banister and called up the stairs. "Heather!"

She discerned a low grunt from behind the girl's bedroom door.

"I'll be back in a few minutes," she said, not adding anything else that could be used against her later, make her fudge an alibi when none was available. She wasn't going to see Jo, which would have been her first convenient go-to for a lie. She wasn't heading back to the shop. And although she was in desperate need of a hair-cut and eyebrow wax, there wasn't a salon in Farringville open once the streetlights came on. The art of the lie. She had honed it over the years, learning a few things along the way from Heather, curiously. Sometimes she thought the kid was better at it than she was.

She opened the closet door and grabbed the hooded sweatshirt—owner unknown—that hung in the overstuffed downstairs storage. Her headlamp, she remembered, was still in the trunk of the Prius. She was zipping up the sweatshirt when Heather appeared at the top of the stairs, a sheet of paper in her hands.

"Would you read my essay before you go?" she asked in an un-characteristic display of neediness.

"What essay?" Maeve asked, a little too sharply to her own ears, and judging from the look on Heather's face, hers, too. Damn it, Maeve thought. Just when they had reached a permanent state of silent, brooding détente. Foiled again.

"Forget it!" Heather said, starting for her room.

Maeve counted. One, two, three . . . door slam. Happened every time. She raced up the stairs, taking them two at a time, and let herself into Heather's room without knocking, finding the girl on her bed, sobbing into the sheet of paper. Maeve sat down next to her on the bed. "What's going on? What essay?"

"My college essay," Heather said, balling up the sodden paper. "For my application."

"To where?"

"Everywhere," she said. "All of my schools are on the common application."

That would have meant something to Maeve if she had been even half awake during Rebecca's own college search, but Cal had insisted that he drive the figurative bus on the search and paperwork, and Maeve had acquiesced gladly. Now she needed to engage; that was clear. She took the essay from Heather's hand and smoothed it out on her lap. She read the title—"My Father's Daughter"—and steeled herself for the inevitable rapture that would spill out before her, Heather's words rhapsodizing about her wonderful father and all he had done for her.

And she wasn't disappointed. Heather's essay started with a story about how her father had taught her to ride a bike and how because of that and the patience he had shown, Heather had learned everything she needed to know about perseverance. Dedication. Love. How being taught by her father how to make lasagna (really?) and drive and care for her younger brother had made Heather the person she was today. How he had cared for her when she got chronic ear infections, spiking fevers. Heather knew what it took to get through hard times—her dad had taught her that, too. She knew what it meant to work hard because she saw her father work hard every day of his life, even now, in his early retirement and in his role as full-time father to her stepbrother.

"You hate it," Heather said. "It's terrible."

Tears blurred Maeve's vision, the paper reading as if Heather didn't have a mother at all. She wiped them away so that Heather wouldn't see how she really felt. "Actually, it's lovely, honey," she said. "There's a typo in paragraph two. It should be *t-h-e-i-r* instead of *t-h-e-r-e*."

Heather laughed. "Oh, man. Rookie mistake." She walked over to her desk and made the correction on her laptop. "Anything else? Does it say enough about me and what I'm like? My English teacher said that it should be a story about me and tell the person reading the application who I am. Give them a window into what I'm like."

"Yes," Maeve said. "It says that."

"It's not too much about Dad?" she asked.

It's way too much about Dad, but I'm a little biased there, Maeve thought but did not say. "It's perfect, honey. Really," she said, the lie catching in her throat slightly, making her cough.

"I think I'll send it to Rebecca to see what she says," Heather said.

"Good idea." Maeve stood thinking back to her dinner with Rebecca and her insinuation that Heather had a new person in her life. "How is everything else going?" Maeve asked.

Heather focused on the essay, making the correction that Maeve had pointed out. "Everything is good."

Maeve looked around the room, wondering if Heather would leave it as it was now when she left, a virtual time capsule of her teenage years. Rebecca had lived more like a Spartan when she was in the house and was the same in her dorm room; the few possessions she had besides her clothes had gone with her to Vassar and returned home during the summer, only to disappear again when she left in September for her sophomore year. "Nothing going on? Nothing new?"

Heather shook her head and crossed something else out on the essay.

"I could use you at the store a little more. Is that okay? Or is soccer taking up too much of your time?"

"I need the cash," Heather said. "I don't want to work my freshman year, so I'm saving. I'm not getting a ton of hours at the grocery store. They just hired a bunch of new people."

That showed a maturity that Maeve hadn't known existed in her daughter. Rebecca had assumed that she would get a monthly allowance in addition to whatever money she had saved, not realizing that paying for an expensive private school was her monthly allowance. Her dream school, her sacrifices to make as well.

They seemed to be communicating well, so Maeve decided to up the ante a bit, asking the question that had been on her mind since her dinner with her older daughter. "Anyone new on the horizon?"

"What?"

"You know. Boys. Anyone new?"

Heather turned and glared at her, any goodwill that Maeve had earned from her comments on the essay gone. "Why would you say that? There's nobody."

"Oh," Maeve said. "I just . . ."

"You just what?"

"I just," Maeve said, "I . . . nothing."

"I'm here every night. I'm doing well in school. You should be really happy with me right now," Heather said, lying back on the bed and putting her arm over her face. "Stop interrogating me."

"I *am* really happy with you right now," Maeve said, underscoring her words with a jocular nudge to Heather's side.

Heather darted to the edge of the bed. "Leave me alone."

As Maeve left the room and went down the stairs, the urgency of her previously planned mission now gone, she realized that all she had done for the past year and a half was leave Heather alone. Maybe that wasn't just *part* of the problem but the *whole* problem.

CHAPTER 26

The next morning, Maeve knew that she would be exhausted later, but she got up early and went back to the street where Taylor Dvorak had gone missing anyway, stumbling around in the dark, which was a great way to describe her life in general, she thought. What had happened to her to make her so focused on things that were dark? What had triggered her obsessions? Driven by something—guilt? responsibility?—she traversed the road where the girl had been last seen, wandering aimlessly, hoping that something would point her in the direction of Taylor's whereabouts.

She should let the police handle it. She knew that, and if the message wasn't her own, it was definitely coming through loud and clear under the guise of her late father. She could hear him in her brain every time she walked this road, his never-modulated, booming voice calling, *Stay out of it, Mavy! You're in over your head!* Jack's faith in the police department, even Farringville's, was unwavering. But he had never met Chris Larsson, who, like Maeve, was definitely in over his head. He had admitted it himself.

Suzanne Carstairs? She was a different story. Behind those seemingly warm eyes lay the heart of a sleuth; Maeve could tell. Maybe a killer. Maeve wasn't sure why, but she felt as if she were looking at a kindred spirit. Another woman whose life was altered by abuse? Hard to tell. If Maeve hadn't had so much to hide, she would engage the chief a little more, maybe grant her a free supply of scones just to get her talking. She would cozy up to her, and Maeve was pretty sure the chief would never see it happening. It was too risky, though, too irresponsible to try to befriend the chief when she had some secrets that she didn't want to get out. Chris didn't count. He had made it abundantly clear that he preferred the head-in-the-sand approach to investigation, the easy "get," the maybe-only-partially-true solution.

Right now, in the early-morning gloom, she was a small woman on a dark and deserted street, something she would caution her girls against, but that she couldn't resist doing. She got back in the Prius and drove up and down the street on a silent quest for God knew what, even continuing on the unpaved stretch of road that ran alongside the little lake—Laurel Lake, as it had come to be known—and driving to the end.

Jack's voice was in her head again. *Nothing to see here. Show's over.*

But the show wasn't over. It was just beginning. She just didn't know it yet.

She went by Barnham's house and parked on his street and waited there, not seeing another car besides his truck, wondering what she was doing. Would she confront him if she saw him? Ask him herself what he had been doing? She didn't have to wonder, because he left her no choice. He appeared at the end of the driveway, looking both ways before peeling out onto the street and driving back toward the place he had been the day before.

But before he could get to Laurel Lake, he took a sharp turn, one that Maeve recognized as the same one she had taken the day she had delivered Donna Fitzpatrick's special cupcakes. She followed him in the gloom, at a safe distance, losing him for a time before she picked him up again at a place she had never seen before, the last vestige of the stone yard, an undeveloped piece of land. His truck could traverse the tough terrain and disappeared over the side of the hole, but the Prius was daintier. She parked at a distance and got out, walking along the side of the road until she could safely peek over the edge and down to where the truck had gone. It was still dark, the moon not offering much in terms of illumination, but it was enough to make out where he was going.

She wondered how this gaping monstrosity had been left to become overgrown and wild. The last house on the street was farther up the road, but surely the inhabitants of this relatively new development weren't pleased with a hole in the ground as one of their neighbors. In the hole, a crater, really, were some porta-potties and a rusted-out truck left over from a time when the homes were being built and the crews needed a place to relieve themselves before plumbing had been installed. She took a safe place behind a tree and observed the activity below, which amounted to Barnham going into one of the few porta-potties that hadn't been overturned and then coming out immediately. Whether he had left something in there or taken something out was something she couldn't see, and while she waited for him to do something else, to give her some indication as to why he was there and what he was doing, he surprised her by getting in the truck and driving back up the hill, out of sight before she had a chance to figure anything out.

She waited until the sound of the truck's engine died out to start down the side of the hill, sliding on her ass most of the way, ripping her pants in the process. Never really sure what she was doing, but always sure of why, she grabbed an errant branch here, an outcrop of rock there and managed to make it to the bottom before looking up and thinking, But how am I going to get out?

She didn't spend time worrying about that, getting out of holes becoming just something else that she needed to do lately, opened the door to the porta-potty that she had seen Barnham go into and poked around the desiccated wads of toilet paper and clumps of dirt that lived at the bottom of it, avoiding looking at the toilet and trying even harder not to breathe.

"There's nothing here," she said out loud, thinking that if the odor of cinnamon had followed her everywhere before, it would be the odor of old, baked-in sewage that would follow her now.

Getting up the hill proved less challenging than she'd thought it would be, but she added a ripped Comfort Zone T-shirt to the torn pants to complete her ensemble. Once in the car, she opened all of the windows and drove through town with the chilly, morning wind whipping through, thinking that a shower with the special gel was in order if she had any hope of not offending every single person with whom she came into contact.

At home, in the shower, she realized that she wasn't ground zero for the disappearance, as she'd thought previously, but she couldn't figure out who—or what—was.

The shower did wonders and she felt well enough to open the store and start her Founders Day preparations; she figured the exhaustion would hit later. That was the life of the small businessperson; you opened when you felt like shit and you put a smile on your face, lest people think that you weren't reliable, weren't open to deliver to them exactly what they needed when they needed it. That birthday cake that you forgot to order? She'd have it for you in two hours and it would be the best birthday cake you'd ever eaten. Need a quiche for a brunch that your wife is dragging you to? Here you go. Just out of the oven.

The store was a bit of a mess when she arrived, the kitchen even worse, but she chose to ignore it for the time being. She went into the front and made a small pot of coffee for herself, looking at the clock. Six thirty. She had had a text from Chris the night before asking if they could have dinner, and she had agreed. It was a full twelve hours until they were to meet, and the thought of it exhausted her. She wasn't sure if it was what had happened with Cal or just the general ennui that is sure to set into a relationship that lasts more than a few months, but her relationship with Chris—Chris, really—was wearing her down. The light, boyish qualities that he had brought to the early days of their relationship, that adorable twinkle in his eye, had turned into a sometimes wooden, heavy demeanor that she just didn't need right now, not when she felt as if everyone looked at her as if she were personally responsible for the disappearance of a girl in town. She knew that she was imagining a lot of that, but it was the way she felt. She realized that she had stopped making eye contact with many of her usual customers, not wanting to engage them for fear they'd look at her with that curiosity, the one that said, "Why did you let that poor girl go home?"

The swinging door that separated the front of the store from the kitchen fluttered slightly, indicating that someone had entered the prep area from the back parking lot. Again, she could hear her father admonishing her to lock the door after herself; did she want to end up a "dark stain on the floor"? It was too early for Jo, but it wasn't too early for Cal, who was always out of coffee and usually on his way home from the gym at this time, or Chris, just about to start his day and eager to see her before he did. She prayed that it was one of them and not someone who had gotten wind of the fact that sometimes she didn't cash out at the end of the day, leaving a few hundred dollars in the register because she was too lazy or too pressed for time to go to the bank and make a deposit.

She looked through the round window in the door, and of all

the people she expected to see, the one she saw would never have crossed her mind.

David Barnham.

He saw her before she could really focus on him, and rather than give her a little wave to let her know that he was just a guy in need of a muffin, he glared at her from across the kitchen, standing in a tense posture at the end of the big prep area. She took a deep breath and went through the swinging door, a smile on her face.

"Coach," she said. "Fancy meeting you here. Out of coffee? Need a muffin?" She wasn't afraid of him, but she didn't want to tell him that—or the fact that he should be a little afraid of her.

"No. None of those things," he said, one hand wrapped around a melon baller, his hand flexing and flexing, as if he thought he could do some serious harm with a cooking implement he didn't realize was broken and was on its way out before he showed up.

"So what is it, then?" Maeve asked, even though she knew the answer.

"Why are you following me, lady? What do you want?" he asked.

"I'm not following you," she said and that "truth," if it could be called that, was as flimsy as one of her crepes when it came off a hot pan. She was also no lady, but he didn't need to know that.

"What do you call it?" he asked. "First you were at the field. Then you came to my house. You weren't lost," he said, holding up his free hand before she could dispute that. "You weren't. Don't lie."

She noticed that he left out the most recent place she had seen him. "And I saw you kayaking in the dark. Don't forget that."

"No. You didn't," he said, and while he didn't seem confused by the statement, he didn't seem clear either. He didn't mention that very morning. He must not have seen her. To her, it seemed like he was trying to figure out how to play this, despite his consternation at her repeated presence, her showing up at places she didn't belong. He had rehearsed. "What do you want?"

She tried honesty; it hadn't been her stock-in-trade of late, and she wondered how it worked. "I'm looking for Taylor."

"So are the police," he pointed out unnecessarily. "Why do you think you can find her?" Disdain was not a good look on him.

Did he really want to know? Did he have that kind of time? Did she? She had found her sister, Evelyn—that needle in a haystack— because as good as she was at keeping secrets, it turned out she was even better at finding things, even better than that at getting to the truth, the heart of the matter. Should she take the time to explain that to him, or would that be a waste of breath? "You wouldn't understand," she said.

"Try me."

"I don't need to," she said. She watched his hand flex on the melon baller. "Put that down," she said, a mother scolding a child. The baller made a clanking sound as it hit the counter. "I understand you're very close to your team. To certain girls," she said, going for broke.

"I'm a coach. A mentor. It's part of my job," he said.

"Is it?" Outside, she could hear the traffic becoming heavier as commuters made their way to that popular early-morning train that started in Farringville and shot like a bullet to the city, making only one stop before it hit Grand Central. People were at the front door. Probably wondering why the store hadn't officially opened. "From what I understand, you're very close to certain girls, closer than a mentor would be. Were you close to Taylor? Was she a special player?"

He didn't respond directly. "And who told you that?" he asked, his face getting red. "Heather? Rebecca?" He shook his head. "I thought she was better than that. That she didn't care. That all she cared about was getting out of here. Getting away from you," he said. "From what Rebecca told me, you were a little pathological with the overprotectiveness."

She tried not to wince, the blow hitting its intended target: her heart. After reading Heather's essay the night before and now this, she wondered if there was enough time left to right the ship that was her relationship with her girls.

Maeve stood her ground at her end of the counter. "Why were you out there?" she asked in the same tone she would ask if the lemon poppy seed or the chocolate chip muffin would be preferable to a customer.

"I'm going to tell you what I told the cops: I was not kayaking. I was in bed."

"Yes, with a Farringville cop, from what I understand." She smiled. "We have something in common, then."

"Lady—"

"It's Maeve."

"You've got a screw loose."

"Maybe so." Behind her, the oven timer went off. "But I know what I saw." She put on oven mitts, her back to him, and pulled out the two trays she had put in earlier. "Muffin?" she asked, sweeping her hand over the tray as if she were displaying precious goods.

"No, I don't want a goddamned muffin," he said. He leaned across the counter as if he wanted to start toward her but had forgotten about the obstacle in his path. "Don't do this," he said, waving a hand around. "Don't go down this road."

"Or what?" she said, wondering just how far she could push him before he lost it completely; he was certainly close by the looks of it.

"Just. Stop."

"Or what? You won't play Heather? I'm sure that's not even a consideration. She hasn't played soccer in over ten years. Frankly, I'm not even sure why you took her on the team. Is she that good?"

"No."

"What, then?" She turned the muffins over onto a large cookie sheet.

"We're shorthanded."

"So you take girls midseason?"

He shrugged. "Why not? It's not like we're going anywhere. Might as well let as many girls play as want to."

Maeve had forgotten: This was Farringville. Everyone was a winner. Everyone got a trophy. Everyone played if they wanted to.

She focused on her muffins. "See, here's the thing you don't know about me: I don't stop. I can't stop. Not until this is resolved." She looked up at him in what she thought was a kindly way, a way to make him feel better about her and her intentions. But he blanched when he met her eye and turned tail quickly, leaving the store.

Maybe what he had said had been correct.

Maybe she did have a screw loose.

CHAPTER 27

Jo stopped in later that day, even though she had the day off thanks to Maeve, who wanted to repay Jo for running things the day before. The purpose of her visit? To complain about motherhood. Again. Maeve wanted to tell her that the baby slumbering in the stroller wasn't really all that challenging as babies went. She reached into the cold case and wiped away a smear of grease that had appeared some time during the day, hoping that by putting her head into an enclosed space, she wouldn't have to listen to more of this. Had she been like this, complaining to anyone in earshot about the "witching hour," the hour when children start to fall apart, their naps being too long or not long enough, their blood sugar plummeting, a time when it was too early for wine but too late for more coffee? It felt good inside this case, Maeve thought, Jo's voice muffled by the glass on three sides.

"What are you doing now?" Jo asked.

Maeve removed herself from the case and held up the bottle of glass cleaner. "Cleaning."

"No. I mean now. After work."

"I was supposed to go out with Chris later, but he canceled," Maeve said, trying not to let Jo see that she was secretly relieved.

He was working overtime, something about the case requiring his attention. She made an attempt to sound disappointed, but even he had remarked that she didn't sound terribly upset. He chalked it up to her exhaustion, the bump on her head.

Whatever he wanted to believe. She had other things to do. Something had occurred to her while she put the finishing touches on the Rotary Club's sheet cake, the process of snapping little florets onto its edges giving her time to think. "You want to help me with something?" Maeve asked.

Jo rolled her eyes and pointed at the baby.

"You can bring the baby," Maeve said. "And I'll tell you everything that happened yesterday on our way to where we're going, because I know you're just dying to know." Maeve had been cryptic, citing a migraine as her excuse for not opening, but Jo knew her well enough to know that she was lying, the truth a much juicier tale that Jo would have loved to hear first thing. But there was work to be done, and Maeve had hung the story out as a carrot to get Jo to complete what she needed her to do before Maeve would give her one little detail of her excursion and the real reason she hadn't come to work the previous day.

Jo rubbed her hands together excitedly. "A good story plus I don't have to go home with Prince Poops-a-lot?" She jumped up and down. "This day just got a whole lot better. We'll take my car." Maeve started to protest, preferring the silent Prius, but Jo held up a hand. "Baby seat."

Jo's car was a used Honda CRV, a car that ate up a lot of gas, spewed a lot of exhaust, and smelled like its previous owner, a guy who had run a short-lived cigar shop in town. Jo had been desperate to find something cheap and reliable for chauffering baby Jack, and this car had fit the bill. The owner was a customer and had asked Maeve if she knew of anyone who needed a car like the one he was selling. Jo had jumped at the chance to have her own set of wheels; her husband used their staid Taurus as his commuter car.

"Does it still smell like cigars?" Maeve asked as they exited the store and went into the parking lot.

"It does," Jo said, opening the driver's door and unlocking Maeve's. "Hold your nose."

But the smell wasn't entirely unpleasant, bringing Maeve back to a time when Jack would host his cop friends as well as some neighborhood guys and they would play poker, poker being a convenient excuse to get together, drink, smoke, and eat large Italian sandwiches from the deli around the corner, sandwiches Maeve heard more than one guy say his wife wouldn't let him eat often. Maeve would hang around and collect the loose change that the men would throw on the table and lose after a bad hand, making neat piles for all of the men who attended, garnering a couple of dollars in dimes and quarters by the end of the night, enough so that she could make her own trips to the avenue to get candy the next day. Here in Jo's car, she put her seat belt on and took a deep breath, the memory of those Friday nights curling over her in imagined, smoky tendrils and bringing back the names of the guys in attendance: Tommy Mulcahy. Eddie Martin. Gene Washington. Marty Haggerty.

She pushed the thoughts of the past aside as she and Jo drove through town. She spied Heather walking along the road that ran in front of the high school, wondering who was in the car that honked as it drove by, garnering a wave and a smile from Heather. The car pulled over, and Heather jumped in, seeming to forget that if she was going to go somewhere after school, she was to let her mother know. Maeve's phone uttered a little ping inside her bag, and she pulled it out, seeing that she had a text from Heather.

Going to the library.

Somehow, Maeve didn't think that was the truth, but what could she do? Commandeer Jo's car and race after the late-model Honda, dark blue, license plate number EJK 413? She shook her head. Half of the village already thought she was a lazy slacker or worse for sending a sick girl home on her own, and the other half was sure she was an overprotective wet blanket of a mother who hovered over her children, suffocating them with her fears. She texted Heather back to be home in time for dinner and threw the phone into her purse and her purse onto the floor, thinking at the last moment that she had one other person she wanted to text.

She grabbed her purse and pulled out her phone again. She wrote to Poole. *Anything on Barnham? Anything on my sister's father?* She hit SEND and then thought of something else. *Anything on why I'm completely crazy and can't leave well enough alone?*

All she got in return was two frowning emojis in response to her first two questions and a smiling emoji to her final one. She didn't take Poole for the emoji-sending type, but one thing she had learned about him was that he was full of surprises.

They stopped at a light and Jo reached back and tickled the baby's feet. Despite her protests to the contrary, Jo adored her long-awaited son, the baby she never thought she'd have, and worshipped him in a way that Maeve couldn't remember having worshipped her own children. Maeve turned around, looking at her father's namesake, wondering if she imagined the mischievous twinkle in the baby's eyes, the throaty giggle every time Maeve smiled. He was Jack, and Jack was in him; of that she was convinced. It was crazy, but she was learning that her crazy thoughts sometimes bore a hint of the truth. And if it made her feel better to think that even a small part of her father lived on in this little man, what was the harm?

The light changed. "Where to?" Jo asked.

"Have you ever heard of Laurel Lake?"

Jo leaned on the steering wheel. "Laurel Lake . . . is that that place out by Settler's Bend?"

"I don't know. What's Settler's Bend?"

"Oh, it's this wooded area where the kids hang out and drink and smoke pot."

Maeve raised an eyebrow. "And how would you know that?"

Jo didn't even attempt a lie. "That's where I find my dealer," she said, as if it were the most natural thing in the world to be a grown woman with a dealer.

"Of course," Maeve said. "Why didn't I think of that?"

Jo started the car as Maeve described the location. "Yes, that's the little lake by Settler's Bend."

"We have places called Laurel Lake and Settler's Bend in this town? Who knew?" Maeve asked. "I feel as if I'm living in a Laura Ingalls Wilder book."

Once they got there, Jo pulled over to the side of the road and turned the car off. "So, what gives?"

Maeve told her what she had done the day before.

"Are you okay?" Jo asked. "And do you really think you should be spending your downtime looking for a missing girl?"

"Yes, I'm fine."

"Maybe she doesn't want to be found, Maeve," Jo said. "Have you considered that?"

"Runaway?"

Jo shrugged. "I am not easily scared, but Trish is a little scary, don't you think? I probably would have hit the road, too." Jo looked out the window. "So you were out here, by yourself, looking for a girl by a lake, a girl that the police can't find." She shook her head. "You know how crazy that sounds, right?"

Maeve ignored the last question and left out the part where she had followed a guy to a porta-potty in the woods. "I don't know."

"What do the police think?"

"Besides that I'm crazy?" Maeve said. "I can tell that they don't believe me. Barnham has a significant other in the Farringville Police Department who is vouching for his whereabouts yesterday morning." She opened the car door but turned back to Jo. "But I know what I saw."

Jo held her hands up in surrender, Maeve's tone defensive. "I believe you, sister." But it was clear that she didn't and that she was only joining Maeve on this journey so she didn't have to go home and deal with a baby alone.

Jo got the stroller out of the back of the car and loaded the baby into it. Maeve marveled at the giant wheels and the way the contraption was easily navigated over the rocky, bumpy terrain, every jolt making the baby giggle with glee. The stroller that she had used for both girls had the handling of a John Deere tractor, but these days, everything was better and made life more convenient where taking care of babies was concerned. They walked along the road, making their way toward Laurel Lake, the little body of water that Maeve hadn't known had a name prior to the day before. They took the path that she had seen Barnham traverse with his kayak and stopped at the water's edge.

Jo pointed to a big tree a few yards away. "Is that the tree you were hanging from?"

"Yes," Maeve said, instinctively looking at her palms, where a few scratches remained.

Jo walked along the little sandy beach with the baby and stopped in front of the tree, calling back to Maeve, "I don't see a sinkhole."

Maeve trotted along the sand until she got to Jo. "What do you mean?" she said, walking up to the tree and feeling around the ground. Jo was right: no sinkhole. In its place was smooth ground, a nice mound of fresh cover where a big hole had been the day before.

"Someone filled it in," Maeve said, looking around the area. She knelt down and touched the ground, letting fine gravel and musky-smelling dirt filter through her fingers.

Jo started back toward the paved path. "You're a weirdo, you know that?"

Maeve ran after Jo. "That doesn't seem strange to you?"

"Nope. What's strange is why you would be out here in the middle of the night wandering the streets looking for a girl who is on every single television channel, whose disappearance is an Amber Alert, and who everyone in the state is probably looking for. Anyone in law enforcement, anyway." She hitched the stroller over a little root and took the baby back onto the road. "Even Doug knows about this, and he's in the city." She turned and looked at Maeve. "Oddly enough, he says Poole's been talking about it, too."

"Poole?" Maeve said. No one knew about her relationship with Poole, not even Jo, and that was the way it was going to stay.

"Yes. Rodney Poole? Doug's partner?" Jo said. "He said Poole has a weird fascination with the story, too, and has talked about it." Jo pushed the stroller toward the car. "You are two of a kind. Too bad he's married," she said.

Not for long, Maeve thought. And they were more similar than Jo would ever know.

"I have a boyfriend," Maeve said. "Remember?"

"Yes, and you should be spending the early-morning hours with him, not running up and down deserted streets looking for a girl you don't even know." Jo turned suddenly, the stroller doing a wheelie and listing the baby sideways. "Is it because people are blaming you?"

"What have you heard?"

"Just what you told me."

"That's it?"

Jo's expression told her that it wasn't, that people were talking and they were saying things that weren't true, repeating the words as if they were gospel. Maeve Conlon was a bad person. She had refused to pick a young girl up at school.

"What do you care what people say anyway?" Jo asked. No one cared less about what was being said about her than Jo. She loved to gossip but didn't care what other people said about her. To Maeve, that was her gift.

"I just do," Maeve said. "Particularly when it concerns a young girl who everyone seemed to have forgotten about."

The baby was getting antsy, his happiness at being outside for a jaunt in his stroller slowly being replaced by hunger or, if his rubbing his eyes was any indication, exhaustion. Jo pulled a lidded cup from a battered diaper bag and handed it to him. He took it from his mother, eyed it suspiciously and flung it a good distance down the street after letting out a primal scream that cut through the silence of the wooded area. Jo ducked.

"Kid has the makings of a relief pitcher," Maeve said.

"Yeah. He gave Doug a black eye two weeks ago when he threw a toy."

Jo strapped the baby, now completely distressed and agitated, into his car seat and not seeing anywhere to turn around, drove down the length of the road to the turnaround at the dead end. There were a few cars parked there, a couple of guys packing up fishing gear and heading home for the day after hauling in some fish; Maeve wondered, were they even edible? What grew in those little bodies of water anyway? The baby wailing in the backseat distracted Maeve but not enough so that she missed two other people standing at the reservoir's edge, one in a smart pantsuit and the other in a sport coat, the two of them talking intently and looking alternately from the shoreline to the wide expanse of water.

They hadn't seemed to believe her yesterday but they now

seemed to believe her enough, apparently, because there was no other reason for Suzanne Carstairs and Chris Larsson to be standing on an almost-deserted beach at dusk, standing close and talking in a way that suggested there was more to this visit than an early-evening stroll.

CHAPTER 28

Maeve pulled into the parking lot of the store the next morning, right after hitting the pothole that Kurt Messer had promised to repair; she usually remembered to avoid it. She cursed loudly as the Prius dipped precipitously into the hole and climbed out, then pulled into her usual parking space, wondering if the village had gotten any of the messages she had left on the DPW's voice mail. She guessed no. Muttering to herself about high taxes and what she deserved as both a citizen and a business owner, she let herself into the store and stabbed at the alarm keypad, her eyes falling onto the bulletin board over her small desk where she tacked up orders for the week, sometimes forgetting to pull down the ones that were already completed. A thought occurred to her, and she threw her purse down on the counter, riffling through the finished orders—the ones that were marked PAID AND DELIVERED—to find the one that she needed.

Thank God for Kurt Messer and his cupcake order. She held the slip in her hand and had started dialing before realizing that the head of the DPW probably wouldn't appreciate getting a call at home at barely six in the morning, despite the hours he undoubtedly kept as head of the group that picked up garbage before the sun came up, cleaned the streets in what seemed like the middle of the night to Maeve, who'd been awakened more than once, and collected leaves when the more diligent residents put them out at the curb. She slid the slip of paper into her jeans pocket, donned her apron, and got to work, checking the clock frequently so that she didn't forget to call later in the morning.

The store was small, and she had been doing this a long time, which was why she could handle the morning rush on her own. She was like a well-oiled machine, making just the right number of muffins and scones, having enough coffee for her thirsty customers and taking time, once that rush had ended, to make some new cakes and quiches; she'd make more when Jo finally arrived near lunchtime. Deliveries were becoming a problem, and letting Jo take on the responsibility of getting the baked goods where they needed to go in a timely fashion was a recipe for disaster because her friend— as sweet as she was—had a very short attention span that could find her meandering the highways and byways surrounding Farringville when a straight line back to the store was really what Maeve needed her to follow.

She sent Heather a text: *Please come by when you can.*

She hadn't seen her daughter the night before, her door shut and music playing softly, indicating that she didn't want to be disturbed. That was fine with Maeve; she hadn't wanted to be disturbed either, tired from the events of the last few days and looking forward to a date with a glass of wine and her laptop.

In bed last night, the Brunello making its way down her throat and warming her to her core, she had spent some time tracing Jesse Connors and his adoptive father, wondering just what a man like Charles Connors had seen in Trish Dvorak, a local girl who was much younger than he was. His graying hair and a lined face spoke to a man in his sixties, a full two decades older than Trish, if Maeve's guess was correct. He went to the gym and was in good shape for a man of any age, and Maeve thought that almost two decades earlier, when the affair had taken place, he had probably been a real catch. Beside him in the photo was a well-put-together wife, the kind Maeve recognized from having lived in Westchester for as long as she had. Toned. Buffed. Facialed. Blond. Maeve wondered whether if she had played the role better, the role of wife to a corporate attorney, she would look like this now instead of the way she really did. Frumpy. Messy. A little dowdy and doughy. Mrs. Connors was not someone Maeve had ever met, but she knew her type. She didn't strike Maeve as someone who would frequent The Comfort Zone, the number of carbs in what Maeve pumped out every day being more than this wraith of a woman could handle.

Maeve still couldn't understand why Trish was struggling financially, and by extension Taylor as well. Obviously the man had wanted to keep his paternity a secret and had gone to great financial lengths to make that happen, but with Trish broke and college looming, something in the mother had snapped, and she was demanding more. From him. From Maeve. From Cal. She was thinking about all of that when Chris appeared in the back of the store ten minutes before she had to open, clearly chagrined that he had had to cancel their date the night before.

He apologized as soon as he walked in.

"It's okay, Chris. I was exhausted last night," she said, handing him his usual: a blueberry muffin and coffee, light and sweet. She worked on a tray of muffins, arranging them to her liking, then carrying them into the front of the store and putting them on the counter. When she returned to the kitchen, he had a hard time meeting her eye. "You look tired."

"I am," he said, pushing the muffin away as if he didn't have an appetite. "Do you know Jane Murdock?"

Maeve searched her overstuffed brain for a face and came up with one. "The owner of Chrysanthemum Jewelry?" Maeve asked. She refrained from adding, *The store with the name no one can spell?*

Chris nodded. Maeve heard someone knocking at the front door even though she still had three minutes before she had to open.

"Yes. Why?" she asked.

"She hired a private company to fix the camera over the store." He paused. "The one that the village abandoned and that we all thought was broken. She just returned from being away and realized she might have something of use to us."

"That's good, right?" Maeve asked, knowing where he was going before he could get the words out.

"Depends," he said, looking up at the ceiling, anywhere but at Maeve.

"Why?" she asked, looking through the window in the door. A line had formed outside the front of the building, and people were waiting to get in. But she didn't recognize them. It was only later that she realized they were media types, begging for a chance to get into the store, to find out what she knew.

"Because we looked at the tape, and the last person seen talking to Taylor Dvorak on the afternoon she disappeared was Heather."

CHAPTER 29

Maeve closed the store at the news, and Chris provided cover as she left the building, on her way to find Heather. It was early, but when Maeve called home, there was no answer, and Heather wasn't responding to texts. She went straight home, hoping she would find her there.

It was already clear that the Farringville Police Department had someone who was feeding information to the local media, so it was no surprise that reporters had shown up at the store at the crack of dawn. While Maeve's involvement in the story hadn't been considered newsworthy, Heather's certainly was. She was now a potential witness, supposedly the last person who saw Taylor before she disappeared, and someone who hadn't mentioned a word about it to anyone. Not her mother. Not her exalted father. Certainly not Chris Larsson or anyone else who had been in the store or around town desperately trying to find an eighteen-year-old girl who had vanished into thin air.

Chris followed Maeve, giving her a gentle beep as she sped from the parking lot and raced toward the house, the sound meant to slow her down. It had the opposite effect, and she ended up at home, leaving her car at the curb, illegally parked, the keys in the ignition. She went into the house and charged up the stairs, practically kicking open Heather's bedroom door. The girl was home and sleeping, her mouth hanging open slightly, a light breeze rustling the curtains in her room. It was peaceful and quiet, the only sound a muffled buzz from the phone under her pillow.

Heather awoke, her only reaction an eyebrow raise at the sight of her mother.

"Get up," Maeve said.

"What?" Heather asked.

Maeve pointed to the door. "Detective Larsson is outside," she said. "Not Chris, not Mr. Larsson, not my boyfriend, but a detective in the village. And you want to know why he's here?" Maeve closed her eyes. "And if you shrug or have some kind of snotty response, I will not think twice before slapping you silly." She didn't think she would do it, but Heather didn't know that. The warning was there. She was not playing, as the kids would say.

Heather waited a beat before responding. "Is this about Taylor?"

Maeve opened her eyes. "What do you think?"

"Do I have to go to the police station?" she asked, her eyes filling with tears.

"Yes," Maeve said and relaxed slightly at the sight of the tears that started to spill onto Heather's cheeks. "You can go with me," she said, looking down the stairs and seeing Chris getting out of his car, starting for the door, ready to begin controlling the conversation that would take place. "But you have to tell them the truth. Everything. That's the only way this is going to end. For all of us."

They walked down the stairs and into the hallway.

Heather nodded and turned to face Larsson. He opened the door and looked at her. "Ready?" he asked, cutting their conversation short.

Before she drove off, she texted Cal: *911. Emergency. Call me as soon as possible.* When he didn't respond immediately, she called his phone, but it went straight to voice mail. In her rearview mirror, she could see Chris, waving his hand to indicate that he was impatient to get to the station and get the questioning under way.

At the station, Chris took Heather away to talk, and Maeve sat in a suffocating room with fake wood paneling, alternately texting Jo to tell her what was going on and checking her e-mail for any messages from Cal or in relation to her business. But there were none; it was almost as if everyone, with the exception of the media, knew to stay away from her. She and, now, her offspring were poison and needed to be avoided. Liars, both of them, they hid the truth from the people they loved and wondered why things didn't turn out the way they planned.

Reporters had been camped out in front of the station house and shouted questions at them as they walked in. *"Heather, where did Taylor go?" "Did you have anything to do with her disappearance?" "How come you never said anything?"* And then over and over until it became something of a mantra: *"Where's Taylor, Heather?"* As Maeve rushed up the steps, she didn't know whether to laugh or cry. By dinnertime, footage of her and her daughter would have run at least eight times, and she would have just as many messages from her sister, excited that she had seen Maeve and Heather on television during the day.

She put her phone away as the second hour ticked by. A brief rap at the door announced Suzanne Carstairs's entrance, the chief in another smart pantsuit and expensive heels. She sat down next to Maeve in the other uncomfortable chair and folded her hands in her lap. "What a shit show, huh?" Carstairs said.

"You could say that."

Next to each other, neither had to look into the other's eyes, and Maeve was happy about that. The other woman sensed Maeve's frustration, her anger. "She's a kid, Maeve. Scared. She wouldn't be the first person who didn't tell something that was important. You know, germane to a case."

"She should have known better."

"Hell, shouldn't we all?" Suzanne said, laughing softly. "If we knew better, then I wouldn't have married a complete ass wipe as soon as I graduated from the academy, and you probably wouldn't have done some of the things you've done."

Maeve stiffened.

"Am I right?" the chief asked. In her voice, or so Maeve detected, was a hint of something else, something not quite as innocuous.

"Yes. You're right," Maeve said, her monotone hopefully giving nothing away. All of the things she had done she couldn't undo, and she lived with that every day fairly easily. It was living with the memories of them, the fallout, that was hard.

"She keep a lot of secrets from you?" Suzanne asked. "And remember, I have a teenager, too. I'm right there with you, sister."

Maeve could see where this conversation was going. By making the connection, Suzanne was building camaraderie, hoping Maeve would tell her what she wanted to know. That her daughter kept secrets. Went out when she wasn't supposed to. Had a mysterious boyfriend Maeve didn't know and, as a result, couldn't keep track of. Maeve, however, could play this game, too. All she did was nod and smile in a gesture of commiseration.

The chief could tell she wasn't going to get anything so changed the subject. "He's a good guy, Larsson. You found yourself a good one."

"Yep. He's the best," Maeve said.

"How does he get along with Heather? They talk at all?"

Maeve continued staring straight ahead. "Why don't you ask him?" she said.

"Oh, I have," she said. "Said Heather is a bit of an enigma." She crossed her legs. "But aren't they all at this age? I know I was."

"Me, too," Maeve said, but there was no commitment in her voice. It was just agreeing for agreement's sake. The room, already stuffy and hot, closed in a little bit, the smell of Carstairs's last cigarette hanging heavy in the air.

"You get along with your mother, Maeve? Or did you give her hell?" she asked.

"My mother died when I was small."

"Oh, I'm sorry." Carstairs looked at Maeve. "You had a cousin who died, too? Am I correct? And then your dad?"

"Yes. Right. All of that," Maeve said, feeling her body go into shutdown mode, only answering those questions that she felt she could without giving anything away.

"All of that. Tragic. Your family's been through a lot, Maeve."

They had. And the chief would never know how much.

The chief popped up out of her seat suddenly. "Well, shouldn't be long now," she said, touching Maeve's shoulder. "We'll get what we need and send her home. Or back to school. Whatever you think is best." She started for the door. "Oh, and Maeve?"

Maeve looked up, having to make eye contact with the chief.

"How long has Heather been dating Jesse Connors?"

Maeve did her best to remain impassive, but the surprise was writ large on her face; she could feel it. "Jesse?"

"Yes, Jesse." The chief held tight to the doorknob. "How long?"

Maeve couldn't lie. There were too many lies and half-truths to remember, and she didn't see any reason to add another one to her growing collection. "I don't know, Chief Carstairs."

"Oh, call me Suzanne," she said, smiling.

"Suzanne."

"No idea?"

"None."

"Huh," the chief said and opened the door. "That's odd. A protective mom like you."

"What do you mean?"

The chief stepped through the door and into the hallway. "Sit tight. Won't be long now, Maeve."

CHAPTER 30

I spend so much time looking outward, fighting the good fight, that I don't even know what battles are right in front of me.

That was the thought that went through her head after she washed her face that night, catching sight of her sunken eyes and slack jaw in the bathroom mirror as she applied moisturizer. Heather was at Cal's, the decision unspoken between both of them when they left the station house, Maeve driving straight to the Tudor and dropping her daughter off, not a word exchanged between them. He knew he was in the wrong having not answered her text or voice mail, his consternation over her rejection having taken precedence over everything else that day. This time, his immaturity had bitten him in the ass. It wasn't Maeve who had an emergency, who needed his help and guidance. It was his daughter and his own pride had kept him from helping her when she needed it.

Good cop, my ass, Maeve thought.

Let him handle it. Let him ask the questions that should be asked. Let him try to get answers from a girl with the personality of a sphinx.

Let him raise her.

That was her final thought as she pulled off her T-shirt and pulled a new one on over her head. She crawled into bed. There had been eighteen messages from Evelyn, each one more excited than the one before, one telling Maeve she looked pretty on television, another saying that she should fix her ponytail. Still another said that she had icing on her backside and she should change her jeans. If she needed honesty, she had Evelyn. For duplicity, she had everyone else.

She thought of Evelyn, how she had neglected her the last few weeks. The next day, after the store closed, she would pick her up and take her to dinner.

Chris had given her a quick glance before she left the station with Heather, and in that glance was a host of unspoken sentiments. "I love you" was one of them. "I'm sorry" was another. For what, she wasn't sure, but she waited for the other shoe to drop, the call that would come saying that she was too complicated and he was looking for something different, something easier. It was coming, the breakup. She was sure of it. She hoped that he would tell her sooner rather than later, like ripping off a bandage instead of peeling it off slowly, so that she could deal with the pain.

There was a knock at the front door, and she raced down the stairs, hoping it was Chris, starting before she even got to the door to beg him for his forgiveness for being who she was and for what she had wrought with her enigmatic daughter. But it wasn't Chris and it wasn't Cal. It wasn't Jo.

It was Gabriela.

It was all Maeve could do not to laugh. She opened the door. "This day just keeps getting better and better," she said, the words falling from her lips before she had a chance to think about what she wanted to say, how she wanted to greet her ex-husband's more recent wife. "You're back?"

"I'm back," she said.

"For good?" Maeve asked, a question Gabriela didn't answer. "What can I do for you, Gabriela?"

"May I come in?" she asked, sounding calmer and more sedate than Maeve was expecting.

Maeve brought her into the living room, her T-shirt and sweatpants in stark contrast to Gabriela's pencil skirt and fitted white blouse. Maeve looked outside and saw Gabriela's little sports car at the curb. "Where's the baby?"

"At home," Gabriela said, taking a seat on the couch. "He's with Cal."

"Nice of him to let me know that this mystery has been solved."

"Yes, he should have told you."

"Heather is there," Maeve said, a caution. The last thing the girl needed after a half day at the police station was a full-out battle between the fiery Gabriela and her idiot father.

"Yes, I know. She was happy to see Devon." Gabriela looked at Maeve, her eyes filling with tears. "Do you have any wine?"

"I do," Maeve said, grateful for the diversion. In the kitchen, she tried to pull herself together so that she could be prepared for whatever Gabriela had to throw at her. Accusations. Emotions. Recriminations. She needed to be ready for all of it.

But when she returned, two glasses of red wine in hand, her former friend only looked at her sadly. "I know the truth, Maeve. So don't feel as if you have to lie."

Maeve took a sip of her wine and waited.

"You see, this is all my fault," Gabriela said. "I let him down. I let myself down. I wasn't the wife I promised him I would be."

Maeve had no idea where this was going, and she was so tired that she didn't care when she thought about it. Gabriela knew. She didn't seem angry at Maeve. So, let's finish our wine, Maeve thought, and go on our way. Let's let life return to normal, what-ever that is.

Gabriela smiled sadly and shook her head. "It's almost as if I had turned into you without realizing it."

Maeve put her wine down. "Come again?"

"The distance that was between us. The walls I had put up. It was like I had put Cal back into the same marriage he had had. The one he escape—" She caught herself, but not soon enough. "The one he decided to leave."

Maeve leaned forward in her chair. She wanted to drink the whole glass of wine down to make this monologue palatable but decided that would be bad. Wine would loosen her tongue, and she might press Gabriela to elaborate on why turning her marriage into the one that Maeve and Cal had had—and enjoyed for a time—was such a bad thing. It had once been great, in that time before Gabriela and her amazing persona had arrived, the one that Maeve came to find was built on smoke and mirrors.

"I need to be better, Maeve. I need to be the woman he married."

"Well, good luck with that," Maeve said, picking up her wine and tilting it in Gabriela's direction. "A toast," she said. "To you and Cal."

Gabriela burst into real tears, not the shimmery fake tears that had filled her eyes when she had first arrived. "Do you still love him, Maeve? Tell me the truth."

"Absolutely not," Maeve said, trying not to burst into laughter. She was unsuccessful.

"So why, then? Why the breach to our friendship?"

"Whose friendship?" Maeve asked, motioning between the two of them. "Yours and mine?" She looked closely at Gabriela. "Are you high? I mean, seriously. Are you on something?"

Gabriela was at a loss for words.

"Because you do realize that you cheating with Cal originally is what broke up our marriage, right? That you sleeping with him and him lying about it was the final straw in our marriage? Or have you forgotten that?"

"He was unhappy, Maeve. Looking for a way out."

"Well, you gave him one." Maeve stood. "I am terribly sorry for whatever it is you think I did," she said, not wanting to give Gabriela the satisfaction of a confession. "But I am going to have to ask you to leave."

Gabriela stayed on the couch, sipping her wine as if they were two old friends catching up. "It was just you, you know. That's what makes it easier to go back. I can forgive him for thinking that he left something here that he still wanted."

"Really, Gabriela. You have to go."

Gabriela looked at Maeve beseechingly. "Please tell me it's over."

This time, Maeve did finish her wine and put the glass on the table next to the chair she was sitting in. "It was over a long time ago." And that was the truth. How to make Gabriela understand that was another story.

"I have to believe you, I guess," Gabriela finally said, standing. With nothing left to say, she started for the front door, but not before downing the last of her wine in a dramatic gesture similar to taking a shot of tequila. "Good wine," she said.

"Thanks?" Maeve said in a questioning tone, not sure how to respond anymore. She walked Gabriela to the door, holding open the screen. "One last thing, Gabriela."

"Yes?"

"If I hear even a hint from Heather that she has been witness to any of your histrionics or Cal's denials, I make sure that he never sees her again. Got that?"

Gabriela nodded, solemn and contrite.

"My daughter is my only concern in this. Not you. Not him. Not even your baby together. Just don't do anything that would upset her."

Gabriela stepped outside, her face illuminated in the porch light, still gorgeous in her early forties, a dewy complexion that Maeve never had and could never replicate at her age. As she navigated her way down the rickety porch steps in her high heels, Maeve called to her.

"And call your friend Tammy! She's worried sick about you!"

Inside the house, Maeve picked up her wine glass and grabbed the bottle of wine that she and Gabriela had started, marching up to her room and putting both on her nightstand. It had been a long day and would probably be an even longer night. She collapsed onto the bed and closed her eyes, the wine glass in her hand. On her nightstand, the landline rang, and she debated whether or not to pick it up.

It was Jo. "Turn on the local news."

"What?" Maeve said.

"Turn on the local news," Jo said again, but by the time Maeve located the remotes, whatever story had Jo so agitated was over. "This is a fascinating story about bulldog rescue organizations, Jo, but I'm tired and want to go to bed."

"Keep the news on," Jo said. "Trish Dvorak is in jail."

"What?" Maeve said, sitting up so quickly that she nearly upended the wine on the nightstand.

"She's the one who orchestrated Taylor's kidnapping."

CHAPTER 31

Before she finally fell asleep, Maeve watched the story three times. Trish Dvorak in handcuffs. Chris Larsson making a statement to reporters. Suzanne Carstairs walking up the stairs to the station house, a grim set to her red lips, not missing a step in her extraordinarily high heels.

Trish hadn't been kidding when she said that she was worried about paying for college. She was so worried that she planned on getting the money any way she could, even if it meant a fake kidnapping plot that would result in her daughter's father, Charles Connors, paying five hundred thousand dollars to the "kidnappers."

According to Chris, Taylor was supposed to go to the Rathmuns', who were housecleaning clients of Trish's, and stay there until the money was delivered. The only thing was, she had disappeared for real.

And for good, it seemed.

"Is this some kind of village of the damned, or what?" Jo asked. "Mothers who would sell their own kid for tuition? Real kidnapping? I thought Doug's job was crazy, but these local cops have their hands full."

Maeve had stared at the screen and watched Chris. They surely did have their hands full, and sometimes it seemed they couldn't get out of their own way. It was a dangerous combination.

Maeve always thought that the strangest things happened in the most bucolic locales. Farringville was proving her correct on that front. The scariest part was that Taylor was missing and the wheels had been set in motion by her own mother. Maeve knew some truly horrifying people—some would consider her one of them if they knew the truth—but that took the cake.

No pun intended.

Maeve texted Heather the next morning to make sure she was going to school and to tell her that that night, over dinner, they were going to talk about everything: her lie of omission about Taylor and the day she disappeared, this new relationship with a kid Maeve didn't know but didn't like already. Once Tommy, the boy-fiend, as Maeve thought of him, had left town months earlier, Heather had lived the life of a monastic, but it appeared that her self-imposed boycott on the opposite sex had come to an end. And she had gone right back to the type of boy that made every mother's skin crawl, only this time, the rumors were far worse than just those usually alleged.

She drove to Rye after work to pick up Evelyn, having let the owners of the group home know via e-mail in the morning that she was coming. Evelyn was waiting at the front door, a little woman in neatly pressed jeans and a long-sleeved polo, her hair combed and lip gloss—an adored item that she went through with alarming alacrity—shining on her mouth. She opened the door when she saw Maeve's car, racing out to greet her younger sister.

"Maeve!" she said, and Maeve prepared herself for the force with which Evelyn would throw herself into her arms. Maeve grabbed her and kissed the top of her head, the older woman being shorter. "Where are we going?" Evelyn asked when she got in the car, making sure to first buckle her seat belt, her feet barely touching the floor mats of the Prius.

Maeve thought about that, wondered how much to say. She decided to tell Evelyn the truth. "We're going to see the house where you used to live."

Evelyn loved an adventure, particularly if it involved her beloved sister, someone she had only known a short time but had come to rely on after her father had died. Maeve would never tell her that Jack wasn't her biological father; he was the only father she had ever known, and he had done right by her, taking her from a horrible institution and making sure she lived a wonderful life right in Maeve's backyard. She wasn't sure Evelyn would understand the difference between biological and adopted anyway. It wasn't a conversation worth starting for many reasons.

"I'm hungry. We should eat," Evelyn said, her appetite a constant.

"Yes, we'll eat. What do you want? What sounds good?" Maeve asked, merging onto the highway, grateful for the flexibility to travel at off hours and to be able to get to today's destination quickly.

"Cheeseburger!" Evelyn said.

Maeve looked over at her, enough of her mother in both of them so that they bore a resemblance to each other. The cheekbones—or lack thereof in Maeve's case—and the softening around their jawlines, the flesh showing their age, spoke to their shared genes. Maeve wondered if those traits would be evident in her mother today, had she lived. Her mother had died young, younger than Maeve was now, so she would never know.

While Evelyn kept up a constant monologue, asking Maeve how every single person that they knew mutually was doing—Jo, baby Jack, Heather, Rebecca, Doug, et cetera—Maeve rehearsed in her mind what she might say to Heather that night once they were alone. Raging didn't work. Neither did disappointment. Maybe she would have to try something that she rarely used with her younger daughter: honesty.

It was worth a shot.

If she were someone else, Maeve would have asked her sister if she remembered anything about the street where she had spent a few years, if anything looked familiar at all, but it was no use. Evelyn remembered odd details about things, but overarching concepts were lost to her, somewhere in her mind, not retrievable.

That didn't mean she couldn't surprise Maeve every once in a while. "That's where the Haggertys lived," she blurted out in the same unmodulated tone that Jack had often used when remembering a lost detail.

Maeve pulled over and parked beneath the shade of an elm and turned to look at her sister, flabbergasted. "You remember?"

But Evelyn was on to something else, remarking on the tallest tree she had ever seen and how the one Maeve had parked beneath paled in comparison. "Do you remember where you used to live?"

"No, Maeve. I live in Rye."

"Did you visit the Haggertys a lot?" Maeve asked. "When you lived here?"

Evelyn was singing a song, another Kelly Clarkson tune, "Since U Been Gone." Her voice was soft and sweet. There was no talk of the Haggertys, just the song. The moment had passed, and there was nothing Maeve could do to get it back.

She never thought of herself as an emotional blackmailer, but walking up to Mrs. McSweeney's house, it was the only way she could describe herself. One hand holding her sister's, Maeve knocked at the front door with the other.

Mrs. McSweeney answered quickly, obviously expecting someone else. The smile on her face was immediately replaced by a frown when she discovered that the person she'd thought would be there when she opened the door was really Maeve and a woman she looked like she recognized but wanted to forget.

"Maeve," she said gently.

"Mrs. McSweeney, this is my sister, Evelyn. The one we spoke about."

The older woman stood inside the door and regarded the two women on her front stoop. "Hello, Evelyn."

They were in a standoff, this much older woman who was as sharp as a tack and Maeve, with only memories of her childhood, and none of her sister. Maeve held her gaze. "She's older now. But you remember her."

Evelyn looked at Maeve, whispering. "I need to go to the bathroom."

Maeve shrugged. "We need to use your bathroom, Mrs. McSweeney."

Mrs. McSweeney opened the door reluctantly, averting her gaze as Maeve and Evelyn walked in. Maeve led her sister to the bathroom, situated exactly where she thought it would be, since her childhood home was a mirror image of this one. She waited outside the door, reminding Evelyn to wash her hands when she was done, even though she didn't need to; Evelyn was fastidious about her appearance and her hygiene, making sure her hair was combed, her clothes were pressed, and her hands were always clean.

Maeve wandered down the hall after a few moments, finding

Mrs. McSweeney in the kitchen. "Do you remember her? I know it was a long time ago. But you must remember something."

Mrs. McSweeney leaned against the Formica counter, looking out the window over the kitchen sink to the backyard. "I told you, Maeve. I remember nothing. I didn't know your sister. I don't know what you're looking for, but I don't know anything."

Maeve heard the water running in the bathroom and knew she only had a few seconds before they would have to leave. "Please."

The woman wouldn't look at Maeve, opting instead to survey the view outside the kitchen window. "There are things that are better not known, Maeve. Leave it alone."

"Leave what alone?" Maeve asked, the door to the bathroom opening and her sister starting down the hall. "Leave what alone?"

Evelyn appeared in the doorway. "Thank you."

Mrs. McSweeney turned, tears in her eyes. "You're welcome."

Maeve beseeched the woman with her own tear-filled eyes before starting for the door. "Please."

Evelyn grabbed the taller, older woman around the waist and hugged her tightly. "You have a nice house," she said.

"Thank you." Mrs. McSweeney kissed the top of Evelyn's head. "And you have grown up into a lovely woman," she said before realizing the indictment in that statement, that she remembered her as a girl. She looked at Maeve. "But now you have to go. I have company coming."

Maeve hesitated at the front door. "Please," she said again, but she knew it was no use. "Tell me."

Mrs. McSweeney surprised her by hugging her, too. "Good-bye, Maeve. Be well," she said before closing the door behind them.

Outside, on the sidewalk that Maeve had run up and down

countless times, she put her arm around her sister's waist. "I love you."

Evelyn looked up at her, her eyes innocent and bright. "I love you, too. And I love cheeseburgers. I'm hungry, Maeve."

Maeve buckled her sister into the car and drove away, watching the neighborhood grow smaller and smaller in her rearview mirror.

CHAPTER 32

"Tell me everything." Maeve was at the kitchen table sitting across from Heather later that night, her rage simmering below the surface but apparent to the girl, whose eyes didn't leave her folded hands. It wasn't the first time she would say those words to her daughter, nor would it be the last. She was ready, finally, to hear the details of the girl's conversation with Taylor on the day she had gone missing and find out why, if Rebecca was to be believed, she continued to have such terrible taste in men.

Heather wasn't her usual sullen self, but she wasn't hostile either. What she was seemed far more concerning to Maeve. She seemed dead inside, without life, a shell of a girl who had lost the ability to feel. She stared across at her mother, words failing her.

Maeve led her along in the story. "You saw Taylor."

"Yes."

"And what did she say?"

Heather traced a circle on top of the old wood table, a knife mark left by one of the girls when they were small and didn't know the lasting damage that one minor act could do. "She told me to stay away from Jesse Connors."

Maeve knew why, but she had to hear it from Heather. "Why?"

"She said he was bad news." She rolled her eyes; she didn't believe that. But then again, where boys were concerned, she rarely did.

"Did she mention that Jesse is related to her?"

Heather looked surprised, a little spark returning. "No. I only found out about that later."

Maeve considered her next questions carefully. "Did she say anything about a party? Something that happened there?"

Heather sighed. "Dating a cop has made you even more annoying. Do you know that?" she asked.

Maeve slammed her hand down on the table, knocking over the ceramic napkin holder that Rebecca had made at day camp, shattering it into what seemed like a million pieces. "Enough," she said, her voice a low growl. "Enough of this."

Heather was not fazed by her mother's outburst. She held her gaze. "You're not the only one who looks for answers," she said, and before Maeve could respond, she was out the door.

Maeve leapt from her seat, slamming into the kitchen table, a piece of ceramic napkin holder getting stuck in her shoe and leaving a rut in the oak floor as she raced to the front door. Outside, the street was empty, the only sound the train going by, its horn blaring in the distance drowning out the sound of Maeve's call for her daughter.

She went back inside and grabbed her car keys, getting into the Prius and driving around the village, coming to rest in a park in the center of town where she knew the kids hung out after school and into the evening hours. It was nine o'clock. She pulled out her phone and called Chris; they hadn't spoken since the day before, both needing physical and emotional distance from the situation.

From each other.

He hadn't looked at her when he released Heather into her care yesterday. She didn't know what Heather had told him, but it was enough to make him want to avoid her. He had been uncomfortable and nervous, so she was glad when he picked up the phone.

"Hi, gorgeous," he said, and there was a smile in his voice. It was faint, but it was there.

"Hi."

"Where are you?" he asked.

"Mathers Park."

"Looking for an adult to buy you beer? A little pot?" he said. "No one over the age of eighteen hangs out in Mathers Park at this hour unless they are up to no good." He dropped his voice to a whisper. "Are you up to no good?"

"No. Not right now." He was going in a different direction with her, flirting a bit to take the edge off of what had happened the day before, but she wasn't in the mood. Anyway, he would be shocked to know what she actually did when she was up to no good.

"So what are you doing there?"

"I don't know." She paused. "Well, I'm looking for Heather."

"She's gone?"

"Left in a huff. I want to talk to her." She peered out the window, spying shadowy teenage figures in the distance but none with the mannerisms or physicality of her daughter. "What did she say yesterday, Chris? Because she's sure not telling me."

He was silent. and Maeve mentally kicked herself for not demanding a lawyer at the time—a real lawyer, someone who wasn't Cal—thinking that while it would have made Heather seem guilty, it would have protected her as well. In some ways, Maeve was the consummate rule follower, accepting what people in authority said or did without question. No doubt about it: Catholic school had done a number on her.

"She didn't tell us much at all, Maeve. If she's keeping something to herself, she certainly didn't let on. She saw Taylor. They had a quick conversation. She didn't mention it to anyone because it didn't seem important. That's all we got."

"Is she in trouble, Chris? Just tell me that."

His sigh filled the space between them. "No," he said unconvincingly, the sigh indicating otherwise. "No, she's not in trouble."

"I should have gotten her a lawyer."

He stayed silent.

"How did you raise such a good kid, Chris?" she asked. She didn't know Chris's son well, but what she did know of him she liked. He was more like Chris than he would probably care to admit, but to Maeve, that was a good thing.

"The same way you did," he said, referring, she thought, to Rebecca. "Vigilance. Saying no more often than yes. Love."

Odd order, she thought, but he was right. And honest. She had tried to lead with love, and it was successful the first time, unsuccessful the second. "Just promise me you'll tell me if there's something I need to know about her. Promise me that."

"Trish Dvorak's confession was a game changer, Maeve. You don't have anything to worry about."

Maeve asked a question that had lodged itself in the back of her mind. "Why did you just find out about the tape? At Jane Murdock's store?"

"We didn't know she had a camera."

Isn't it your job to know those things? she wanted to ask but couldn't. "And she didn't think to let you know?"

"People aren't suspicious by nature, Maeve. They don't think the worst. They don't realize that they may have information that we need. It's that simple."

He was dead wrong, but she would never say that. She was suspicious. She thought that other people were just like her.

"Really," she said.

"Really." The next stretch of silence went on longer than she cared for. "Okay." He was cooking; she could hear the sounds of water running, a pot being put on the stove. "Come over. I'll make you dinner."

She had things to do and places to go. "No," she said. "Thank you. I'll see you tomorrow." Before he could ask again, and she knew he would, she hung up, knowing where she was headed.

CHAPTER 33

The person who answered the door was not expecting to see Maeve; that was clear. Tall, wearing a lavender polo shirt and expensive jeans, his feet bare, he regarded Maeve with a question on his face, respect in his voice. "Can I help you, ma'am?"

Okay, Junior, she thought, let's not lay it on too thick. "Hi. I want to talk to you."

He stood inside the immense foyer that fronted the house, his hand on the doorknob. "Is this about the Relay for Life?"

"What?" Maeve asked. "Relay what?"

"Yes. Relay for Life? Team Connors?"

"No," Maeve said, shaking her head. "It's not about Relay for Life. I'm looking for my daughter. Heather Callahan. I'm her mother," she added unnecessarily, trying to reconcile two competing thoughts in her brain.

He's bad. The police think so. But he looks like butter wouldn't melt in his mouth. She knew better, though. The bad ones always looked like that.

Tommy, the former boyfiend, was up front about his wayward

habits. He had the requisite tattoo, the DUI on his record, the sullen disposition of the teenage rebel without a cause or a clue. But this kid standing before her, six feet three inches of well-fed, well-bred Anglo stock, was a specimen to which she was not accustomed, at least where Heather was concerned. Just where had he come from, and why was Heather interested?

"I'm sorry, Mrs. Callahan, but Heather isn't here."

"When's the last time you spoke with her?"

He looked up at the ceiling, thinking. "A week ago? We're in the same English class."

"Last week?" Maeve asked. Out here on the grand stone porch, she felt small and insignificant. "I thought you were dating," she said before taking the time to measure her words.

"Dating?" he asked, his large white teeth appearing in the most charming approximation of a smile. Only problem was that it didn't go up to his eyes, his eyebrows never moving to join in on the hilarity. "No. We're not dating."

"Why?" Maeve asked.

"Why what?"

"Why aren't you dating?"

He looked confused, as if he had just been presented with a four-syllable word on the SAT, something that would be a formality, likely, his acceptance into Brown or Dartmouth or Boston College assured, a conclusion Maeve jumped to based solely on the existence of the lavender polo shirt. "I don't know." He stammered a bit. "I wouldn't call it dating."

"Well, what would you call it?" Maeve asked.

"We're friends."

What she wanted to ask, she couldn't; she already looked crazy. *Did you abuse that girl? Do you know where she is? What was it? Was she going to talk? Tell the whole story about what happened at that party! Is that what it was?* She stood there instead, her mouth hanging open slightly, the words on her lips but unspoken.

They looked at each other, this entitled boy and this rumpled woman, neither sure what the other was capable of. Heather wasn't here, and that was all she needed to know. Although part of her wanted to get inside the house, wanted to see Charles Connors and ask him how he had conceived a child with Trish Dvorak, there was no way she was getting past this kid who seemed to have leapt off the pages of *The Preppy Handbook*. Behind him, his mother appeared.

"Can I help you?" she asked, a touch of a Scottish brogue in her voice.

"I'm Maeve Conlon. I'm looking for my daughter."

She smiled, but like her adopted son, not sincerely. "Well, she's not here, Mrs. Conlon." She stood next to her son, putting a protective arm around his waist. "There's no one here but us."

"Do you know my daughter?"

"I don't."

"The police think your son does."

"Mom, Heather is in my English class. But that's it."

Mrs. Connors smiled again. "So there you have it."

"The police seem to think they're dating," Maeve said. On the porch, it was getting cold, but it didn't appear that she was going to be invited in.

"The police?" Mrs. Connors said. "Why would the police be involved?"

"Taylor Dvorak? Her disappearance?"

At the mention of the girl's name, the woman's face turned hard. "Which has absolutely nothing to do with us." She turned and called out, "Charles!"

Charles Connors appeared at the top of the staircase in the foyer and, at the sight of Maeve, raced down the stairs. "What are you doing here? I thought we settled everything the last time we spoke."

"You know her? You've spoken to her?" Mrs. Connors asked, looking from her husband to Maeve.

"Just that once, Genevieve." He looked at Maeve. "Please leave us alone." He closed the door, Mrs. Connors's angry, blotchy face the last thing Maeve saw before she heard the dead bolt slide across inside.

"I'm sorry I bothered you," Maeve said to the closed door, thinking that if she didn't get off their porch and out of their neighborhood, it wouldn't be a stretch to assume that she, too, would end up in the Farringville police station, this time for trespassing. She jogged to the car and hopped in, keeping an eye out for a police car coming this way, but all she passed was commuters whizzing home on the narrow rural roads, and one deer who seemed to have lost her way.

Back at the house, spent from the day, her argument with Heather and her confrontation with the Connors making her bone tired, she sat on the front porch steps and looked down toward the river. Her house was old, like all of the houses in the neighborhood, and that alone kept it affordable. She wondered if in years this whole area would be gone, the landed gentry returning and razing what was once old Farringville and making it new again, every house facing the beautiful river. In her hand, her phone vibrated, and on its face appeared a message from Heather:

Staying at Dad's.

Maeve had no way of knowing, but she wondered if implicit in those three words existed the end of her relationship with her daughter. She was tired and being dramatic; she knew that.

But in her mind and in her heart, she saw no way to mend what was rapidly becoming a flawed and very broken relationship with a girl who kept more secrets than Maeve imagined she could count.

CHAPTER 34

Maeve felt guilty at how well she had slept the night before and actually felt a smile break out on her face when she saw Mark Messer, the sun barely up, filling in the pothole that had nearly swallowed the Prius several times over the last few months. She got out of the car and walked over, surprising both of them by giving him a big hug. This was what her life had come to: joy at predawn pothole filling.

"What do you want, Mark? I'll make anything to thank you."

He had the face of a boy, but she knew he had turned twenty-two so was technically a man. She was a mother and figured she would always see the child underneath the older features of people she had seen grow up through the years. "Oh, it's okay, Ms. Conlon. I'll grab a muffin when I'm done."

"You'll grab as many muffins as you want," Maeve said, turning to go into the store. "Is this your regular shift? At five in the morning?" she asked.

"No," he said, smiling. "My dad said that if I didn't come out here and fill your pothole today, I shouldn't bother coming to work today."

"I'm sorry, Mark," Maeve said. "That's my fault. It's just that I thought I'd lose the Prius more than once driving in here and not paying attention."

He tamped down some gravel with the flat side of his rake. She wondered how he could see what he was doing; the only light he had was a flashlight in his pocket that he turned on intermittently to see his handiwork.

Inside the store, Maeve prepared to open, getting scones and muffins ready for the busy commuter rush. The media had moved on since the drama of two days earlier, not interested in her or her daughter, moved on to some other salacious story, another juicy detail related to another sordid or tragic tale. Focused on Trish Dvorak and her ham-fisted plot to get her daughter's father to give the girl what she deserved. Had the woman ever heard of a lawyer? Clearly she had one now, but there were others out there who would have loved to sink their teeth into a case involving a destitute woman and her daughter and the wealthy estranged father who lived in the same town.

Desperate times. Maeve knew that sometimes they existed, even if she couldn't always condone the desperate measures.

That morning, it was just her and the sound of the wonky oven that only she knew how to massage into working order every day, the occasional tamping down of the gravel outside as Mark continued his work on the hole, the feeling of dough beneath her fingers, the smell of cinnamon all around her. It was almost as if everything were normal and her life happy, the people in it content. She knew that wasn't true, though, and the thought of that made her focus on the dough on the butcher block, the only thing that kept her from thinking dark, unsettled thoughts.

She never heard Mark leave as the crush of commuters descended upon the store before leaving for the station. The kid had left without his muffin, she thought. She was circumspect to her regulars about her absence the day before, citing a bad headache to a few, a nasty fall to others. Anything but what it really was, that her daughter had been picked up by the police and questioned in a girl's disappearance.

Nine o'clock rolled around, and she took a minute to breathe, pouring herself a cup of coffee and sitting on a high stool behind the counter to peruse the paper before going back to work. The back door opened, and while she would have been surprised to see Jo arriving early to work, she was even more surprised to see the woman standing before her.

"Trish," Maeve said. "Shouldn't you be in jail?"

She seemed thinner than she had when Maeve had first seen her at back-to-school night, and now, days after her daughter's disappearance, broken as well. Maeve motioned toward a stool on the other side of the counter, but Trish continued to stand.

"You must think I'm a horrible person," Trish said, opening a conversation Maeve didn't want to have and not answering Maeve's question.

"I don't judge," Maeve said, which sounded better than the truth: *I shouldn't judge. I can't judge.* She had done some terrible things, but in her own mind, they were justified; maybe Trish felt the same way. "But was that really the only thing you could do? A fake kidnapping?" Maeve asked, getting deep into it with the woman quickly.

"You don't know, Maeve. You have no idea," she said, looking around the kitchen, a place for her eyes to land so that she didn't have to look at Maeve. "The things he always promised. The way we'd eventually be together. That's what I wanted. That's what I deserved."

Maeve closed the paper, looked through the hole in the kitchen door to see if anyone had come in without her knowing. "He told me he gave you a lot of money. That it's gone."

"Did he tell you why?"

Maeve shook her head.

"Did he tell you that Taylor had several surgeries as a baby to correct a heart defect? Did he tell you that?"

"No."

"That I had to declare bankruptcy?" Trish asked, escalating, gripping the sides of the counter to stay upright.

Maeve pulled the stool out from under the counter. "Here. Sit," she said, going into the front of the store to wait on a lone customer while a cup of tea steeped on the counter for Trish. She rang up the order and went back into the kitchen with the tea and a scone and placed them in front of the distraught woman. "Eat something. Please."

Trish picked at the scone and blew on top of the scalding cup of tea. "It's hard being known as the town slut, Maeve."

"I've never heard anyone say that."

"You haven't, but I have. A single mother with a child who has no father. This town thinks it's progressive and hip, but it's like 1950 all over again."

"I think you're overstating that, Trish. I don't think anyone cares that you're a single mother."

"You think you know because you're divorced, but it's different. Cal lives in town—"

"Oh, yes, Cal," Maeve said. "Who you tried to get money from."

Trish looked up at Maeve. "I was desperate. I don't know how many ways to say that, Maeve."

"You stole from me."

Trish looked down at the table.

"Charles actually gave me the money back," Maeve said.

"He's a regular prince."

"There's financial aid, Trish. There are loans. There are ways to pay for college," Maeve said.

"Which is all well and good, but I have nothing," she said slowly so that Maeve couldn't miss her point, pushing the scone away. "And my daughter had nothing. It's not fair."

Maeve folded the paper and threw it in the trash. She knew in her heart that their situations were different, and although she wanted to kill Cal on a daily basis, there was one thing that he hadn't done, and that was abandon his children financially or emotionally. He was there for them and cared for them, and while he often made parenting a pissing contest, she couldn't dispute that he loved them and wanted the best for them. "It's not fair, Trish. It's not fair at all."

The tears that Trish had been holding back finally came, and with them a torrent of emotion that Maeve was uncomfortable witnessing. She got up and hugged the woman, feeling every bone in her emaciated frame as she shook with anger and sadness, and all Maeve could think was: He threw you away. And with that thought, anger and sadness flooded her body as well, but one emotion took hold more than the others.

Rage.

She took Trish's face in her hands and looked at her. "We have to find her. By whatever means necessary."

Trish nodded, although she didn't know what Maeve meant. "Someone has to help me," she said, and Maeve hugged her again, thinking that she was just the person for the job.

CHAPTER 35

After Trish left, Maeve was grateful for the influx of customers who came into the store so that she didn't have to think about the encounter anymore. Making small talk, boxing up cakes and quiches, and answering the phone took her mind off the thought of Trish and what she had done. When Jo came, she went into the kitchen and sat at the counter, wondering what she would do next. In the pocket of her apron, her cell phone rang, and she saw the number of the only person she wanted to speak to: Rodney Poole.

"Maeve Conlon?" he asked, as if they had just met.

"Hiya, Poole. How are you?"

"I'm good. Another day in Dodge City."

"Here, too. We've had some drama."

"Oh?"

"Cops picked up Heather two days ago."

"You should have called me. I could have helped you with that."

"You must be sick of hearing from me."

"Never. Now tell me what happened."

"Heather was caught on tape talking to Taylor on the day she disappeared."

"About what?

"Dunno. No one is saying."

"Even the boyfriend?" he asked, and she knew he was referring to Chris.

"Mostly the boyfriend." She took a sip of her coffee. "Did you see the news?"

"About the mother? Yes."

"Surprised?"

"Nothing surprises me, Maeve. There are bad people out there. You know that."

"She had no choice, Poole. It was a bad, bad thing to do, but she had no choice."

He fell silent, and she knew better than to try to fill that space with chatter. He would speak when he was ready. "I've got nothing for you, Maeve Conlon."

"About my sister?"

"Yes. I wish I didn't have to say that."

"It's okay, Poole. This may be a secret that died with Jack. Obviously he wanted it to."

"So why do you want to know?"

"I like to be the one with the secrets. I'm not great at having other people hold back from me."

"Very astute, Maeve Conlon. Extremely self-aware."

She heard him curse under his breath. "Everything okay?"

"There are two types of people in this world: those who use the shopping cart return area and those who don't."

"You thinking about shooting someone?" she asked.

"That's your department, my warrior queen." She heard him call out to the offender with a gruff "hey!"

"I'll let you go, Poole. Sounds like you've got your hands full. Thanks for your help."

She knew having him find out anything was a long shot, but she figured she'd try, wondering if she could reconcile herself to the fact that she loved her sister as much as she did, even though there existed this huge question mark between them, one that Evelyn had no idea haunted her younger sister.

She looked up at the ceiling. "Who was he, Jack? And why didn't you want me to know?"

In the kitchen, the back door slammed, which meant one of two people had arrived: Chris or Cal. She prayed that it was the former, not enthusiastic about talking about Cal's marital problems with everything else that was going on.

But it was her ex who stood inside the back door, the baby asleep in the stroller, a pacifier dangling from his slack lips, snoring gently. She couldn't stop the words from coming from her mouth. "Oh. It's you."

"And it's you," he said in return. "I heard you talked to Gabriela."

"Indeed."

"And what did you say?"

"I mostly listened."

"So I guess you heard about what a terrible husband I am," he said.

"I already knew that." She enjoyed the sour look he got on his face. Just what did he expect exactly? Kindness? Compassion? "She told me that she was afraid she was turning into me, and that's the only reason she's not angry at what happened between the two of us."

"But you didn't confirm anything."

"I confirmed nothing," Maeve said. Behind her, on the way, the old phone, which had surely been there since the 1970s, its cord dirty and tangled, rang, waking the baby, who set up a mournful howl in protest. "I listened. That was it." She made her way to the phone as Cal threw an envelope on the counter.

"Here," he was saying as she picked up the phone. "Here's the check Heather needs for that extra course she wants to take at the community college."

"What course?" Maeve asked before saying, "The Comfort Zone," to whoever was calling her. "And why didn't you give it to her last night?" she asked, her hand over the receiver. "I assumed she went to you. She texted me that that was where she was headed," Maeve said.

And as he said, "I didn't see her last night," Judy Wilkerson was saying, "Heather never came to school," and Maeve slid down the wall, feeling the floor beneath her turn to an ocean of sadness and grief, her ability to stand deserting her in one emotional tidal wave of terror.

CHAPTER 36

Chris Larsson, the man she loved but wouldn't trust now with finding a missing cat, snapped his notebook shut. "So the last time you saw her was right before we spoke last night?"

"Yes," Maeve said. "She texted me that she was staying at her father's, but she never showed up."

Cal was sitting at the counter, his head in his hands. Maeve picked up the baby and fed him a cookie to keep him quiet, knowing that sugar was not on the list of approved ingredients that the child could eat and not caring. "What do we do, Chris?" she asked.

"Leave it to us, Maeve," he said, and while she knew that that was the answer he had to give, she wasn't confident that it was her best choice.

After they left, Chris taking his two uniformed colleagues with him, Cal departed with the baby, now wailing lustily, in need of a nap or organic baby food. Maeve texted Jo, telling her the store would be closed for the rest of the day, but not telling her why.

Then she texted Poole.

His response was short. *See you at your house.*

And then, as she arrived, running through the front door and screaming Heather's name, *Don't touch anything.*

There was nothing to do but wait. She had never cleaned up the broken glass from the night before, a reminder of their last encounter, her and Heather's, so she got out the broom and dustpan and swept everything into a neat pile, discarding it in the trash can, covering a half sandwich that Heather had made yesterday and never finished. The tears came fast and blinded Maeve, causing her to miss the trash can with her second delivery of broken glass and dirt, the contents of the dustpan drifting to the floor, creating another silty mess.

She was sitting on the floor of the kitchen, her back against the door, the dustpan beside her, when Poole showed up, his kind face the only thing she needed to see, his calm presence grounding her in what was real, what was true, what needed to be done.

"Cops say anything about coming over, looking at her room?" he asked, taking her hand and helping her into a standing position.

She shook her head, not wanting to speak for fear of the tears coming again.

"Good. I'm delighted in their ineptitude," he said, cracking himself up. "Let's go. Show me before they figure out that they need to be here."

"I don't have much faith in the cops on the force," she said, feeling immediately that she had somehow betrayed Chris, "but I think the chief is a little sharper."

He followed her up the stairs. "Then we don't have much time."

Heather's room looked like it always did: stuffed with clothes, books, and a variety of other items, but tidy in its own way. Poole walked over to the tall dresser right inside the bedroom door. "You mind?" he asked, pointing to the top drawer.

Maeve shook her head. Once, she had done the same thing,

searching through the drawers in the hopes of unlocking the key to the secrets that Heather held close and being none the wiser when she was done. Poole pulled a pair of purple rubber gloves from his pocket, gingerly picking his way through multiple pairs of underwear, bras, single socks, T-shirts. The next drawer revealed pajamas and a rogue pair of pantyhose that Maeve had bought the girl when she attended an eighth-grade dance, a few years before. Beneath that, sweatshirts. Below that, a drawer full of jeans.

He was single-minded in his work, not disturbing too much, feeling around under the jeans for any items that didn't belong. Maeve sat on the bed, watching him, wondering how this had become her life, how she sat in a room, her daughter missing, a detective who had once let her get away with murder now her trusted confidant, the only person who knew her darkest secrets.

He turned, and in his hand was an envelope. "Let's see why she's filing things away with her jeans, Maeve Conlon." He opened the envelope and dumped the contents on Heather's bed. Out slid a couple of screen shots, two photographs, and another envelope, the flap tucked inside. Maeve looked at Poole.

"Facebook screenshots," he said. "Nasty stuff."

The screenshots were taken on a date in July and mentioned Taylor. The slut. The whore. And a lot of other words and phrases that Maeve didn't know but that were clearly not flattering or kind. She looked up at Poole. "Awful."

"And this one?" he said, holding one of the photographs. "Know these kids?"

"Yes," Maeve said. "I do know that one," she said, pointing to Jesse Connors. "And yes, that one, too," she said, pointing at Tim Morehead. "The other one's a henchman."

"Henchman?" Poole said, raising an eyebrow.

"That's the only thing I can think to call him," Maeve said.

The other photo, which Poole slid into view, was the three boys' names written on some institutional wall somewhere—Maeve guessed the high school—with the words RAPIST LIST written in black marker above the names. "So Rebecca was right," she said, feeling sick that in wanting to keep her daughter's name out of the investigation, she had kept key information to herself.

Poole read her mind. "Trust me, Maeve. They already know."

"So how come that's not in the media? How come I haven't seen anything about that?"

"They connected?"

"They have money. At least the Connors do."

"That may be it," he said.

"Are you so sure they know?"

"They're cops. They know."

She laughed in spite of the situation, more from the thought that the Farringville PD could know something before the two of them did than out of any sense of hilarity over the situation. "I don't know, Poole. That's not a given."

Poole picked up the items and looked at her. "Let's go downstairs. That poster is giving me the creeps," he said, pointing to a poster from one of the more disturbing Harry Potter movies.

They sat at the kitchen table, the envelope between them, not wanting to open the last piece of the puzzle for fear of what it might reveal.

"Coffee?" she asked.

He shook his head, pulling the flap open on the envelope and taking out a letter and unfolding it carefully. He spread it out on the table in front of them.

Behind them, the screen door flew open, and Jo burst in, talking before she saw that Maeve had a guest.

"What is going on with you?" she asked, her footfalls heavy in the hallway. "Closing the store two days in one week? That's no way to make a living. We've got bills to pay, sister!"

Maeve turned to face her. Jo stopped short in the kitchen door-way. "Rodney?" She looked from the older man to Maeve. "Rodney Poole? What's going on?"

If I told you the truth, you'd never believe me, she thought, but instead of voicing what could only be described as fantastical, she went with the next best thing: a lie. "My cousin's murder. New evi-dence," she said.

"Doug never mentioned anything about that," Jo said.

Poole said, "I'm working a different angle."

"If I were you, I'd work no angles," Jo said, looking at Maeve. "You know how I feel. I don't care who did it, and I hope that asshole rots in hell." She looked at Poole. "Sorry. That's just how I feel."

"I understand, Jo," Poole said. He was quick on his feet, making the whole thing seem normal. "I didn't tell Doug, because it's just a waste of our time. But I had to ask Ms. Conlon here if it had any legs." He swept all of the photographs into a pile and made a neat stack. "Sorry to take up your time," he said to Maeve. "This is over now. I'll see myself out."

Jo watched Poole walk down the hallway to the front door, and when he was gone, out of earshot, she turned to Maeve. "What is going on?"

"Heather is missing," Maeve said, and the stress of that, along with the tension of acting out what she felt was a pretty convincing play for Jo involving Poole, brought the tears again, fast and furious this time.

Jo sat in the chair that Poole had just vacated and put her head in her hands. On the table, Maeve's phone pinged loudly, and a quick glance at the screen indicated that Poole had texted her already, his number but not his name visible.

Give it all to the pd.

But she didn't want to; she wasn't sure why.

They hadn't had a chance to look at the note that was in the second envelope, and Maeve didn't want to open it in front of Jo; she pushed everything to the far edge of the table, away from her friend's prying eyes.

"Maeve, this is bad. Two missing girls . . . ," Jo said, trailing off. "Now that I'm a mother—"

Maeve held up a hand. "I know. Stop."

Jo didn't know what to do, had no clue what to say, so she got up and started cleaning Maeve's kitchen, putting on a kettle of water to make tea. The Farringville police, namely the chief, Larsson, and one uniformed cop, arrived sooner than Maeve expected, showing up on her front porch mere minutes after Poole had left, his quick visit seeming like something Maeve had imagined.

Jo leaned back from the sink and looked down the hall. "More cops."

Maeve eyed the photos and the note in the envelope. "Jo, do me a favor? Let them in?" she asked.

Jo dried her hands on a dish towel and started down the hall. Maeve had only a few seconds to open the note and read it.

She had less time once she read the note, the cops now in her hallway, to shove everything back in the envelope and put that between two of her favorite cookbooks on the shelf above the table.

She tried to bring her breath back to normal, her voice to a calmer cadence, but the words on that note, anonymously written and coupled with the photographs that she and Poole had looked at, had shaken her to her very core.

The note was short and to the point: *Get them.*

CHAPTER 37

"How's your relationship with your daughter, Maeve?" Suzanne Carstairs asked in the same tone as if she had said, "Do you like shrimp?"

"If you're thinking she ran away, she didn't," Maeve said, but she didn't sound convincing even to her own ears. Chris Larsson stood behind his boss, his arms crossed, a look that combined concern and confusion evident on his face. Jo had disappeared, not wanting to be part of this line of questioning, giving Maeve her privacy to discuss whatever it was that needed to be discussed with the police.

"Well, we have to consider that possibility. You argued before she left?" the chief asked, knowing full well that they had because that's what she had told Chris not two hours before.

Yes. But that's nothing new. "Yes. We argued. You have a teenage daughter. You argue?"

The chief laughed. "All the time." She looked at her notepad. "We've checked out all of the usual haunts. But we'll keep looking."

Chris looked at a spot over Maeve's head, anything not to look directly at her. "We'll need to search her room, Maeve."

"Of course."

"Take anything that might be of interest."

Maeve willed her gaze away from the bookshelf above the kitchen table and nodded.

As the two officers walked down the front hallway, they were greeted by Cal, who noisily protested the search of Heather's room, something that didn't surprise Maeve. While the three discussed the reason for the search—which to Maeve was evident and didn't require explanation—she texted Poole to let him know what the note said. When he didn't reply after a few minutes, she put her phone in her pocket and went out to the backyard to get away from the noise, heading for the picnic table that she should have put at the curb for pickup years ago but still sat under the shade of a big tree, every year becoming more decrepit and splintered, probably a haven for carpenter ants. She sat atop the table and looked out at the little slice of river that could be seen when the leaves started falling, eventually becoming a mulched mess beneath her feet.

Behind her, she heard the rusty gate swing open; she was expecting Jo and a barrage of questions. But there was only one.

"Mom? Am I in trouble?"

Maeve didn't know whether to laugh or cry, so she did both. Seeing Heather brought up contradictory feelings. On the one hand, she could have killed her. On the other, she wanted to tell her to run the other way, that the police were inside, that they wanted to talk to her and wouldn't let her go until she told the truth.

After Heather told her story, no one was really sure what the truth was, but one thing was clear: Heather wasn't where she said she had been.

Stacy Morris—the girl Heather professed to have spent the previous night with—was a worse liar than Heather. "Yes, she was here," she had told Chris Larsson when he questioned her, but her mother, Donna, another divorcée in the village who had once tried to bond with Maeve over their single status, had no recollection of seeing Heather Callahan in her house the night before. She did admit that a bottle of wine and an Ambien may have clouded her recollections, or lack thereof, but no, to the best of her knowledge, Heather had not been there.

Chris threw his hands up. "I don't know what to tell you, Maeve." They were in her kitchen, him standing by the back door, looking as if he wanted to make a quick getaway from the house and Maeve— and stay away forever. Maeve sat at the kitchen table, the envelope with Heather's photos and the note tucked in between her Jacques Pepin cookbook and *The Joy of Cooking*. Cal had gone home, the drama over, at least for now, leaving Maeve, as always, to deal with the fallout of another situation involving her youngest, his middle.

Maybe that was it. Heather was a middle child now. Didn't middle children traditionally have issues with fitting in with the family, not knowing their place? Maeve would have to search for yet another overpriced self-help book that would help her figure out why her daughter had turned into a secretive, sullen, moody cluster of cells.

"I'm worried about her" was the last thing she said to Chris before he left.

"You should be" was his response.

Heather was in her room, and Maeve was steeling herself for the inevitable fight that would ensue. She didn't say anything about what she and Poole had found, keeping that information to herself. She just didn't have the energy for it. She texted Jo, letting her know that everything was back to normal and Heather was home. She sat at the edge of the couch, preparing herself for when Heather emerged from the bedroom, but when she did finally come down, after forty-five minutes or so, Maeve was even less prepared for what her daughter had planned.

Heather had packed a bag, larger than any bag that Maeve had ever seen her pack for an overnight at her Dad's, and appeared at the bottom of the steps after the door slammed and Chris Larsson went back to the station house. Maeve didn't need to ask where she was going or why; it was clear that she was moving out and heading to Cal's for good.

"What did I do?" Maeve asked.

Heather couldn't look at her, facing instead toward the wall, her back to her mother. "I can't live here anymore with you."

"Why?"

Heather slumped a little bit, her spine caving in as she resisted the urge to cry. "You're not here," she said.

"I'm here now."

"No. You're not here. Even when you're here," she said. "It's always something else. Evelyn. Chris. Now Taylor. You're never here."

"And Dad is?" Maeve asked, feeling as if her insides were being crushed, making it hard for her to breathe.

"Yes. Dad is," she said and hoisted the bag over her shoulder.

"Where did you go last night?" Maeve asked.

"In a few months, you won't be able to ask me those questions, and I won't have to answer them."

"Because you'll be eighteen?" Maeve asked.

Heather nodded.

"You're going to go out on your own? Live your life?" Maeve asked.

"I don't know, but you don't need to know where I was last night. I was fine, by the way."

"You're dating Jesse Connors," Maeve said, and the look on Heather's face, as usual, was inscrutable, unknowable. Maeve thought she'd make a great CIA agent.

"No. I'm not," Heather said, shifting the bag from one shoulder to the other.

"The police said you were."

"The police don't understand hooking up," she said.

It always came back to that, Maeve thought. Grown-ups just don't understand.

"And I feel as if you're doing your own investigating in your own way," Maeve said.

"I don't know what you're talking about."

"I just want you to be safe," Maeve said.

"You've made that clear. About a thousand times."

Outside, Maeve saw Cal's minivan at the curb, but she didn't follow Heather outside or speak to her ex-husband, whose smug face she could see even at this distance, even with a screen door and the length of the front walk between them.

It was a long time before she moved, the day turning dusky and finally dark, and it was only the phone ringing in the kitchen that got her moving. "Heather?" she said when she reached the phone on the sixth ring, hoping that the girl had had a change of heart, that they could work things out and Maeve hadn't been catapulted into living life alone too soon in this big house.

"No, Maeve, it's Kurt Messer."

"Kurt, hi. Thanks for fixing the pothole," she said. "You really didn't need to send Mark out at five in the morning."

"He came out at five in the morning?"

"Yes. Too early. But thank you." She wondered if this was a personal call or if the store phone had forwarded the call, something she had programmed it to do after hours. Sometimes people thought of things late at night—for instance, they needed a cake the next day and had forgotten to order one—and she didn't like to miss those calls. "What can I do for you?" she asked, her voice sounding tired and weak to her own ears.

"Founders Day. Do you remember I said I'd have a party the day before for the crew?"

No. "Of course."

"Can I place my order now, or would you prefer that I come in tomorrow?"

She looked around for a piece of paper, Heather's envelope sticking out from between the cookbooks, reminding her that she had to think of what to do with that information. "Now is fine," she said. Founders Day was this Sunday, and she hadn't given a thought to what she would make or, even more of a worry, how she would make it in time. Jo was going to have to do double duty, and she wouldn't like that. She didn't even enjoy doing single duty, although her latest stint at the bakery was far more productive than her last. Maybe motherhood had changed her.

"Got that?" Kurt asked.

"I've got it," Maeve said. "Thanks so much for your business, Kurt."

"You sound a little off, Maeve. Is everything okay, or am I being too personal?"

"Not being personal at all, Kurt," she said, resisting the urge to both cry and tell him everything—how she felt responsible for Taylor's disappearance, how one of her daughters hated her and wanted nothing to do with her, how she had killed one man and had a hand in another man's death yet felt nothing inside when she thought of both those instances. "Just teenage drama." That was the understatement of the year.

"She's a nice girl, Maeve."

"Who?"

"Heather. A lovely girl. You've done a very nice job there." His voice dropped to a whisper. "I lost a daughter, Maeve. Car accident. And not a day goes by that I don't think of her and wonder what she'd be like now. Now that I know Heather, I wonder if she'd be as wonderful as your girl."

"Heather Callahan?" Maeve asked, wondering if she had stepped through a portal into a different world where people thought that her recalcitrant and moody daughter was a "lovely girl" she had done a "nice job" raising. "You must be thinking of Rebecca."

"No, I'm thinking of Heather, Maeve," Kurt said, letting out a little laugh.

"How do you know her? From the store?"

"No," he said. "From Mark. They're spending time together, Maeve, and I couldn't be happier."

CHAPTER 38

She would deny it. Maeve was sure of that, so there was really no reason at all to try to talk to Heather about this new relationship. She had denied dating Jesse Connors and would deny even knowing Mark Messer.

"Therapy," Maeve said, surprising herself with the sound of her own voice and the word spoken. Therapy wasn't something her people did. They drank. They raged. They stewed. And eventually, when all of that was done, they swept whatever it was under the carpet, never to speak of it again.

When she had a moment to think, a second to look into it, they were going to therapy. She'd have to prepare herself mentally for what she would hear from her daughter, but it had to be done. There was no way out of this situation unless they had someone to listen to them both, mediate the conflict.

It would be a last-ditch effort, one she loathed the thought of, but something she would have to do.

The next day at the store, she texted Cal to make sure that Heather had moved in and stayed there, as she said she would, something he confirmed with one word.

Yes.

So they weren't speaking either, she guessed, Cal in a snit about whatever it was that was troubling him currently. Alone in the store, she sat at the counter in the kitchen, waiting for the scones to bake, and wrote out a list of things she would need to do for what she thought was the most ridiculous event ever to be scheduled in Farringville: Founders Day.

Sure the village was old, and yes, the immigrants who had settled here had found a delightful little tract of land right beside the Hudson River, but what was the town celebrating exactly? That it was a bedroom community that gave rise to a bunch of new, giant homes that didn't fit in with the old-world grandeur of the east side of the village? That the taxes were making it so people like Maeve wouldn't have a chance in hell of staying here once she was retired, if she could ever do that? That the threat of bigger stores—the Starbucks and the Smashburgers and the Whole Foods— that threatened to encroach on the real estate would put people like her out of business in no time? That the one major business that had allowed people to live comfortably had been sold by its owner, leaving its former employees to scramble and find work elsewhere?

She laid her head on the counter. Settle down, she told herself. She was spiraling out of control mentally, and she knew that feeling. It wasn't a good one.

Jo was early that morning, showing up not long after the morning rush. "You look like death warmed over."

"How so?" Maeve asked. "How warm exactly?"

Jo eyed her from across the kitchen. "Wow, someone woke up on the wrong side of bed this morning."

"Heather moved out."

"To Cal's?

"Yes, to Cal's. She's too young to get a hotel room, Jo," Maeve said, hoping to laugh it off but sounding bitter and resentful.

Jo walked past her into the store. "I think I'll just leave you alone for a while. I think you need to stay here. Customers don't enjoy crabby bakers."

She took Jo's advice and stayed in the kitchen. After making batter for four dozen cupcakes, some of which she would freeze in anticipation of the weekend's festivities, she went online and reread the story about the girl who had gone missing in Prideville the year before, noting, when the story came up, the similarities between Caroline Jerman's case and Taylor's.

She was seventeen.

She had long, dark hair.

She had played soccer.

She had left work to take the five-minute walk home, disappearing somewhere between the Rite Aid on Route 3 and her house.

Maeve slammed her computer shut and pulled open the door between the kitchen and the front of the store. "Can you hold down the fort?" she asked Jo.

"Yes," Jo said, gesturing to the empty space. "I think I can handle servicing no customers."

No customers. On her way out to the car, Maeve thought about that and how between the hours of eight and two, hardly anyone came in anymore. The railroad guys were regulars, but even their numbers seemed to have dwindled. She had heard once that any press was good press. Bad press, contrary to the prevailing theory, seemed to be hurting her bottom line.

No customers, she thought again. It didn't matter. At least not right now. She got into the Prius and headed into the village, the place where the high school kids gathered to have lunch and blow off a little steam before heading back to class. A Mexican takeout place was Heather's favorite, and although Maeve bristled at the amount of money she spent on the food, she knew it was marginally healthier than the Chinese place or the sandwich places that dotted either side of Main Street.

Maeve parked in Mathers Park and took the short walk into town, scanning the throngs of kids for a glimpse of Heather. After fifteen minutes, just about ready to give up, she saw her coming out of the Mexican place with a bottle of water in one hand and a bag of food in the other. She was on the other side of the street, by herself, not noticing her mother until Maeve raised a hand and got her attention.

Maeve could tell that her first inclination was to pretend not to see her mother, but she looked both ways before crossing, as Maeve had taught her a long time ago, darted out into the street after a car passed by, and trotted over. Without pausing, she walked quickly toward the park, Maeve trying to keep up with her long-legged daughter.

"I know no one wants to be seen with their mother during lunch," Maeve said when they finally arrived at a picnic table.

Heather opened the bag of food. "Are you hungry?"

Maeve inspected its contents. Two tacos, an order of rice and beans, tortilla chips. "Kind of."

Heather handed her mother a taco, picking at hers in silence.

"How did we get here, Heather?" Maeve asked, her anger dissipated and in its place, bewilderment tinged with sadness.

Heather shrugged, putting a piece of shredded lettuce in her mouth.

"I'm hoping we can get back on track."

"And what track would that be?" Heather asked. "The one where you're either nonexistent to me or completely up my ass?"

"See? This is what I'm talking about," Maeve said. "We have to be able to have a conversation without employing the nuclear option."

In spite of herself, Heather laughed. "What does that even mean?"

"Nuclear. Bombs. Explosions. Blast off," Maeve said. "Is that not a term you kids use these days?"

"No one uses that term, Mom," Heather said.

Maeve could see that the fight had gone out of her; her defenses were down clearly. "Heather, what are you doing? In terms of Taylor?"

"What do you mean?"

"Are you dating Jesse Connors?" Maeve asked, steeling herself for the answer in the he-said, she-said situation that existed.

"Not really," Heather said.

"Do I even want to know what that means?"

"I flirted with him a little bit, tried to figure out what he knew."

"About what?"

"About Taylor," Heather said, as if that was completely obvious.

"Why did the police tell me that you were dating?" Maeve asked.

"Why do the police say anything?"

"Did you tell them you were dating?"

"Not really." Heather toyed with the plastic fork that had come in the takeout bag. "I wanted them to talk to Jesse some more. It was the only way I could think of to . . ."

"Get him?" Maeve asked. Before Heather could respond, she held up a hand. "I found the note. I found the photos. I kept them. Just how deep into this are you, Heather? And why you?"

Heather balled up the taco into its foil wrap and pushed it into the bag, her hunger gone. "Why me? Because I like Taylor. I felt sorry for her. She doesn't really hang out with anyone. And those guys . . ." She trailed off.

"What?"

"They're awful."

"Why didn't you go to the police?" Maeve asked. "Come to me?"

"She said she was going to disappear for a few days, and then she was really gone. I got scared," Heather said. "So I thought I'd look for her on my own."

"But the Jesse thing . . . ," Maeve started.

"Just a hunch. I heard what everyone else heard. I wanted to see if it was true."

"And did you ask him?" Maeve asked.

"I tried. He shut me down." Heather looked dismayed at the thought, shouldering the responsibility of finding a girl who had been tossed aside by almost every male in her life.

Inside, Maeve felt her heart break just a little bit. As much as Heather wanted to run from her mother, it was becoming apparent to her that they were more alike than either would admit. She said the words she should have said to herself before the whole thing started, the words that Chris had tried to articulate time and time again. "It's too much for you, Heather. You're just one girl. You can't do this alone."

"I know that now."

"Did you tell the police?" Maeve asked. "Chris?"

"I told them about that last day, what Taylor told me. But nothing else. It would just get too big, make us both seem guilty of something we didn't do."

Yet. Something they hadn't done yet.

A couple of tables away, a group of young mothers sat, some with babies in strollers, others with toddlers playing in the sandbox in the playground. Maeve could hear snippets of their conversation, the complaints about lack of sleep, the picky eaters they had birthed, the absence of help from their working husbands. The long days. The baths and the meals and the boredom of being home all day with kids.

Little children, little problems, Maeve wanted to say. She looked back at Heather, and in her face she could see the girl she once was, the "dark gypsy," as Jack used to call her, brooding and silent but the one who laughed the loudest when her mother tickled her and kissed her the longest at bedtime. "Oh, honey," Maeve said. "You're in over your head."

Heather looked at her phone. "I have to get back to class. What should I do?"

Maeve thought for a moment. "Don't do anything. Let me think." They both stood. "Come here," she said, and Heather accepted the hug, wrapping her own arms around her smaller mother and holding her tight. "We'll figure this out," Maeve said. "I promise."

"You sound sure about that."

Heather didn't know what she was capable of and Maeve wasn't going to tell her. She changed the subject to something more innocuous.

"How is soccer?" Maeve asked. "Does your joining the team have anything to do with this?"

"Yes and no," Heather said.

"That's specific."

"Taylor asked me to join, so I did it as a goof."

"When did you become friends with Taylor?"

Heather shrugged.

"And soccer?"

"And what?"

"Do you like it?"

Heather shrugged. "It's okay.

"And Coach Barnham?"

"What about him?"

"What's he like?"

"Sometimes nice, sometimes an asshole. Plays favorites. What does Rebecca say?"

Maeve tossed their trash in the bin. "Pretty much the same."

"He's super upset about Taylor."

"Really?" Maeve asked.

"Calls her a special girl."

Maeve froze by the garbage can and wondered: innocuous platitude or something more sinister? There was only one way to find out.

She watched Heather walk away, and instead of taking her own advice—*don't do anything . . . let me think*—she got into her car and pulled out of the parking lot, a new destination on her mind.

CHAPTER 39

She drove to the other side of town, going back to where it all started, where she had first pulled the thread from the mysterious spool and gotten nowhere, back to David Barnham's manly cabin in the woods.

It's him, she thought, and her palms started itching, letting her know that she was missing her gun. She wished she had it, but that ship had sailed; no more weapons for her. She had promised herself that she would straighten out, be a person who didn't opt for shooting when threats would suffice. She didn't know what she was going to do when she got to Barnham's house, but everything was pointing to the soccer coach's involvement in Taylor's disappearance.

It's you, she thought, as she pulled up silently on the street that fronted the cabin, climbing out of her car and walking through the dense woods, wondering where Cosmo might be stashed for the day. He seemed perfectly nice, as animals went, but boy, did she hate dogs. The pickup wasn't in the driveway, and as she approached the house, peeking in a living room window, there was no sign of the dog, no barking, no movement inside.

She walked around to the back and put her hand on the screen door. There was no turning back; she was in the muck of this thing and wanted to see it end, one way or another. She took a deep breath and tried the back door, finding the handle turning easily in her sweaty palm. In the kitchen, a half-empty pot of coffee sat on the counter, two mugs beside it, a plate with the remnants of an egg sandwich on the other side.

The house smelled of pine and something else, something that she recognized as dog. Dog hair covered the cushions that protected rush-seated pine chairs, and a fine layer of dust collected by the baseboards, mixed together with what could only be strands of Cosmo's hair. There were strands of medium-length brunette hair as well, one here, another there, suggesting the presence of the cop Suzanne Carstairs had mentioned the first time she had been at Maeve's bakery, when Maeve was convinced that she had seen Barnham testing the depth of Laurel Lake. She picked up a hair that had become suspended on the rung of one of the chairs, turning it over in her fingers, noticing its gloss, its beautiful texture. Her own hair wasn't like that; dirty blond, it was dry and flyaway, somewhere between curly and frizzy, and always in a state of messiness. This hair in her hand was the hair of someone who took care of herself, who liked to be pampered and groomed. She dropped it on the floor to become one with the dog hair and the dust.

She worked quickly, looking through drawers in the kitchen, finding the usual things one would find in the proverbial junk drawer, something every house had: a corkscrew with a cork firmly embedded in it, a few slotted spoons, a whisk, some rubber bands, an Allen wrench. In another drawer were some ratty dish towels and Ziploc bags—lots of Ziploc bags—that had been used, washed out, and put away for another day. The third drawer housed some papers, which Maeve riffled through quickly. The water bill. A small phone book. An envelope that held a thick sheaf of papers and bore the insignia of the U.S. Marshals Service.

A photo of the team, and some other photos of individual girls. Before she could figure out if Taylor was one of the solo subjects— or, almost worse to consider, Heather—she froze.

Next to her ear, she heard the click of a gun, a bullet sliding into its chamber. "You should have asked which cop when you were told that he was sleeping with someone on the Farringville force."

Maeve tried not to let the fear show. She was usually the one holding the gun. "Yes. I should have, Chief Carstairs."

"Want to tell me what's going on here, Maeve?" Suzanne Carstairs asked, a plush robe cinched tightly around her waist, her glossy hair a little disheveled.

Before Maeve even knew what was happening, she was sitting in one of the kitchen chairs, her hands cuffed behind her back, something she really didn't think was necessary. The Chief had other ideas. Namely, that Maeve was guilty of breaking and entering and was, most likely, nuts. Who knew what she was capable of? That was the look etched on the chief's face, a woman who could produce handcuffs with alacrity, despite being in a robe and nothing else, if the expanse of bare leg was any indication. "Well . . ."

"And don't lie, Maeve. I can spot a liar a mile away."

"Interesting. Your boyfriend lied to you about being at Laurel Lake, yet you chose to believe him." Maeve held the chief's gaze. "Or you weren't here. One or the other."

Carstairs chose to ignore Maeve's taunt. "Start at the beginning."

"You know everything that I know. There's another missing girl, and she's a dead ringer for Taylor Dvorak. She played soccer."

"Oh, so we're back to that? Soccer?" Carstairs shook her head.

"So we have a girl who has long brown hair and played soccer, so David Barnham killed them both?"

"Is Taylor dead?" Maeve asked. "Is that other girl dead? Do you know?"

Carstairs grimaced, realizing her mistake. "We don't know. I misspoke."

"He appeared out of nowhere, your boyfriend, and he has close relationships with some of the girls."

"He's a coach, Maeve. That's his job. And he's been here for several years. You know that."

"So why is he here? To have parties? To invite girls over to his house?"

Suzanne put the gun in her lap. "You've been spending way too much time in front of your oven, bakery girl. David Barnham is a soccer coach, plain and simple. And what makes him a good soccer coach is that he has rapport with his athletes."

"He's a good soccer coach?" Maeve asked. "Really?"

Suzanne smiled. "Well, you've got a point there." She pushed a crumb from the edge of the table onto the floor. "And let me tell you, none of those girls are complaining about having attention from their hot coach."

"That's how you think of him? As a hot coach?"

"If the cleats fit . . ." She trailed off, laughing at her own joke. "Really, Maeve. Do you think I'd be dating a guy who was acting inappropriately toward high school girls? Do I look like I need to go that low?" she asked, sweeping a hand over her body. "Trust me. If he were up to no good, I'd kill him."

If Maeve's hands hadn't been cuffed, she would have tucked in the shirt that had ridden up over the waistband of her jeans, exposing a swath of flabby midsection. Instead, she looked at a spot over the chief's head rather than take in her toned and enviable physique.

She remembered the chief patting her midsection, suggesting she didn't exercise. Nothing could be further from the truth unless she lived on a steady diet of coffee and cigarettes, which was entirely possible.

Maeve leaned in close, and the chief's hand closed around her gun again. "Tell me the truth. Was he here that morning?"

Suzanne used the gun to point at Maeve's hands. "What is it about this situation that gives you the idea that you can ask the questions?"

Maeve looked down. "Sorry."

"Now why don't you tell me a few things? First, what's going on with your daughter and Jesse Connors? And where did she go the other night?"

"Nothing is going on with my daughter and Jesse Connors. As for the other night, I wish I could tell you that, but I can't."

"Or won't?"

"Can't."

Carstairs eyed her, carefully crossing one leg over the other. Maeve was right: She was naked beneath the robe. "Okay. So let's try this. Why are you here again?"

Maeve was resolute, something she hoped was written on her face, despite the fact that her insides felt like overcooked spaghetti noodles. "I think your boyfriend knows something about Taylor's disappearance."

"Because of the kayaking," Carstairs said, sighing. She was tiring of the conversation, and Maeve wasn't sure she could convince her that something was amiss.

"Because of the kayaking. And the girls. The parties. He has a fondness for Taylor that I'm not sure is entirely pure. But mainly the kayaking."

"Oh, we're back to that."

"I know what I saw."

"And I know what I saw." The chief stood up. "This is exhausting. *You,*" she said, pointing the gun lazily at Maeve, "are exhausting."

On the counter, a cell phone rang, and the chief picked it up. "Hi . . . Not sure," she said to the person on the other end. "What do you want me to do?" She listened intently. "Got it." She put the phone down and started for the hallway. "So, I'm going to get dressed, and then you and I are going to go down to the station."

"Why?" Maeve asked.

The chief looked at her, a bemused smile on her lips. "Because that was, as you refer to him, my boyfriend, and he wants to press charges." She let the smile grow wide. "Ever been to jail, Maeve?"

CHAPTER 40

They were in the car when Jo let out the feeling she had been holding in since arriving at the Farringville police station an hour earlier. "Maeve Conlon! You are out on bail!" She banged the steering wheel, scaring the baby in the backseat, the kid setting up a howl. Jo reached back and patted his knee until he calmed down. "Seriously. I thought I'd be the first one in jail. Not you."

Maeve learned that the wheels of justice turned quickly in Farringville. She leaned her head against the headrest and closed her eyes. Chris hadn't been in the station when she was brought in in handcuffs, nor had he arrived when she had been booked. So either he was working a case or he had been warned: *Your girlfriend is here. The one who is making you fat. Don't come in.*

Jo had been the first person she thought to call. She could only imagine the histrionics, the knight riding in on his white horse, if Cal had been the one to come get her. She would never live it down. She had already lost emotional and almost physical custody of Heather; a rap sheet would seal the deal permanently.

"Just take me home," Maeve said when she had the energy to get the words out.

Jo maneuvered the car out of the parking lot. If Maeve hadn't been in such a terrible state of mind, she would have enjoyed the spectacular river view that greeted them as they headed away from the station and toward her house. "Breaking and entering, huh?" Jo asked as they rounded the corner toward the main drag. "What exactly were you doing?"

"I guess I let myself into the guy's house, and that was not a very good decision on my part."

Jo raised an eyebrow. "What the hell?"

"I wish I could tell you, Jo, but it just sounds ridiculous. The whole thing."

"Something tells me your boyfriend isn't going to be pleased when he finds out he's dating a felon."

"Well, I hope it's not a felony. That won't be good."

"Maybe the guy whose house you broke into will decide not to press charges."

"The door was unlocked."

"Don't matter, girlfriend." Jo waited at a red light, tapping her fingers on the steering wheel. "This is about Taylor, right?"

"Right."

Jo looked over at Maeve, her lips pursed. "You going a little crazy, friend?"

"Crazy?"

"Yeah. Crazy. As in, you don't sleep enough and you work too hard and you're starting to see things where they don't exist?"

Maeve turned toward the window and looked out at the street outside. The world was normal and lovely, with people walking and talking, the coffee shop abuzz with the after-school crowd, the local restaurants gearing up for the dinner rush. She *was* going a little crazy, but she would never admit it. She felt as if she couldn't walk among these people because of the baggage she carried with her, and in that moment, that realization made her sad.

"I've seen you like this before," Jo said.

Maeve didn't respond. *You have?* she wanted to ask but couldn't, knowing where this was going. *And what was that like?* she wanted to know but didn't ask.

"You get crazy. You get obsessed. And it's good for no one," Jo said, driving through the light, hanging a right at the traffic circle. "Especially you."

"Can we talk about this later?" Maeve asked, exhaustion covering her like a warm blanket. She knew she'd be home in a few minutes, but she wanted to stay in this car for a long time so she could fall asleep to the hum of the engine, the sound of the baby sucking his thumb contentedly in the backseat.

The house was empty when they arrived, as Maeve knew it would be. "Want me to come in?" Jo asked, looking up at the old Colonial, the emptiness of it telegraphing out to the street.

"No," Maeve said, wondering if she had the strength to make it from the car to the front door. She was embarrassed—humiliated, really—and didn't know if she'd recover from this one. The entire Farringville Police Department would know that Chris Larsson's girlfriend, the Cupcake Lady to many in town, had let herself into someone's house, gone through his personal things, and been arrested by his girlfriend, a woman who just happened to be the village's police chief. It was going to be in the local paper's police blotter for sure, and she would never live this down, no matter how many perfectly constructed, Thulian-crossed-with-salmon-frosted cupcakes she made, no matter how many Comfort Zone quiches were sold that bailed out a husband who was supposed to make dinner on a certain night for a certain overworked wife. She looked at Jo.

Jo reached across the space between the two seats. "Come

here," she said, gathering her best friend into her arms and waiting for the inevitable onslaught of sobs that should have accompanied a trip to jail. A normal person would cry.

But there were no tears, because Maeve knew she wasn't normal. Maeve laid her head on Jo's shoulder and stayed there for a few seconds before breaking away. "Thank you. I'll give you the money tomorrow. Is that okay?"

Jo pulled back. "Sure. Tomorrow is fine."

Jo's face gave away what she felt inside: Maeve was losing it, and she was bearing witness to that. Maeve rearranged her features into an expression that approximated something normal, something with which Jo would be familiar, and smiled. "I'm fine, Jo. Don't worry. I'm done with this."

"With Taylor? With what has happened?"

"With everything," Maeve said. "It's not my fault."

"It was never your fault," Jo said. "There's no reason on God's green earth why you should feel responsible. Now that witch Judy Wilkerson? That's another story."

Maeve hadn't thought about her in a while. "Yes. She has a lot of explaining to do."

"Her little punk-ass grandson can build as many schools in Mississippi as he wants, but he'll still be the kid who rear-ended Doug's car and then denied the whole thing."

"What?" Maeve said, sitting up. "Her grandson?"

"Yes. Tommy or Todd or Timmy Morehead."

"Tim Morehead."

"Whatever. Kid looked Doug straight in the face and said he hadn't backed into him in the grocery store parking lot when Doug saw the whole thing." Jo looked back at the baby. "Not that the big dent doesn't give the Taurus a little street cred, but what kind of kid lies to a cop's face?"

"I don't know," Maeve said, thinking of Judy Wilkerson and her ability to lie without blinking. Must be a family trait.

"Had a friend with him who lied, too."

"Preppy?"

Jo looked at her. "Yeah. The Connors Kid."

Jo slumped in her seat, changing the subject back to what was rapidly becoming Maeve's least favorite: her own state of mind. "I hate seeing you like this. You're not responsible for everyone, Maeve."

Maeve was defiant. "I know that."

"I don't think you do."

Behind her, the baby gurgled in agreement with his mother, and something about hearing his little voice in the backseat softened her, making her think back to the time when she was in the driver's seat and one of her babies was in the back. "Thanks, Jo. I'll pay you back tomorrow," Maeve said again before getting out of the car. "And thanks for everything." She got out and stood on the sidewalk, the car door still open. "I love you, you know. I just wanted to tell you that. In case I didn't get the chance again."

"Why wouldn't you get the chance?" Jo asked.

Before Jo could ask any more questions, Maeve slammed the car door and went inside, closing the door to her house and herself off to the world outside.

She had barely reached the second floor when she heard a knock. She started talking to Jo before she reached the door. "I really just want to be alone," she said, flinging it open to find Charles Connors standing on the other side, his expression telling her that this wasn't a social call.

CHAPTER 41

She didn't let him in, letting him stew on the other side of the door, the screen between them. "What do you want?" she asked, her antipathy toward him greater now that she knew Trish's side of the story.

"It was bad enough that Taylor's disappearance announced to the world that I was her father, and a negligent one at that, but now the police are spending a bit more time with me and my family than I would like," he said, a man used to getting his own way, making things happen on his terms.

"Maybe they are asking you questions so that they can find your child, Mr. Connors."

"A child that you were too busy to help," he said.

Knowing what she knew now, Maeve was less inclined to absorb that emotional blow. Of all of the people at fault, she was way down on the list. The man in front of her held a spot at least five or six rungs above her on that ladder. "Why are you here, Mr. Connors?" she asked.

"You and your daughter are causing trouble for my family, and I won't tolerate it," he said.

Maeve smiled. He had underestimated her and would regret it

if this went any further. "Or what, Mr. Connors?" she asked. "You'll bring the full force of your team of minions upon me?" She opened the door to the porch and stepped outside. "Here's one thing you should know about me and my daughter: Unlike you or your son or your nephew or whoever he is to you, we tell the truth. No matter what the cost." And while that wasn't necessarily true, it had the intended effect of knocking the wind out of his sails a bit, his furious blinking a sign of that.

"He's my son. I don't know why you can't understand that."

"Adopted."

"Yes, adopted."

"While you had a daughter in the same town whose paternity you would never acknowledge. I've always said that this town has a lot of secrets, but that one takes the cake," Maeve said. "No pun intended."

"Whatever it is you think you know about my family, Ms. Conlon, is likely far off base," he said. "Jesse is the child my wife and I could never have together."

"And Taylor?"

"She was not." He turned, attempting to leave, his mission of intimidation, of getting Maeve to back off, not having been at all effective. "Please leave my family alone, Ms. Conlon. That's all I ask."

Maeve followed him down the porch steps. "I just don't understand it," she said. "How you could leave that girl."

He turned back to face her again. "I have a wife I love. I made a mistake. It's as simple as that. I set the girl up for life. And Trish ruined that."

"The surgeries. Taylor's illness. That's why Trish doesn't have any money."

He let out a laugh, more of a bark, really. "Is that what she told you? That the baby was sick?"

Maeve felt a little queasy, not sure who she was supposed to believe, who she could trust. "Yes."

"She blew through the money I gave her and then more money that I gave her later. She has a problem. Gambling," he said. "As insidious as drugs, as bad as alcohol, although there's some of that, too."

"Why should I believe you?" Maeve asked. On the sidewalk, she stepped aside to let a neighbor and her dog pass, the neighbor giving Charles Connors the side eye. Maeve didn't have many visitors, and certainly none as handsome and imposing as the man standing next to her.

He didn't respond directly. "Taylor will get a trust at age twenty-one, when she is an adult and on her own." He looked up at the sky. "God willing."

"But you wouldn't pay for her to go to college."

"Yes, I would," Connors said. "I would, and I told Trish that. The extortion was her idea. There was no way I wasn't going to get that girl out of this town and away from her mother."

"You could have sued for custody."

He smiled, patronizing her. "You think you have all of the answers, don't you?" He put his hands in the pockets of his checkered golf pants and looked up at the sky, dotted with cumulus clouds. "What is that you said? People are telling lies about you?" He put a hand on her shoulder. "We have that in common." He started for his car, idling at the curb.

"Nothing you've done makes sense," Maeve said.

"I'm sure there are a few things you've done, Ms. Conlon, that no one but yourself would understand."

He waited for her to respond, but she didn't, couldn't. He was right, but there was no way she would let him know that.

"I think you know something. You or your son," she said. "Your wife."

His response came quickly. "My wife knows nothing."

"I think you all do."

"Think what you want. The truth is usually farther from your grasp than you think." He opened the car door. "Just leave us alone."

CHAPTER 42

The next morning, Maeve opened the store and set about getting ready for Founders Day, which was coming up sooner than she would have liked, making more batches of cupcakes than she had ever made in one day. Jo handled the front of the store with ease, checking on Maeve periodically but understanding that her role that day was strictly retail. Maeve could hear her bantering with customers and upselling them on items they hadn't known they wanted when they walked into the store. Maybe she was getting the hang of this bakery thing after all.

Jo brought a piece of quiche in at lunchtime and put it in the microwave, placing it in front of Maeve when it was hot. "Eat," she said.

"I'm not hungry," she said. "And I hate Founders Day."

Jo leaned against the desk and folded her arms across her chest. "Any word from Chris?"

Maeve shook her head, focusing on the bowl of frosting in front of her.

"Well . . ."

"Well, nothing," Maeve said, interrupting Jo midthought. "I

screwed up. I embarrassed myself and him. If I never heard from him again, I wouldn't be surprised." She thought about Rodney's words in relation to his own dissolving relationship. *There's no good part with me.* She was starting to feel the same way about herself.

"Need help back here?" Jo asked.

"No," Maeve said, icing her fiftieth cupcake of the day. It was beautiful, just like the forty-nine others she had iced before this one.

"Make sure you eat," Jo said, going back into the store.

Maeve didn't have an appetite. She picked at the quiche before dumping it into the garbage pail and pulled out a stool, sitting and regarding what she had accomplished in the short time she had had in the kitchen that morning.

"Pretty impressive."

She hadn't heard Chris Larsson come through the back door, nor the noisy screen slamming behind him. As always, he'd taken care to come in and not disturb her. She looked at him, at a loss for what to say.

He held up a hand. "Don't say anything."

"There's nothing to say," she said. "Except that I'm sorry."

He looked flustered, not ready to hear that she was at fault, his expression suggesting that he had expected defiance, defensiveness. "Well, okay." He put his hands in his pockets, looking around the kitchen. "Do I want to know what this is about?" he asked. "Why you felt the need to break into the coach's house, go through his drawers?"

"I didn't break in. The back door was unlocked."

He looked up at the ceiling, exasperated. "Maeve, you know better than that. You know what you did was wrong."

"Taylor. I want to find her." Although she willed herself not to cry, it was too much to keep in. A tear slid down her cheek, landing on her apron.

"We all want to find her," he said, his voice cracking. "It's all I think about. I don't sleep. And when I do catch a few minutes, I see her face. She is someone's daughter."

"That's all I think about, too."

"Why do you think you can do what we can't?" he asked, and written on her face, she knew, was the doubt she had about him and what he was capable of. How she knew that he would never find Taylor Dvorak, that she was his needle in a haystack, one he would never locate. She watched his body go slack, his face showing sadness because the woman he loved felt he was incapable of greatness, of doing the one thing that needed to be done. "Worse than the arrest, and worse than thinking that you've been out there on your own, possibly messing up our case, is the fact that when you look at me, all I see is doubt."

"I don't doubt us," she said.

"Not us," he said. "Me." When she tried to protest, he held up a hand to stop her. "It's right there," he said, reaching out and touching her cheek just below her eye. "It's been right there all along."

"Where do we go from here?" she asked when it was clear that he was done talking.

"That's why I'm here, Maeve." He moved his mouth a few times, choosing his words. "We don't go anywhere."

"We don't?" she asked, her voice sounding weak at the realization that the best thing she had right now—a relationship with a normal guy—was over.

"I helped you when you were looking for your sister. I even tried to defend you when Judy Wilkerson said what she did. I have tried to deal with the secrecy and your family issues and everything else that goes along with loving you." He smiled, but it was tinged with sadness. Regret. "I do love you. But this is all just too . . ."

"Complicated?" she asked.

He nodded. "Complicated."

Outside, it was a beautiful day. Inside, the kitchen suddenly seemed gloomy and dark even though sunlight streamed through the window over the sink, casting a glow over Chris Larsson that showed her just how this would never work out. He was simple and true, with not one secret to share. And she, cast in a shadow thrown from the big shelf by the back door, was none of those things, someone who held her secrets close and who realized, at that very moment, that they would be what finally destroyed her.

"Please leave this alone, Maeve. I can't understand why you put yourself in the middle of this, but now, you're just a hindrance," he said.

"I thought you didn't know big words," she said, the joke falling flat by the disappointed look on his broad, honest face. She handed him a cupcake. "Here. Try this. For Founders Day."

He held the cupcake in his big, meaty hand, with no intention of eating it in front of her. "Maybe we can try this again some other time?" he said, waving the cupcake between the two of them.

"Maybe," she said. But she knew the truth: It was over, and it would never start again. She would see him around town, and it would be awkward and strange, two people who had shared everything once and who now lived separately, moving on without each other. "I'm really, really sorry, Chris." It sounded lame to her ears, but it was all she had. "I never meant to hurt you."

His face crumbled into what seemed like a million pieces. "My heart feels broken," he said, words at odds with who he was most of the time: big, strong, stoic.

Mine, too, she wanted to say, but he was gone, and there was no one to say it to.

CHAPTER 43

Jo clapped her hands together. "Are you ready for Founders Day?" she asked when she arrived at work on Sunday morning. "The day that gave us our beloved Farringville?"

Maeve had been at work since four, putting the finishing touches on the cupcakes for the celebration as well as Kurt Messer's order.

Jo continued. "Where big guys with even bigger dogs will search for that one special someone, the woman with just the right tramp stamp."

Maeve looked up. "What are you talking about?"

Jo wasn't finished. "Where the smell of roasted meats and caramelized onions will tickle your culinary fancy, delighting your senses for hours after you've departed. And why? Because you'll never be able to get the smell out of your nostrils no matter how hard you try."

Maeve hadn't laughed in a long time, and it felt good. "You've given this a lot of thought."

"Not really. I've just been to a lot of small-town festivals and celebrations. They are all the same."

Maeve boxed up the last of the cupcakes and three quiches, tying up the boxes with several layers of red-and-white string. In any other town, the local DPW guys wouldn't eat quiche, but Farringville wasn't like any other town. Not every town had The Comfort Zone.

Jo went into the front to gather supplies for their booth: napkins, plates, some money from the cash register. Maeve sat up on her stool and surveyed the work that she had done, taking a moment to breathe. She would be surrounded by hundreds of people that day, but she would feel more alone than she had ever felt; she knew before even stepping foot on the main drag that her loneliness was just beginning and would only get worse with time.

Inside her pants pocket, her phone vibrated. She looked at the screen.

Poole.

Mrs. McSweeney has passed. Natural causes.

And with her, Maeve thought as she clutched the phone in her hand, went any knowledge she had of my sister, her birth, her parentage. It was gone, just like the girl from Prideville the year before, and Taylor now. Maeve didn't respond at first, silently putting the phone back in her pocket and trying to forget that there were certain stories that would never have a happy ending.

After a minute of thinking about everything that had happened, she couldn't help herself. She pulled her phone out again and thanked Poole for the information, asking another question.

Why would someone have mail from the U.S. Marshals?

His response didn't come quickly, but when it did, it left her more confused.

They are a Marshal themselves. Or Witness Protection.

It made no sense. David Barnham wasn't a U.S. Marshal, not that Maeve could discern. Did they do undercover work, placing guys like him in positions like soccer coach? It seemed unlikely but what did she know?

Witness Protection.

She shook her head. Both scenarios were completely preposterous, even more so than her believing that he had something to do with those missing girls.

She and Jo loaded all of the cupcakes into the back of both their cars and headed for the center of town, where cars were allowed for just a few hours before the street would be closed off to traffic. When they were done, they parked their cars in the police station parking lot with the other vendors.

Jo looked at Maeve as they got out of their cars. "Well, this isn't too uncomfortable."

"I'm going to forget that you said that, Jo, and pretend that it is totally normal to be out on bail and parking in the police station lot."

"Suit yourself," Jo said. "I just love irony."

When they got back to the booth, they set up the display of cupcakes and waited for the parade to start.

"Don't look now, but there's the happy couple," Jo said. "Three o'clock."

Maeve turned to her right and saw Cal and Gabriela walking along, the baby in his stroller, his parents' arms entwined, Gabriela's head on Cal's shoulder.

"Jeez, it's after Labor Day. Put away the white jeans, sister," Jo said.

"She's not from here. I'm not sure they have that rule in Brazil."

Jo put a hand to her brow, shielding her eyes from the sun. "Is she even wearing underwear? Who does that? The sun is shining. We don't need to see that. Not on a day for families."

"Who does what?" Maeve asked, her eyes trained on Suzanne Carstairs, walking along the parade route, one hand on the gun on her hip as if she were suspecting trouble from the group of preschoolers who marched alongside her, oblivious to her presence, her guarded stance.

"Goes outside without underwear. To a town fair, no less," Jo continued putting boxes under the table while ranting. "Go commando at home. Not outside."

"Huh?" Maeve asked, getting a glimpse of Chris Larsson in the distance, his eyes trained on the parade and its marchers.

"Forget it," Jo said, clapping in time to the ragtag group of musicians the Farringville High School called its marching band. "Are they playing '99 Problems'? Amazing," she said. "I didn't realize you could turn Jay Z into a marching band song." She whistled through her fingers. "Well done, guys! Playing like bosses!"

Maeve watched as the band went by, Suzanne Carstairs and Chris Larsson coming closer together, landing on a corner near where Judy Wilkerson and a boy who looked vaguely familiar to Maeve stood. Chris clasped a hand down on the boy's shoulder, smiling when the kid looked up at him, while Carstairs spoke quietly, all the while with a smile on her face, to Judy Wilkerson. Her hand left her hip, and she put an arm around Judy, while Chris walked in the other direction with the boy.

"Madison, Mississippi," Maeve said, but Jo was too busy singing along with the marching band to notice that she had said anything. "Not Connors but the other one."

Jo turned. "What did you say?"

"Nothing," Maeve said, looking down at her cupcakes. When she looked up, everyone was gone, the kid having been spirited off with Chris before anyone had noticed a thing, Judy Wilkerson in the wind as well. All she could see when she looked across the street was Gabriela's perfect ass, packed into tight white jeans.

Jo was right: no underwear.

The soccer team was making its way down the street behind the marching band, Coach Barnham and his team waving as if they had just won the World Cup. Heather wasn't with the team, as far as Maeve could see, but every other girl seemed to be.

"They need a new sax," Jo said, still listening to the marching band. "The kid on sax is a disaster."

In the crowd, Maeve saw Jesse Connors moving among the people watching the parade, looking over their heads, likely looking for his cohort, who had gone off with Chris Larsson somewhere.

"Trombone is okay," Jo said, keeping up her critique of the jazz band.

"I need to go to the bathroom," Maeve said, coming out from behind the table.

"Already?" Jo said. "And you didn't recently push a giant baby out of your hoohah. You'd better get that looked at. You may have a problem."

But Maeve was halfway down the street already, not listening to Jo's rant about the damage caused to the urinary tract by one large newborn. She scanned the crowd but didn't see Chris, Carstairs, or the people they had snatched from it. All she could see was parents with little kids, all with balloons touting the celebration, and teens wandering the streets with pockets full of cash to spend on crappy food and even crappier souvenirs. They were out of the house for the day, and that was all their parents cared about, the Farringville parent alternating between completely overprotective and almost neglectful.

She wandered the streets for a little while, losing herself in the crowd, not seeing the boy or the woman among the revelers. The chief and her lead detective were nowhere to be found either. She spotted Kurt Messer in front of a tiny upscale restaurant that had opened six months previously; he and the owner were chatting about the festivities, the owner wondering if this was something the town would do every year.

"Well, I hope not!" Kurt said, letting out a big guffaw. "We can't afford the overtime." He saw Maeve and beckoned her over.

"Maeve, hello. Do you know Thom Prendy?"

Maeve shook hands with the owner. "Nice to meet you. I own The Comfort Zone."

"I've been wanting to talk to you," Thom said. "I'm not happy with our pastry chef. Wondering if I should just go local and pick up from you."

Maeve smiled. "Sounds like a good plan to me. Come on down when you get a chance, and we can talk."

Kurt put a hand on Maeve's shoulder. "You can't go wrong with anything from Maeve," he said. "Her food is outstanding."

"Thanks, Kurt," Maeve said. "Do you want a job in public relations?"

Kurt let out another booming laugh. "Only if I can have a title like director of sales and marketing," he said. "Then again, I've got my hands full keeping this village clean, Maeve. But I'll do my best on a freelance basis." He looked over her head. "Parade's ending. Gotta go. Maeve, I've left the back door open so you can leave my order in the kitchen. Anytime after four?"

"Sounds good, Kurt. As soon as things settle down here, I'll be over." She turned to Thom. "I'll talk to you soon."

She went back to the booth, where Jo was selling cupcakes like they were going out of style. "How many did you make?" Jo asked.

"Four hundred," Maeve said, pulling an apron out from under the table and pulling it on over her head. "As soon as we're sold out, we're done," she said, over the idea of Founders Day and its attendant misery. She wasn't comfortable out in the open like this; she was sure the entire village knew that she had been arrested and was no longer dating Chris Larsson. Bad news—salacious news—traveled fast. Good news traveled less quickly. It was the way of a small town.

Mark Messer approached the booth, and Maeve handed him a cupcake. "Enjoy, Mark," she said.

"Hey, Maeve," he said. "Thanks. Where's Heather? I haven't seen her around."

Now wasn't the time, but it was on the tip of her tongue to ask him about their relationship, how long it had been going on, what it was like. Did they go on dates? Had he met Cal? Did anyone besides him, Heather, and his father know that they were dating? Instead, Maeve shrugged. "I don't know, Mark. She's around," she said, leaving out the part where it had been days since they spoke. Not even a text. Maeve could only be sure she was fine based on the fact that she hadn't heard otherwise from Cal. If there was a problem, she'd know about it. Unlike her for the last several years, he wouldn't tackle anything on his own, leaving his life with his new wife and son unblemished by the travails of raising two teenage girls.

"If you talk to her, would you let her know that I was looking for her?" he asked. "She's not responding to my texts."

Join the club, pal. "I will." Maeve watched him wander down the street, a black plastic bag looped through his belt, on duty for the day. Sure, he was a little old for Heather, but he was a nice kid, by Maeve's standards. As she watched him, she admitted a little class consciousness to herself. Had she seen her daughter dating a DPW worker? Or someone more like Jesse Connors with his allegedly faulty moral compass, someone who looked good to the outside world but who seemed to have his share of skeletons in his closet? It didn't matter. Heather wouldn't admit to having dated Jesse and probably wouldn't admit to dating Mark either. They weren't speaking, so Maeve couldn't ask her even if she wanted to.

The cupcakes were gone by two. Jo looked at Maeve. "As second-in-command, I am making an executive decision that we are officially closed."

"That was the deal," Maeve said, taking off her apron and balling it up. She threw it into an empty box and, using a knife she had brought from the store, started to cut up the other boxes for recycling. "Where's the baby today?" she asked, as she made a neat pile of cardboard.

"Doug's mother is in town, so she and her precious baby are spending the day together."

"That sounds nice."

"And by precious baby, I don't mean Jack. I mean Doug," Jo said, rolling her eyes. "Calling Dr. Freud! Old guy would have had a field day with those two."

Maeve stacked the cardboard behind the table. "So you can help me make the delivery to Kurt Messer's?"

"You've got me for as long as you want me."

Maeve smiled. "So, wine after?"

"Most definitely," Jo said.

They left the cardboard on the table under the tent and walked to their cars, agreeing to meet at The Comfort Zone to pick up Kurt's order.

They worked quickly, the thought of opening a bottle of wine after the workday something that reminded Maeve of the old days when it was just her and Jo, milking any opportunity to get together to socialize after a long day at the bakery. The baby had complicated things, which didn't come as a surprise. And after the week she had had, Maeve needed her friend.

At Kurt's house, the back door was open, just as he had promised. Maeve arrived first and started moving platters of cookies and cupcakes from the car; Jo had the quiches. In the tidy house, grander than Maeve was expecting the head of the DPW to own, the counters gleamed with a high gloss and the stainless appliances were spotless, without a fingerprint in sight. Kurt kept his house as he did the village: clean, picked up, and neat.

Maeve put the platters on the counter and walked around the kitchen, waiting for Jo to arrive. She peeked into the living room, seeing a large stone fireplace against the far wall, photos arranged above it, showing Mark as a child as well as the daughter that Kurt had mentioned having lost. Behind her, she heard the door slam as her eyes focused on the largest photo in the room, a photo of a girl in her teens, smiling on the beach, her brother at her side.

Jo stepped into the room. "Wow, she looks a lot like Heather."

CHAPTER 44

Maeve begged off the second glass of wine by professing exhaustion.

Jo looked disappointed, whining, "But I never get out any-more." She stared into the bottom of her glass and then looked at the half-empty bottle, giving Maeve a not-so-subtle hint that she didn't want the night to end.

"I'm shot, Jo," Maeve said, yawning to prove her point, adding a groan at the end to underscore just how tired she was.

"Well, okay," Jo said, getting up reluctantly from the couch. She stretched. "I guess I'm kind of tired, too, and I'm sure tonight is the night that Jack decides that a three-o'clock round of peek-a-boo is in order."

Maeve stood on the porch and watched Jo drive away in her smelly, secondhand car, waiting exactly ten seconds after the tail-lights disappeared into the inky night to go back into the house and grab her laptop, doing a search on the accident that Kurt Messer had told Maeve about a few days earlier.

Sixteen years ago, a time when Maeve was busy taking care of the girls, in a marriage that still had a lot of life left in it, the Messer family—widower Kurt and the two children he was raising alone, teenage daughter Caitlin and son Mark—had been in a two-car accident on the parkway right at the Farringville exit, a crash that had left only three survivors. Kurt and Mark had been questioned and released; Kurt's inability to control the car coming around a curve was the likely cause of the accident, though no charges were filed.

There was one survivor in the other car, a two-year-old named Jesse Connors. An autopsy revealed that his father, Bennett Connors, had been intoxicated way beyond the legal limit.

The only reason the story was even relevant, that Maeve could find something about it so many years later was that a stone that had been laid anonymously at the site and that had stayed there for many years, had washed away in a recent storm, landing on the lawn of a Farringville resident five miles from where the accident had occurred, a testament to the force of the raging water that had flowed through the town that stormy weekend.

That and the fact that Bennett's family was now involved in another matter, this one concerning his brother's illegitimate daughter.

There was a photo of the Messer trio, a professional shot in which the absence of a mother loomed large but Jo was right: Caitlin Messer looked just like Heather. And a little like Taylor. And even more like the girl who had gone missing from Prideville. Not a lot to go on, but just enough. Maeve closed the computer and breathed in deeply.

I used to be the woman who had the gun.

I used to think I would have a mission and that it would be to save the innocent souls.

I'm not her anymore.

She stood. "Or maybe I am," she said aloud in her big, empty house, grabbing her wallet and keys and heading out the door. One thing she knew for sure was that every single person involved in this case—her daughter included—had lied, and she felt as if only she could get to the truth of the matter. It was probably stupid and probably beyond her capabilities, but she had to try.

The other side of town, the side where houses were big and spaced far apart, where Taylor Dvorak's car had been found, seemed even darker than where Maeve lived, closer to the heart of the sleepy village, where lights could be seen from the railroad and the sound of commuter trains whizzing by was something she didn't even register anymore. Out here, you could be in your house and never hear a sound from any other house, from the occasional car that sped past; the houses were set back from the road, private in a way that Maeve had never experienced. Her Bronx neighborhood was one where you could get away with nothing—oh, except abusing a little child for years if you were her cousin, Sean Donovan—as everyone in the neighborhood seemed to hear and see everything and would let your father know if you punched Dermot O'Brien in the face (he'd called you a "fat cow," after all) or if you had declined helping Felix McElroy with his math homework (he just wanted to copy the answers). No, back here, no one would hear a thing, and not a soul would know if you were happy or sad, depressed or elated, sharing everything with the world or keeping a secret.

Maeve parked on the road and stared up at Kurt Messer's large house, waiting to see if his after-party was still in full swing, if he still had an errant guest or two. But curiously, the house was dark. He must have run out of beer, she thought, because in her own experience, there was no quicker way to end a party than to run out of booze. Or it was the boss's party and the guys had made a polite showing but had headed into town for the real party, at a local place in the village where beers were cheap and the jukebox was loud.

Something wasn't right here, or anywhere in this neighborhood. It was ground zero for the police department's investigation, yet they still didn't know anything, and Maeve wondered if they ever would. In her sneakers that still weren't broken in, her heart beating a little too quickly in her chest, she walked up the driveway, under the cover of some tall trees that lined each side, and approached the house. She was right: Not one light was on in the house, not a sign of life inside.

I'm in luck, she thought. Whatever had started here was over, and the house was desolate. She moved a little to her right and was thinking about going back inside when a floodlight bathed the yard in bright, LED illumination, as if night had ended and day had begun. Without thinking, she dived behind a big stack of wood, logs for Kurt to use when winter fell on Farringville and the temperatures dipped into the teens. From behind the wood, she listened, her back up against the scratchy bark, and heard the sound of heavy footfalls approaching.

"You should have died that day. Not her," the voice said. Kurt.

A moan followed that proclamation, and when Maeve peered around the edge of the wood stack, hearing the voices farther in the distance, she saw the back of one man hauling another man in a fireman's carry over his broad shoulders.

"Do you know what you've done? What you caused?" he asked.

The floodlight's power extended just as far as the edge of the grass, and by the time Maeve looked to see who was out there, their bodies were merely silhouettes in the moonlight. The man, who Maeve was sure was Kurt, flung the person he was carrying to the ground with seemingly no regard for his welfare and kept walking, past an old picnic table and another stack of wood, behind which he disappeared. In the distance, Maeve could see a rotting tree house, the steps missing risers, the floor sagging in the middle. She watched as Kurt, standing beneath it, pulled a rope from the ground and lifted a door.

"Jesus," Maeve said before she could think to keep her mouth shut. It was clear what was about to happen, and she was powerless to stop it. She pulled her phone from her pocket and texted Chris Larsson her location and a message straightforward and simple because there wasn't more time: *SOS. 911.*

Kurt dragged the tall, lanky boy along the grass, and when he arrived at the door to whatever lay beneath, he pushed him in, slamming the door shut and walking toward the house, brushing dirt from his pants, clapping his hands together to dislodge whatever still clung to them. He came closer, and as the flood reengaged and lit up the backyard, Maeve realized she was wrong. It wasn't Kurt.

It was Mark.

And as he passed the stack of logs, where she sat unnoticed, he started talking on his phone, his voice different now, normal. The voice that told Maeve how much he loved her cupcakes and the one he used when he called her daughter.

"Hey, Heather. So glad you answered. I've been trying to get you. Want to grab a quick bite? You know, celebrate Founders Day?" He laughed. "I know. It's not a place where I would live either, but it's all we've got right now. Pick you up at your Dad's?" He waited. "Oh, okay," he said. "I get it. I don't feel like answering twenty questions either. See you at the usual spot." Another second. "I love you."

Her insides crystallizing in a compound of fear and intense dread, Maeve waited until she heard his footfalls on the driveway fade away before sprinting across the backyard and toward the tree house, trying to stay in a spot that didn't engage the floodlight. At first, she couldn't find the door, its shape not visible under the grass, but then she saw a thick piece of sod, a little greener than the rest of the grass, tamped down on top of the door. She lifted the grass, surprised at her own strength, and observed the rope that lay beneath it. The door was another story, an old hatch cover from a boat, or so she thought, the light from the moon doing nothing to make things clearer for her, to make her understand why, when she finally did pry the door open and look down into the gaping maw of hell, all she saw was evil.

CHAPTER 45

Jesse Connors wasn't dead, but he wasn't conscious either.

Taylor Dvorak was alive and awake, though, and she screamed when she saw Maeve's face, her own visage recognizable even under a layer of dirt and blood. Maeve leaned in as far as she could, her eyes landing on things she didn't want to acknowledge, a stack of bones in one corner, a skeletal hand sitting in the dirt. "Taylor, you need to stop screaming," she said, although what she wanted to do was join in, take the opportunity to just go completely insane with the girl and never return from the mental abyss. It would be easier that way, easier than leaning into this tableau of death, trying to figure out a way to get both the girl and the unconscious boy out of this hellhole. She reached in and took the girl's hand, a mistake; Taylor had adrenaline flowing through her veins and was stronger than her several weeks underground would have led Maeve to believe she would be. She struggled with the girl for a few seconds, the cell phone in her pocket falling into the dark hole, the screen lighting up as it cracked and then went dark. She wrested her hand out of the girl's and stood, closing the trapdoor to block out the screaming, which filled the night and disrupted the silence she would need to focus on the plan. In the stillness, she heard a car pull up the drive-way and watched, from across the wide expanse of lawn, Chris Lars-son get out of his Jeep, alone and moving as if he were just arriving late to a barbecue rather than responding to Maeve's 911 text.

She wanted to call out his name, but something stopped her—the other form that appeared on the driveway and started to speak to him, Chris imploring whoever it was to put the gun down, to come to his senses, to be reasonable.

His voice grew loud. "I'm just here to see your father," he said, the lie leaving his lips.

"He's not here," Mark said.

While Mark was occupied with Chris, Maeve crept back to the stack of logs, hoping she could get to the house to find Kurt, a phone, or, even better, a gun. The men were still talking, Chris still trying to reason with someone Maeve now knew was completely out of his mind, someone who pretended by day that he was nice, helpful, but who by night and any other time he felt like it was ca-pable of horrible, evil things.

Someone who hid his true identity in plain sight.

"I don't understand what's going on here, Mark," Chris said. "I don't know why we're having this problem."

"Get off my property."

"Well, see, now, I can't," Chris said. "You've got a gun, you're holding it on me, and that presents a problem. I'm a police officer, Mark," he said in a tone that suggested he was talking to a child, some-one mentally incompetent, which Maeve guessed he was. Mark was out of sight beyond the edge of the garage, but Maeve could see Chris moving toward him, going closer than she thought he should, her instinct telling her not to do that, not to put his hand on his waist and touch his own gun, not to make the movement to take it out, not to try to be the hero here.

When she heard the shot ring out, and saw him crumple to the ground next to his Jeep, a car in which they had steamed up the windows several times, she stifled the gasp that nearly escaped her parched throat.

Mark came into view, nudging Chris's motionless body with his shoe and then placing what was a very large shotgun against the closed garage door. He knelt down, his breath coming out in ragged chuffs, and attempted to pick the larger man up and toss him over his shoulder, but gave up after a few tries, coming to the conclusion that dragging him was his best bet. Blood leaked from a gaping wound in Chris's midsection, and Maeve prayed—to her mother, her father, to anyone who was dead and would listen—that he was still alive.

Mark gave up halfway to the cellar in the ground under the tree house and was directly in Maeve's line of sight. She stopped breathing until he resumed his trek, Chris's body limp, the blood draining from him, and waited until he was at the tree house before running in a straight line to the driveway and to the gun propped against the closed garage door.

He was on her as if there hadn't been half a football field between them, the sound of his breath close behind indicating that he was nearly to the spot on which she stood, the spot where she turned, stood her ground, and pointed the gun. He looked surprised and put his hands up, smiling as he did, not knowing a few things about her.

Jack Conlon raised a girl who could shoot.

And Jack Conlon raised a girl who believed that sometimes, wrong in the eyes of the law was right in the eyes of God, or the universe, or whoever you believed in.

Jack Conlon raised a girl who didn't flinch when others might, who made split-second decisions along with others that were more thought out.

And lastly, Jack Conlon raised a girl who didn't close her eyes when she shot, making sure that it counted and she could see the soul leave the body of the person whose life deserved to be taken.

She dropped the gun, marveling at how one minute Mark Messer was danger and evil personified and now, with half his head missing, he was a threat no more.

CHAPTER 46

"I don't believe you," Suzanne Carstairs said, and it wasn't the kind of disbelief at what Maeve had done and what Carstairs and her entire police department couldn't do.

She didn't believe Maeve's story even though everything Maeve had told her was the truth, right down to when she shot Mark Messer in the head. She left out the part where she didn't feel a morsel of regret.

But it was the truth, for what it was worth. From the inside of what had been Chris Larsson's cruiser, she watched as Kurt Messer's body was carried out from the house. If she had figured out what was going on in the nick of time, he had figured it out just a bit sooner. Mark must have shot him before going on to kidnap Jesse Connors and punish him for . . . what? Raping Taylor Dvorak? Being in the car that caused his sister's death? Maeve didn't know, and she was too tired to ask.

Carstairs repeated what Maeve had told her.

"Something like that," Maeve said. "It's all kind of a blur right now." In the darkness, she could see the pain on the chief's face. She would feel that pain, too, but right now, something approaching shock mixed with disbelief had her thinking that Chris Larsson would come lumbering toward her, putting his big, beefy hands on her face, now blazing hot, and give her a kiss. A long kiss. One that would go on forever and would let her know that she had opened her heart enough to be loved by this kind, simple man, that she wasn't as complicated as he thought and could make him happy.

That there were good parts with her.

"He raped her, didn't he?" Maeve asked. "Jesse Connors."

The chief stayed silent for a few beats. "Not him. The other one. Judy Wilkerson's grandson. We think. Couldn't prove it. Jesse was there, though. Not sure he did anything to stop it, although he claims he did." The chief pulled a cigarette out of her bag and left it unlit, putting it between her lips. No one but a professional smoker could talk with a cigarette dangling from their mouth; the chief was one of them. "Lucky for Morehead we picked him up or he'd be in that cellar, too, right now. Maybe worse."

Maeve turned fully in her seat. "Morehead?"

"Bunch of assholes. With good attorneys. He said, she said. Works every time," Carstairs said, a tear slipping down her cheek.

"But there were witnesses," Maeve said. "Social media . . ."

Carstairs held up a hand. "Stop right there. It's done. No one saw anything, would go against these kids. Happens all the time, Maeve. Taylor had no one to stick up for her."

Except Heather, Maeve thought. She turned back around, faced the windshield, looked out at the flashing lights atop the police cars, turning lazily in the fog. "You speak from experience."

She nodded, the glow from the myriad police lights on the street casting a greenish tint to her skin. "I do." She reached up and hastily wiped away the tear. "Anyway, I don't know why you were here . . ."

"Cupcakes. Picking up my platters."

"Right. Cupcakes. Platters," Carstairs said, shaking her head. "What a bullshit story."

"I'm sorry about your boyfriend," Maeve said, and there weren't enough words to say just how sorry she was. It sounded empty, emotionless, and she guessed it was. She had been wrong. "I'm sorry about Chris," she said in the midst of a heart-wrenching sob.

"Nice guy," Carstairs said. "Not sure he's the greatest cop, but a really nice guy." She tapped the steering wheel, drumming out a methodical beat. "Isn't cut out for this line of work, I don't think. Has too much heart. A lot of soul."

Maeve nodded. That much was obvious. She wondered when the numbness would go away and when she would feel the weight of everything that had just happened. She hoped never. "Is he going to be okay?" she asked.

Carstairs looked out the window. "Hope so."

The chief didn't speak for a while. "Assholes," she said finally.

"Who?"

"Teenagers."

Maeve had to laugh in spite of the situation, but as soon as it came out, a sob followed. And then another one, and one more, until the car was filled with the sounds of her crying, raw and wretched, emotion that she hadn't felt in a long time making itself known. I'm here, it was saying. And I'm not going away.

Carstairs waited until it subsided before asking Maeve another question. "You done with County?"

Maeve nodded. She had spent two hours talking to a man who reminded her of her father, down to the perfectly parted, slicked-to-the-side old-school haircut, a man who believed her story more than the local chief. There was no way that this little woman, all one hundred and twenty pounds of her, her face freckled and sweet, had gunned down a murderer herself in cold blood, not feeling an iota of shame or guilt before, when she had made the decision, or after, when the deed was done.

"Self-defense, I suspect," Carstairs said.

"What else would it be?" Maeve asked. "You saw what went on here."

The chief started the car. "I'll take you home."

Before they reached her street, Maeve tried one more time to figure out one of the remaining pieces of the puzzle. "Your boy-friend?"

"I hate that term. I'm a little long in the tooth to be calling someone my boyfriend."

"Barnham."

"Yes?"

"Witness Protection."

The chief tried not to flinch, but she wasn't as good as Maeve in the lying department. "What made you say that?"

"I don't know." They pulled up in front of Maeve's house. "Any chance you can get him to drop the charges?"

"Maybe if you stop saying things like Witness Protection."

Maeve felt that she was right, but she let it go. She had bigger mysteries to solve, including one that involved Heather. She thanked the chief for the ride. "I'm sure I'll be seeing more of you."

"You can count on that," Carstairs said. "Maybe try baking a little more, perhaps take on a renovation project at the house here?" She leaned over and looked out the passenger-side window. "Looks like it could use a coat of paint."

"I understand."

"That might go a long way toward clearing up the mess you're in with my boy—"She stopped herself. "Well, you get it."

"I do."

"You killed a guy, Maeve," the chief said, looking straight ahead.

More than one, Maeve thought.

"How does that feel?"

Maeve smiled, even as she felt the wet on her cheeks. "It feels okay."

Maeve stood on the street and watched the chief drive away, not sure she had the strength to mount the short set of steps up to the front porch. She tried her legs, but they were uncooperative; she sat down on the first step and waited until the dizziness and weakness passed before getting up again and lumbering up the rest of the way.

The front door was unlocked, something Maeve hadn't remembered when she left and there was a light on in kitchen, the one over the sink. A glass of milk, half-drunk, sat on the counter. With newfound energy that she hadn't had previously, she raced up the stairs to the second floor and found the door to Heather's room ajar, the girl asleep in her bed.

Maeve stood in the doorway, solving the mystery that had previously been unsolvable.

She was the last person to have seen or talked to Taylor.

"Get them."

Mark Messer.

Jesse Connors.

Maeve resisted the urge to brush the damp hair that had plastered itself to the girl's forehead, remaining in the doorway and watching her sleep. If she closed her eyes, breathed in the scent, it could be years earlier when things were simpler and life had its own predictable rhythm. It would be when the big bed in there was really a toddler bed, two actually, with two tiny, lovely little girls asking for one more book, another glass of water.

"We love you, Mommy!" they would cry in unison as she pulled the door almost shut, waiting on the stairs to hear what they talked about. They would debate who loved Maeve more, who was the better daughter. Who was just like her, and who would be the best baker.

"I'm just like her," little Heather would say to her sister when she didn't know Maeve was listening. "I'm going to be just like her when I grow up." At three and four, it was the best thing she could think to be, not knowing that in several years, it would be the sentiment that would make her cringe, cause her to do everything in her power to distance herself from Maeve and her own emotions.

I'm just like her.

Maeve came back to the present and looked at the girl, sound asleep, sleeping more deeply than she ever had.

You are just like me, Maeve thought.

I just wish that weren't true.

CHAPTER 47

The day that Coach Barnham quit the team, leaving Farringville in his wake, Heather also quit the team, citing a lower-back problem.

Like father, like daughter. Cal constantly complained about lower-back pain and had once thought that medical marijuana was the answer, rather than the services of a good chiropractor.

Chris Larsson was still in the hospital. She had visited once, and when it was clear that whatever that had been between them had vanished into thin air, was more gone than the day he had broken up with her in the store, she had left, hoping that he would do as Chief Carstairs was going to suggest and take early retirement, putting the unpleasantness of being a small-town cop—something he hadn't signed up for—behind him.

He was a nice guy. He would find a nice girl to love him, someone who didn't come with as much baggage and have as many secrets as Maeve did. It was small comfort as she lay alone in her bed at night, wondering how everything had turned so dark and so deadly. She finally concluded that it was her; she brought those things to every life she touched, or so it seemed.

It was a few days later, days of uneasy détente in the house, when Maeve pulled the envelope out from between her cookbooks, leaving it on the kitchen table in front of Heather, who regarded it coolly while eating a bagel.

"I still have this," Maeve said.

Heather shrugged.

"Get them?" Maeve said. "How did you think you were going to get them?"

Heather put her bagel down. "Yes. I wanted to get them. For what they did."

"For raping Taylor?"

"For that. For ridiculing her. For letting it happen." She pushed her plate away. "And if I had known about her mother earlier, I would want to get her, too."

Trish Dvorak had instructed Taylor to go the Rathmuns' house, which as the housecleaner she had a key to, until they got the money. They never got the money, and Mark Messer found Taylor first.

"You know what, Mom?"

Maeve stood by the back door, focusing her attention on the overflowing garbage in the bin rather than see the look on her daughter's face. It was a look she saw every day when she regarded her own reflection. It was resolute and determined. Fearless. Righteous. "What?"

"Bad things should happen to bad people. That's the way the world should work."

Maeve froze, half bent over the garbage can, her back to her daughter. "Don't say that, Heather."

Heather stood and put her plate next to the sink. "I'll say it because I believe it."

Maeve turned. "So you were going to get them? How?"

"I just wanted them to tell the truth. To let everyone know what they had done." She stared at her mother, no trace of the little girl she once was evident on her face. "To get what they deserved."

"But then Taylor went missing."

"And I tried to find her." Her tough facade crumbled only slightly. "Mark said he would help me."

"But he had her almost the whole time."

The petulant teen returned. "I know that now," she said as if she were talking to someone of limited intelligence.

"Why did he take her? That other girl?"

Heather wasn't sure how much to say.

"Why?" Maeve asked. "And what did you find out? Anything?"

Heather was calm, and it was that calmness that troubled Maeve the most. She had been that calm, too, once, right after she had shot and killed a man who had made her early life miserable. "I didn't find out as much as I wanted to. As much as I needed to. I tried with Jesse but I didn't get anywhere." She paused. "As you know."

"This was never your responsibility, Heather," Maeve said. She could have been talking to herself, the words washing over the girl without taking effect. And it wasn't lost on her that the advice she was giving was advice she should have been taking.

The newspaper lay folded on the kitchen table; Maeve had brought it in from the sidewalk but hadn't had a chance to read it. Heather reached over and unfolded it, revealing the story of why Mark Messer kidnapped two girls—one long deceased and beside whose bones Taylor had lived for sixteen days. It was creepy and horrifying, and if it was true, and Maeve wasn't sure it was, the local media not being above making things up for ratings and sales, it was something that she would never entirely believe because it was unthinkable.

She looked at Heather, whose expression was flat, emotionless. "This can't be true."

Heather nodded. "But it is. He was trying to bring his sister back."

CHAPTER 48

There were two things Maeve still didn't know and might never get the answers to:

Who Evelyn Rose Conlon's father had been.

Why, if there were witnesses, Tim Morehead got off months ago scot-free for raping a teenage girl.

Money, some people said.

Connections, said others.

True, Judy Wilkerson's father had been a chief in Farringville long before Suzanne Carstairs arrived on the scene, but did he really carry any weight anymore? Apparently so. They were an old Farringville family, and that, more than money, more than status, assigned you a certain credibility in this little tiny village.

Lack of evidence was a prevailing theme and theory among some townspeople, even with veiled references to the attack having been on Facebook.

He said. She said. No one knows the truth. They were good boys, people said. Their families were institutions in Farringville.

Yes, Taylor was back, but she wasn't talking, and as a result, the case was dead, despite Chief Carstairs's tenaciousness, her personal history, her willingness to take this as far as it needed to go.

Maeve wondered about all of it, but not that much, because trying to get her life back on track, back to a more normal rhythm, was all she cared about.

She kept a watchful eye on Heather, but there was nothing other than genetics to explain why her daughter felt that she had to become so deeply involved in something that was none of her business and way out of her league, not to mention incredibly dangerous. Maeve tried, and failed, to get her to understand that some things were better left to the professionals and that her involvement had just jeopardized everyone involved.

The same could be said for herself.

She put on a clean shirt and jeans, tucked her feet into a pair of clogs, and drove away from her house, not looking in the rearview mirror as she did, knowing what it looked like, bad paint job and all. She headed south.

You can go home again.

Whoever said that you couldn't was wrong. Maeve parked on her old street, where she and Jack had lived for so many years, just the two of them, happily for most of the time, despite what Maeve had endured, in silence, as a child. Maeve walked up and down the street, unnoticed, taking in the fall colors, the row of houses, the little well-tended yards. Her cousin's house was at the end of the street, and she assiduously avoided that. There were new people there now, but it still held memories of hurt, both physical and mental, and she wanted to avoid going down that prickly memory lane.

Poole had been surprised when she had suggested meeting at a place on the same avenue where her mother had died. Been killed, really. To say that she had died—after telling Maeve "Be back soon"—

was an understatement. She had been mowed down by a drunk Marty Haggerty and left to die in the street, her clothing torn and tattered, a pool of blood surrounding her body. Maeve had heard all of the gory details, ever watchful, always hearing what she shouldn't as she lay in her bed, a floor above where the mourners had come to support Jack, but really to hear what had happened. One thing about her childhood neighbors: They loved a tragedy. The more tragic, the better.

"Will you be selling the house?" one had whispered, hoping to get in on the ground floor of the amazing deal that a brokenhearted Jack would make, only to be roundly rebuffed by her father.

"What will happen to the little girl?" another had asked, wondering if Maeve would be shipped off to live with a relative who was a mother with her own children, people not confident that a grieving Jack could raise a daughter while working as a policeman.

And then later, when what they thought was an appropriate amount of time had passed, "My sister . . . she lives in Poughkeepsie. Lovely girl. Beauty in her day. Makes the best Irish soda bread this side of County Cork." But Jack wasn't interested. He had a woman in his life who needed his undivided attention, and that was his little Mavy, the most perfect girl in the world. It was just the two of them, and that was the way he liked it.

That, and he would never find a woman to love the way he had loved Claire, despite the child she had conceived with another man.

Poole was waiting for her in a bar on the avenue, one that Maeve remembered being kind of dodgy in her day but that had been turned into a proper pub, right down to the brass bar she was still too short to rest her feet on. She climbed up on a bar stool and ordered a glass of wine, remembering in that instant that Poole didn't drink.

"Sorry," she said. "I forgot."

"Not a problem," he said. "About three years in, I decided that I was going to have a very boring life if I couldn't hang out in bars with the guys." He smiled. "And the occasional girl."

"Divorce final?" she asked.

"Not yet," he said. "But that door has closed. She lasted as long as she could. I hope she finds someone who makes her happy."

"Did she make you happy, Poole?"

He looked down. "I'm not sure anyone can make me happy." He looked at her. "What do you think, Maeve Conlon? Your guy make you happy?" He realized, too late, what he was asking, that the relationship had ended.

She thought about it. "He did."

A look passed across his face. "Sorry. I . . ."

"It's okay," she said. But it wasn't. It never would be. There would always be that lingering feeling that the end of their relationship had been her fault alone. He had made her happy, but as Poole had once said, and she now believed about herself as well, there were no good parts with them, her and Poole alike. Just sadness and grief at what they never had a chance to be. Happy. Whole. Content.

He understood. She could see that. She could also see a glimmer of hope in his eyes, something she needed to shut down.

"That's not what this is about," she said, reminding him. "It never was."

"Wasn't it?"

She couldn't handle the weight of what he was implying. There were other, weightier topics to discuss. "My sister. Marty Haggerty?"

He didn't look surprised that she had figured out the truth. Something on his face told her he always knew she would. "I never wanted you to know."

The bartender delivered her wine, an interruption that gave her a chance to gather her thoughts. Around them, the bar was abuzz with the after-work crowd, the people disembarking express buses and the commuter rail, darting into a warm place where they could slough off the stress of the day before going home to an even warmer, cozier house, she expected. She took a sip of her wine, looking down at the coaster that was placed beneath the glass. HAPPY DAY! it cried in a jaunty typeface. But it wasn't a happy day. It was never a happy day when you discovered that a sister you had only known for six months was the daughter of the man who had killed your mother. Maeve wasn't sure she would ever have a happy day again. "How did you find out?"

"That old lady? McSweeney?" he said. "I flashed the badge. Asked her what she knew. She knew it all." He paused. "That day when we saw each other? I followed you to her house, wanted to see what you had up your sleeve."

Maeve downed the wine and asked for another one.

"Easy there," he said, pushing the empty glass toward the edge of the bar. "And how did you know?"

"My sister doesn't remember much. But she remembered being there. She remembered their house. It just made sense."

He nodded. "You're a smart cookie."

"I guess I should have known, Poole. I guess I should have guessed that this one would have a tragic ending, too." She thought about it. She had known the minute that Evelyn had recognized the Haggerty house. She traced it back. That was the moment she knew but didn't want to acknowledge at the time.

"They're not all tragic endings," he said.

"They're not?" she said, angry. "In my world, they seem to be." She laughed. "I'm turning into Job, Poole, right before my very eyes."

He leaned in, placing a hand on her knee. Anyone who was watching would have seen a woman with tears in her eyes being comforted by a handsome, kindly man, one who clearly adored the small woman and would do anything for her. He kissed her lightly on the lips, and she relaxed just a little bit, letting herself be taken into his warm embrace. "I'll help you get through this, Maeve Conlon," he said.

"With one condition."

He raised an eyebrow.

"That you stop calling me 'Maeve Conlon,'" she said.

He laughed, the first real laugh she had ever heard him emit. "Deal."

"Can I tell you something?"

"There's more?" he asked.

"There's a lot more. I'm responsible for more death than the actual angel of death, Poole."

"Job. The angel of death. Been reading your Bible a lot, Maeve?"

She watched two other people at the end of the bar, laughing and chatting, and wondered why she and Poole couldn't be like them. "I don't know if you remember, but a guy died at the dam two years ago. In my town."

He knew where she was going; she could tell by the knowing look on his face. "You were there."

"I was."

He waited for more.

"He was abusing his child. A little girl. Her name was Tiffany. He broke her arm."

"Like your cousin did to you."

She didn't remember telling him about that specific incident, but he knew somehow. That knowing was what they shared. "I couldn't stand it, Poole."

"So you made him disappear."

She did. And now, a little girl and her younger sister were living somewhere else, hopefully safe and sound. Maeve would never know.

"Good riddance," Poole said. "Feel bad about it?"

Maeve thought about that. "Nope."

"My warrior queen," Poole said, the respect evident in his tone.

Her wine appeared, but she didn't drink it. "If I drink this, I won't be able to drive home," she said, feeling the effects of the first, hastily consumed one. "Walk me to my car." She threw some money on the bar and got up.

Outside, they kept a distance between them that would suggest that they didn't know each other, not ready to make what they felt public. Theirs was a tenuous relationship, one that would have to build over time. "I wonder where it was," Maeve said as they walked along the avenue. "The exact place where my mother died." She had thought about that a lot over the years.

"You don't want to know that," Poole said from his spot in front of what Maeve had known to be a five-and-dime when she was a kid but was now a shop that only sold olive oil. She wondered how it stayed in business, if the people of this neighborhood needed that much olive oil to sustain them. "Some things you're better off not knowing."

Maeve turned her back to the avenue and stood on the curb near the bus stop. "This is the bus I used to take to the city. The real city. Manhattan. I thought I'd live there one day. Who knew that I would move further away and that this was the closest I would ever get? That I'd be a kid here and never come back?" Behind her, down the street, the bus approached. People would get off and maybe go into the bar that they had just left, happy to be out of the "city," even though they lived in its environs. That was a funny thing about the people in the boroughs; they never considered themselves part of the main borough where everything happened all day, all night. They considered themselves, their particular borough, different, distant from where everything else was happening.

"You were where you were supposed to be," Poole said.

"So philosophical, Poole," she pointed out. "You know, Poole, the whole philosophy thing aside, I think we might be made for each other." She was only half kidding.

"How so?" he asked, even though it was clear that the proclamation made him profoundly happy.

"Somewhere in our shared pain, we might be able to find happiness," she said. "I'm starting to believe that."

He reached out to take her hand, and she let him, feeling her small palm nestled within his larger, calloused one. Working-man hands. That's what Jack would have called them.

There was her grammar school and the place where she got on the bus to go to high school. "That's where I busted open my chin," she said to no one, remembering taking a step off the curb and hurting herself, Jack bundling her up and flagging down a police cruiser on the street and whisking her to the emergency room, holding her down as they put three enormous stitches in her chin. She sometimes looked at the scar and laughed. Of all of her scars, that was the only one that was visible, and it was one she had gotten all on her own.

She continued down the street. Unlike any other man she had been with, he didn't feel the need to speak to fill up the silent spaces; he just needed to be near her. That was enough. No talking, no laughing, no asking questions. They were just beside each other, and it was all he needed.

"I'm enjoying this trip down memory lane, Maeve," he said, "But I have to go."

"Back to work?" she asked.

"Back to work," he said and put his big hands on her face, drawing her in for a kiss.

When she pulled back, she looked at him, the man who now held her heart. "You were wrong, Poole."

"About what?" he said, smiling the biggest smile she had ever seen on his face.

"There are a few good parts with you. More than a few, maybe."

CHAPTER 49

It was a lot to think about, a lot to absorb, but in spite of all of that, one thing continued to trouble her.

It wasn't the fact that David Barnham seemed to have disappeared without a trace himself. And it wasn't the fact that he had mail from the U.S. Marshals in his kitchen junk drawer. It wasn't even the fact that despite his nebulous background, the rumors about him, he had managed to con a seemingly bright and suspicious woman in the person of the local police chief.

It was what had happened that morning she had followed him, why David Barnham had been out at that lake, testing the water's depth.

Start at the beginning, she thought, laughing to herself as she drove down the dirt road to the little patch of beach, still a little giddy from her meeting with Poole, or maybe a little insane, given what she had learned. It felt wrong to be happy with all that she had wrought. She had already been back to the giant crater at the edge of the neighborhood built on the backs of people who had labored for Charles Connors, making him rich beyond anyone's wildest imagination. There was nothing there, the rank porta-potties still reeking but empty, nothing to indicate that David Barnham had ever hidden anything there. There was still Laurel Lake, though, and what had happened that morning, a morning that seemed like it had been yesterday and a thousand years earlier.

She had struck up an uneasy alliance with Suzanne Carstairs, their fates linked together by everything that had transpired. Suzanne had stopped in at The Comfort Zone right before Maeve had closed that day, eyeing her suspiciously.

"You look guilty," she said, taking a big bite of a cupcake. "Like you're up to something."

Carstairs was good. Maeve felt her cheeks go hot. She figured that this one time, she would tell the truth. "I'm thinking of going kayaking tonight."

Carstairs gave her the once-over. "You kayak? At night?"

"Yeah," Maeve said, laughing. "Laurel Lake. Seems like as good a place as any."

Carstairs had regarded her for longer than Maeve would have liked, finally breaking the silence by updating Maeve on a subject she had no business being updated about anymore. "Chris did retire. Officially," she said. "Heading up to the Finger Lakes."

The thought of him in a remote area, on a lake somewhere, gave her peace.

"You've got a mole in your department," Maeve said.

"Yeah, we've got roaches and chipmunks, too," Carstairs said.

"No, a mole. Someone feeding stuff to the media," Maeve said.

"You think?"

"I know," Maeve said. "Too many coincidences, too much media knowing things before they could. I just think it's weird. I think it's one of yours."

"I'll be sure to check that out, Maeve," Carstairs said. "Anything else?"

"Yeah," Maeve said, going for broke. "Why did you lie for him?"

The chief was silent. "That's a little more complicated."

"How so?"

"Let's just say that I didn't think I had." She looked at Maeve and Maeve decided not to press it. There was something beneath the surface of her answer that hinted at things better left unsaid.

They had left it at that, the chief diving into another cupcake before Maeve closed, following it up with a cigarette in the back parking lot before getting in her car and driving away.

Now, at Laurel Lake, Maeve surveyed the landscape, walking to the water's edge. She would never know how deep the water was because she would never venture out in one of the County-sanctioned boats at its edge. Sure, she had once had a gun, but without the benefit of a wetsuit—and an ability to actually swim—she would dream of getting in the chilly water to see if there was something down there that Barnham wanted.

She'd never know.

The sinkhole, once filled in with fresh dirt and smoothed over, if she had thought about it, could have been the work of Mark Messer, but she'd never know that either. Who else had access to a lot of dirt and a large rake to fill in a hole? Landscapers? Gardeners? She had had to beg and plead with Kurt to get the pothole fixed, so a big hole in the middle of a deserted beach certainly hadn't been on anyone's mind, particularly the DPW's. Maybe he had had sinkholes to fill. She stared out at the water and considered everything she knew, coming to the conclusion that what she knew amounted to exactly nothing.

"I knew you'd be back."

She turned at the sound of the voice. David Barnham walked down the beach, soccer shoes on his feet, the requisite warm-up clothes on his body. His hands hung at his sides, and in his right one was a gun slapping lazily at his thigh.

With all that she had done, with all that she had been through, it wasn't lost on her that this might be where it all came to an end, out at the edge of town on a little stretch of beach whose name she hadn't known a few weeks earlier, a woman and a guy with a gun.

She was used to it being the other way around.

"Where have you been, Barnham?" she asked.

He shrugged. "Around. Here and there."

"That sounds like a whole lot of ridiculousness. You've got to come up with something better than that," she said. "How did you find me? Did you follow me?"

"You're not as smart as you think." He used the gun to point over his shoulder. "Back there. The transmitter. I'll get rid of it once I get rid of you."

"You had a tracker on my car?" she asked.

He didn't respond. "What is wrong with you exactly?" he asked, moving closer in the gloom, training the gun at a spot right in the middle of her forehead, squinting. "What makes a woman like you get into other people's business?"

"Well, it's a good thing I do, don't you think?" she said, shoving her hands deep in her pockets, her fingers grazing her phone.

"Let me see your hands," he said.

She pulled them out of her pockets and held them in the air.

"Let's not be dramatic," he said.

"What are you hiding?" she asked, keeping her hands up.

"You really don't want to know," he said.

"Try me."

He considered that, wondered how much he should say. "Just money. Nothing else."

"Now who's being dramatic? If it's just money, who cares?" she asked. "You put money in the water?" He must have owned stock in Ziploc.

He ignored her question, inching closer, looking as if she might spring at him and break his neck. She was good, but she wasn't that good. Plus, her jeans were too tight, the result of having consumed more than her fair share of loaf breads over the past few weeks, and there was no way she was springing anywhere. Waddling, maybe. But springing? No chance in hell.

There was something, though, and not even that deep below the surface, that gave her a measure of satisfaction at the idea that this guy, whatever he had done, was terrified of her and of what she might do. She smiled at the thought.

"Why are you smiling?" he asked.

"No reason," she said. "Listen, if you're going to kill me, could you just tell me what's going on so that I can die knowing that I was right about something? Just this one time?"

"Why don't you seem scared?" he asked.

"Because I'm not."

"Someone is holding a gun on you and you're not the least bit terrified?"

"Not really," she said.

"Why not?"

It was her turn to shrug. "Seen a lot. Been hurt a lot. What you do to me can't be any worse than what's already happened."

"Death?"

She thought of her mother and of Jack's contention, all these years since her death, that yes, they would all be reunited one day.

She had believed her father because there was no reason not to. If it wasn't true, and the lights just went out, the pain going away forever, that was one thing. If it was true, well, that was the best thing that could happen.

It was a win-win in her opinion.

She tried another tack. "Why here? Why Farringville?"

"It's as good a place as any to get lost, don't you think?"

"But you were never going to stay lost," she said. "That was a problem."

"It wasn't until you got involved." He came closer and grabbed her by the hood on her jacket.

"Were you sleeping with any girls on your team?" she asked.

He laughed. "Um, no. But thank you for asking. It's flattering to think that I could seduce a bunch of teenagers. I read a book on team building. They said to have parties."

"With girls?" Maeve asked. "That sounds kind of messed up."

"Well, maybe not girls, but I figured it couldn't hurt," he said. He realized that talking about team building wasn't the purpose of their unexpected meeting. "This is scintillating but we have other things to discuss. Like why you're crazy."

"Before we get to that, what about Suzanne Carstairs?"

"Great girl. Lots of fun. We had a good thing going." He motioned toward the water with the gun.

"That morning. The morning I saw you. Why were you here? Where were you going? What were you hiding? Why did she lie for you?"

"You've got a lot of questions. I've told you everything you need to know."

"The construction site. The porta-john. What was in there?" she asked. "Why did you go there?"

He was tiring of her questions. "Let's go." He waved the gun menacingly, and if she hadn't known his background, she would have thought that he didn't really know how to use it.

"Where?" she asked.

He pointed to the water, and right then, she decided that there might a fate worse than death, than being shot in the head.

Drowning.

An upside-down canoe rested at the water's edge, the little waves brushing up against it making a soothing noise. Barnham pulled a pair of handcuffs out of his pocket and grabbed her wrist, slapping one cuff on and fastening the other to a tree branch. The branch was much higher than her head, and Maeve listed uncomfortably, one foot touching the ground with just the tips of her toes. She watched as Barnham wrestled with the canoe with one hand while trying to keep his gun trained on her. Her new phone, in the opposite pocket from her free hand, was useless to her, her one hand not being dexterous enough to punch in a number.

Why hadn't she paid closer attention to the girls when they texted and video chatted and used technology that remained an elusive ideal to her? When she was little, Jack had told her that one day, you would be able to call someone and see their face on the phone. That day was here. It was a smartphone world, and she was a rotary phone.

This is rich, she thought. I'm going to be killed by a guy who can't get a canoe into the water while a perfectly good phone sits in my pocket.

She watched him a little longer. "I see what the problem is!" she called. "It's chained to that tree over there." Maybe that would take him some time to undo and she could figure out how to call someone.

See, Mr. Killer Man? I'm nice and helpful. Please don't murder me. And please, maybe, get distracted so I can get away? Make a run for it, a run by a middle-aged lady having the same chance for success as that one time she tried to make a chocolate soufflé during a heat wave.

He looked up at her, mystified. "You are an insane person."

In the distance, a car pulled up beside the beach, the sound of a door closing something she never knew would sound so good. She craned her neck but couldn't see who had arrived, but Barnham could. He raced to the tree, unlocked the handcuff, and pulled her in front of him like a human shield, pushing the barrel of the gun into her temple.

"Hiya, David!" Suzanne Carstairs walked gingerly on the beach in her high heels, picking her way around a cluster of roots here, a rock there. "You left without saying good-bye." She looked at Maeve. "Kayaking, my ass."

"I'll kill her. Don't move," he said.

"Wow, you've got some balls there, my friend. A U.S. Marshal on the run from the Marshals themselves. But that money you stole from El Gato really didn't get you far enough away," she said.

Jo hadn't done a follow-up presentation on the El Gato story since her first recitation all those weeks ago. The minute Carstairs said the name, Maeve remembered that day in the store, how the local police blotter had been devoid of juicy stories, how Jo had turned to the *Times* for some entertainment.

"Sure, he's dead now," Carstairs said, "but you must know how many people are out there who would just love a chance to torture you to death."

"I didn't steal that money. He gave it to me. To get gone."

"Both of you?" she asked.

"Both of us," he said.

Carstairs shook her head, sad at that thought or others; Maeve wasn't sure. "That morning. I lied for you but I didn't know it. Did you drug me?" she asked.

"You slept like a rock that night, honey. Best night's sleep you'd had in years, you said."

"I trusted you."

"You might be in the wrong profession, Suzie-Q," he said.

Maeve saw the cop's face change, the sadness turning to anger.

"Who's David Barnham?" Maeve asked.

"Me. Lots of people. A kid who died in Kansas. Someone who couldn't be traced."

Maeve was more confused than ever.

"And the money?" Suzanne asked. "Why now?"

He pushed the gun into Maeve's temple. "This one. Poking around. It was getting too hot."

"What are you, a freaking moron?" Suzanne asked. "With that kind of scratch, *you* get gone. For good. Immediately. You go to Turks and Caicos. Venezuela. Thailand. You don't come to a place like Farringville, for god's sake."

He pulled Maeve tighter, and his grip around her neck pressed against her windpipe. She struggled for air, the pinwheels dancing in front of her eyes letting her know that it was only a few moments before she blacked out completely.

"I was hiding in plain sight," he said. "It's a thing."

Carstairs pulled the gun from her pocket and pointed it at him. "Let her go."

The gun in his hand was wiggling against Maeve's temple, his whole body, pressed tightly against hers, trembling.

"One more time," Carstairs said. "Let. Her. Go."

The click of his gun sounded a lot louder than it normally would have, but everything was heightened now. The little waves lapping the shore of Laurel Lake sounded like a tsunami, Barnham's breathing like a tornado, her own heart like a loud metronome, keeping time with the world. She prepared herself for the inevitable, hoping against hope that Jack was right and that he and Claire would be waiting for her when it was over and that all of the lost time would be found, and all of the love she had been denied would envelop her like a warm blanket, the likes of which she hadn't felt since she had just given birth and a nurse presented her with a cotton throw that had been heated. Would it be like when she had held her children for the first time, the blanket around her body keeping her warm, their breath on her cheek warming her very soul? Or would it just feel safe and comforting? She figured she was about to find out.

Maeve heard the shot and felt his body go limp, the butt of his gun thumping her head noisily and with force, but it was only when she collapsed herself, seeing his body at the water's edge, that she realized what had happened. Suzanne Carstairs put the gun on a rock and walked toward her. Her face plastered in the wet sand, the tiny waves caressing her head, Maeve closed her eyes.

"Hang on, Maeve," her new friend said, crouching beside her after taking her former lover's pulse. "You'll be fine."

"You're quite a shot," Maeve said. "Almost as good . . ."

"As good as who, Maeve?" the chief asked, her face close to Maeve's.

"I'm so tired," Maeve said.

"I know."

"I promise never to butt in where I don't belong," Maeve whispered, her throat tight and sore. The things she had done had taken their toll, and not just on her. It was time to stop.

"And I promise never to use Match.com again," Carstairs said. "You think I can get my money back?"

Maeve coughed. "I don't know."

Suzanne let out a rueful chuckle. "He was supposed to be my perfect match."

CHAPTER 50

A perfect match.

Maeve looked out at the ocean and took a deep breath of the tangy Key West air. In the condo a bottle of wine was chilling, a thick steak on the grill. She was worried about his cholesterol, and he was worried about her blood pressure, but they were navigating the ins and outs of getting older with ease. Now that they were together, nothing seemed too monumental to be conquered.

The steak had been her idea. "Are you trying to kill me?" he had asked, half joking, as they both knew what she was capable of.

"No," she had said, ruffling what was left of his hair. "Never worry about that."

He waved to her from the porch that sat high above the sand.

She shielded her eyes. "Dinner?"

He flashed her a thumbs-up.

On the porch, she looked out at the ocean. "Key West is beautiful this time of year."

"Key West is beautiful every time of year," he said. "You sure you can't stay?"

"You know I can't," she said. It was a conversation they had had many times. "But I'll visit."

"Many times, I hope."

"As much as I can."

Her girls were both in college now, and things had changed for her. Heather had settled closer than Washington State and Maeve was happy to visit Boston when she could. She was alone in a big house now, running a business that was profitable but physically taxing; she wasn't getting any younger. Neither was he.

"You can retire, you know," he said.

"I wish I could. Let me get Heather out of college first. Then we'll talk."

He looked to the beach, to the families playing with their children in the dying light, the couples strolling along the water's edge. "How is Heather?" he asked.

"A little too much like me for my liking."

"In what ways?"

She followed his gaze out to the water, to the father dragging a small child by the arm to a nearby blanket, his face contorted in anger. It wasn't fun and games; it was exhaustion and exasperation. Maeve kept her eye trained, waiting to see if the situation escalated. "In every way." I'm done with that, she thought to herself, hoping that it was really true, that she could leave those ways behind her.

"Watch her, Maeve," he said.

"You think this stuff is inherited?" she asked.

He poured a little more wine in her glass, looking longingly at the rose-colored liquid. "Not sure." He put the bottle in the ice bucket next to the table. "Keep an eye on her."

Maeve would. Maeve kept close tabs on her, as close as she

could given the distance. Heather seemed happy and content, and it didn't seem like an act. Maeve hoped it wasn't.

"Stay," he said again, reaching out for her hand.

"I can't, Poole. You know that."

One more day and she would be back in Farringville. Back to her normal life, whatever that was.

But for now, she had this. And maybe later, there would be more of this, more comfort and warmth and all of the things she had been missing in her life but never stopped to acknowledge.

She looked out to the beach; the family she had been watching was gone, and she relaxed a little more, wondering if she could make that part of herself disappear just as she had made some awful men disappear. Did she want to?

She looked across at Rodney Poole, the man who had let her go, who understood, as Heather had once said, that bad things needed to happen to bad people. He was part of that old life she had. Would he be a reminder? Would that be a bad thing?

"What are you thinking about, Maeve?" he asked.

She got up and went around to where he sat, folding herself into his lap. "Maybe about all of the things we could do together."